HIJINKS WITH A HELLHOUND

A Hidden Species Novel

LOUISA MASTERS

Hijinks With A Hellhound

Copyright © 2021 by Louisa Masters

Cover: Booksmith Design

Editor: Hot Tree Editing

I'm a one-and-done kind of hellhound. I don't catch feeeeelings…

Once upon a time, my first and last relationship taught me that romantic love isn't enough to stop your boyfriend from trying to kill you. Been there, done that, got the T-shirt. My awesomeness is now strictly reserved for one-nighters and casual hookups. Sure, my friends seem to be matching up in romantic bliss, but screw that—I'm not interested.

Besides, things are heating up at the Community of Species Government, and I'm right in the thick of it all. Those bad guys are going down—and not in the good way. They might seem to have the drop on us now, but we're going to turn the tables on them. Even if it means going on a mission with Aidan Byrne.

I'm still not happy about the way Aidan handled things with my bestest bestie a few months back, even if he did turn out to be right. Plus, there's something about him that rubs my fur in the wrong direction. He's the kind of guy who thinks karaoke is only for college kids and looks down on me for licking my own balls. He also thinks that just because he's the species leader, he's in charge.

Too bad for him, I've never backed away from a challenge… even if it is unnervingly sexy and really bendy. A hookup won't lead to feelings… right?

Community of Species Government - CSG

Malia - God, Head of State of the Spiritual Plane
Percy Caraway (felid shifter) - the Lucifer: Head of State of the Physical Plane

Senior Investigation Team:
Sam Tiller (human/felid shifter) - Team Admin, Gideon's boyfriend [Demons Do It Better]
Gideon Bailey (demon) - Sam's boyfriend [Demons Do It Better]
Elinor Martin (hellhound)
David Carew (sorcerer)
Lily Heath (succubus) – killed by Tish
Andrew Turner (vampire) – Noah's boyfriend [One Bite With A Vampire]
Alistair Smythe (hellhound)

Noah Cage (human) - CSG intern, Andrew's boyfriend [One Bite With A Vampire]

Aidan Byrne (felid shifter) - Shifter Species Leader
Jun Chew (hellhound) Oregon Pack Leader
Riona (felid shifter) Oregon Clan Leader

Coalition for Community Advancement - CCA
Terrorist organization responsible for genetic manipulation experiments

Dr Francis Tish (sorcerer) - Lead scientist; Sam and Noah's childhood doctor

CHAPTER ONE

Alistair

I JUMP up the front steps to my BFF's townhouse but slow as I approach the front door. His perpetually grumpy asshole boyfriend has a nasty habit of activating their privacy wards to keep me out, and I *do not* want to run face-first into them and bounce back into the street again. That shit *hurts*. It wouldn't surprise me if he did it on purpose—he's the type of guy who gets his kicks from inflicting pain on others.

Well… not really. He's actually a good guy, just crabby. And he does seem to like tormenting me. But my bestie loves him, so I gotta tolerate being kicked out of their house at three in the morning and having him put up the wards when I just want to grab some breakfast. Some people have no concept of hospitality.

I let myself in through the front door—it's locked, but hello, I'm a hellhound. No lock can stop me—but pause in the entryway. After that one time I walked in on them right before, er, *completion*, they've been pretty stringent about putting the wards up before sex, but Gideon threatened to cut my dick off and feed it to me if I ever again walked in on them fucking, so I like to be doubly sure it's safe. Also, can I just say, how rude is it to have sex in the living room when you know you have friends who might want to visit?

Shameful.

Anyway, there are no suspicious noises, and the sex smells all seem to be at least a few hours old, so I head on through to the kitchen to find something to eat. I can hear the shower running upstairs and someone closing a drawer, which means they're still getting ready for work. Running a little late this morning.

I'll make breakfast for us all!

The kitchen is fully stocked, as Sam's kitchen always is, and I help myself to a cup of coffee from the half-full pot while I consider my options. I'm really in the mood for pancakes, but they're not in my cooking repertoire. For some reason, every time I make them, they end up either charred or raw in the middle. It's very sad. Instead, I stick bread in the six-slice toaster and pull out the bag of oats that Sam buys just for me—well, he used to buy it just for me. Since his transformation from human to shifter, his metabolism has been working over-time, and he's come to appreciate the filling properties of a big bowl of porridge.

The first lot of toast has popped, and I'm stirring the oatmeal on the stove when Gideon comes in. He glares at me as he prowls over to the coffeepot and refills the mug in his hand.

"Some of that had better be for Sam," he growls. I've known quite a few demons in my nearly two centuries of life, and he's the only one who seems to feel he needs to live up to the human expectation of demon behavior. Although, when I mentioned that to

Sam, he gloomily told me that apparently it's a family trait. Sam hasn't yet met Gideon's family, just spoken to them on the phone, but they aren't the warmest people.

Poor Sam. Even if he did choose to hook up with an anal-retentive asshole who likes to rearrange people's cupboards and torture poor, unsuspecting hellhounds.

"Of course some is for Sam," I proclaim. "I *love* Sam. He's my bestest BFF in the whole world—"

"Yeah, yeah," he grumbles, grabbing the toast and putting more bread in. Two shifters and a demon can put away a lot of food, and twelve slices of toast plus porridge will not be enough.

Hmm. Maybe…

"I was going to make you pancakes, but you remember what happened last time," I say innocently. "Would you like some porridge too? I can make more."

He blinks at me over a mouthful of toast and peanut butter. I can't blame him for being surprised—he doesn't know I'm a master manipulator, and last week I did refuse to share my four-pound bag of M&Ms with him and then yelled at him for five minutes for being a best friend stealer.

Finally, he swallows and says, "No… thank you. I can make my own pancakes."

I shrug, like this doesn't matter at all to me, and say, "Sure."

He seems suspicious, so I keep up a steady stream of small talk about how much I'm looking forward to spring and seeing people's gardens in bloom as he gets out a bowl and cracks the eggs into it. Only four, which is a worry.

"Good morning," Sam declares breezily as he

wanders in, empty mug in hand. "Alistair, no food left at your place?" He wanders over to the coffeepot.

"Are you implying that you don't want to have breakfast with me?" I place a hand over my heart as I lift the pot off the stove with the other. "I'm hurt. How could you hurt me this way? How can our friendship mean so little to you after all these years of devotion and—"

"Fucking hell, I almost wish he'd go back to talking about the damn flowers," Gideon mutters, and I grin.

"I knew you were listening! You pretended you weren't, but I could tell. You love spring flowers just as much as I do, don't you? You're just a big softy inside. Maybe it's buried way down deep—very deep—okay, so we'll need an excavator to find it, but you *do* have a heart, and mmph—"

Sam's hand clamping over my mouth interrupts me midsentence. "Stop now before he murders you. I won't protect you." I make big sad eyes at him, and he drops his hand with a sound of disgust. "Why do the puppy eyes always work on me?"

"It's evil hellhound magic," Gideon says. "You need to guard against it."

I gape at that bit of horrific slander, but Sam laughs and goes over to grab a slice of the now cold toast. "Are you making eggs?" he asks, peering into the bowl, and Gideon shakes his head.

"Pancakes. Want some?"

I'd like to point out here that he never offered *me* any. Me! A guest in his home. See what I meant about hospitality?

"Yes, please," Sam says. "Pancakes and porridge sounds perfect."

I shoot him a pleading look behind Gideon's back, and he rolls his eyes. "Make enough for Alistair, too, since he was kind enough to make me porridge. In my kitchen. With my ingredients."

"Thanks, Gideon, I'd love some! So nice of you to offer." I hand Sam his bowl of porridge with one hand and the maple syrup with the other, then grab my bowl and a container of blueberries and join him at the kitchen table.

Gideon turns around and gives me a very level, very dry look. I smile back. "Tomorrow," he tells me, "I'm leaving the wards up."

I shovel in a spoonful of porridge because I'm starving—I really did run out of food—then pout at him. "But then I won't be able to get in."

Sam coughs.

"That's okay," I declare magnanimously, "I'll just call when I get here. Or maybe I can stay over tonight. That would be fun. Just remember, no sex while I'm in the house. Your soundproofing is good, but not that good, and hellhound noses smell *everything*."

"Anyway," Sam says hastily and way too loudly, "what's your schedule like today? Are you in the office or out?" Sam, Gideon, and I all work on the same team for the Community of Species Government—CSG. It's actually something I'm insanely proud of, being one of the youngest members of such a senior team and reporting directly to the lucifer, but I try to be cool about it, because that's the kind of guy I am.

"In," I tell Sam. "I'm working out in the gym this morning with Noah, and then Percy"—the lucifer—"wants to see me."

"What did you do?" Sam demands. It's hurtful.

Although maybe warranted.

"Nothing! I swear. He didn't sound mad. It's probably just a check-in or something. We never did get a chance for a three-month review since I started this job."

Sam still seems suspicious, which wounds me deep in my heart, and since I'm definitely sure I've done nothing wrong—well, mostly sure—I stare deep into his eyes and say, "How can you doubt me like this? Don't you understand that true friendship is based on—"

"Just eat, Alistair," he says resignedly.

I give an offended sniff and settle in to enjoy my porridge as Gideon begins cooking my pancakes.

It's so nice to start the day with friends.

"MOTHERFUCKING SCUM-SUCKING DICK EATER!" Noah shouts.

"You can do it!" I encourage him from across the room. There's no way I'm getting any closer while he's in this frame of mind. He may be a twenty-year-old human who just relearned how to walk and is still ridiculously weak from loss of muscle mass, but he's still one scary motherfucker. He survived being the test subject of an evil sorcerer scientist, lived in hiding right under his enemies' noses—in their compound!—for nearly a year, then basically taught himself to manipulate existential magic in a way nobody knew humans could. And when he was taken captive again by that same sorcerer, he managed to teleport himself to safety from another dimension—a feat that should be impossible. So yeah, stay away from pissed-off Noah.

It's only been a few weeks since we thought we would lose him to the extreme malnourishment that was the result of that teleport. The going theory—because we don't know for sure—is that human teleporting uses so much energy that his body basically cannibalized itself to provide it, leaving him almost a skeleton. Some top medical sorcerers were working on him, though, and even though he's still got a lot of muscle left to build, his life is no longer in danger—and his tongue muscles are back in top form. We're all taking it in turns to work out in the gym while he does his physio sessions, partly to keep him company, and partly as a protection thing. After all, Dr. Tish, his former captor, might try to come back for him.

"Shove it up your ass, Alistair!" he replies savagely, intensely focused on the exercises his therapist is making him do.

"I'm only trying to be supportive!" I whine, starting another set of reps. Although really, I quite like having things shoved up my ass.

Noah says something through gritted teeth that not even my hellhound hearing can make out, but given the murderous expression on his face, that's probably just as well. I'm sure it would hurt my feelings, and then he'd regret it later and have to deal with the crushing pile of guilt as well as everything else he's got on his plate.

I finish up my workout and watch quietly as Noah strains through the last of his. It's hard for me to tell, because I've never been good at judging human strength capabilities, but he seems to be doing really well. Since the last time I was here, he's definitely made progress. Part of that is probably because Andrew is constantly shoving nutrient-rich protein bars in his hand.

Speaking of Andrew…

Right on cue, my phone vibrates in my pocket. The team has talked at great length about our oldest member's inability to stop fretting over Noah—it's out of character for the ordinarily laissez-faire eight-hundred-year-old vampire. On the other hand, when you've waited nearly nine centuries to fall in love and then your love is almost killed doing something that's supposed to be impossible, it stands to reason that you might become a little paranoid.

I pull out my phone and read the text.

ANDREW:

How's it going? Is he nearly finished? Does he need me to come and help him with his shower?

I roll my eyes.

We still haven't finished that conversation about why you were KEEPING SECRETS from me, your beloved secondary best friend.

Again with this crap? Just tell me how Noah is. Should I come down there?

It's shocking how you managed to keep your feelings for Noah HIDDEN from us all for so long, especially me, your beloved secondary best friend.

I'm coming down there.

Noah's fine. He's swearing like he invented the words and nearly done. Now let's talk about how deception is a terrible thing for a secondary best friendship.

Does he need me to come and help him with his shower?

And what even is a secondary best friendship?

Do you remember what happened last time you insisted on coming to help with his shower? I'm not asking him in case he decides to turn that wrath on me. If he needs help, he'll say so.

How can you deny our secondary best friendship like this? You wound me. It's like a knife right through my heart.

I'm not denying anything—yet. I just don't know what it is. Did you make it up or is it some weird hellhound thing?

MAKE IT UP??? Make up only the second most powerful type of friendship there is? Oh, if only I wielded that kind of power!

Okay, it's been fun, but if Noah doesn't need me, I actually do have work to do. Stay biped while he's in the shower in case he falls or something—DO NOT let me hear about you chasing your tail or licking your balls while my boyfriend needs help.

You're just jealous you can't lick your balls.

"Is that Andrew?"

I look up at Noah. He's standing in front of me, sweaty and mussed, while his physio is putting away the equipment they used.

"Yep." I turn the phone around to show him. "Don't worry, he's not coming down unless you ask him to."

Noah shakes his head. "I love him, but sometimes I want to smother him with a pillow the way he's smothering me with concern."

I smile. "Aww. You should have that printed on one of those fancy wall stickers and put it on the wall in your bedroom. You could have the outline of a heart around it with the heading True Love."

He rolls his eyes and huffs, but there's a tiny hint of a smile on his mouth. "I'm going to shower."

I fall in step beside him, slowing my usual pace to match his slightly shaky one. "Me too. Although your vampire Daddy says I'm not allowed to shift and lick my balls in the locker room in case you need me to—"

He stops so sharply that I take two more steps before I even realize and turn back. There's a look of horror on his face that has me scanning for the threat.

Nothing.

"What?" I ask, and he sputters.

"I… what… I don't even know where to start! Wait, yes, I do—don't you *ever* call Andrew that again. My *vampire Daddy*? What the fuck have you been snorting?"

"Oh, come on! What else should I call it? He's a much older—much *much* older—man who insists on taking care of you. And he's a vampire. It fits perfectly."

His glare is terrifying, even though I can see the slight tremor racing through his exhausted muscles. I prudently take a step back. He hasn't been using the magic during his recovery, since nobody's sure if it would hinder him, but I'm fully aware he's capable of throwing fireballs if he wants to.

"He insists on taking care of me because I almost *died*, you nutjob, and I still barely have the strength to get through the day." His expression changes suddenly, and he sighs. "Maybe I shouldn't smother him after all," he concedes. "You're still an asshole, though. Do you really lick your own balls? And in a public place?"

Snorting, I offer him an arm to lean on as we continue to the locker room. It's not far—the staff gym attached to CSG is small—but he's pushed himself pretty hard this morning and probably needs to sit down for a bit. "You only wish you could lick your own balls. All you people who can't do it seem to talk about it an awful lot. And, dude, when I'm in canid form, they're right out there for everyone to see anyway—what does it matter if I'm licking them or not?"

He just shakes his head, seemingly lost for words. It's so true, though. Other species talk about hellhounds licking balls *all the time*. We don't ever bring it up—we just do it. Even the cursed cats—felid shifters—get all weird about it, and they're capable of doing it themselves.

I don't think I've ever seen a felid licking their balls, though. They've gotta, right? I mean… why would anyone waste that ability? Maybe they're just squeamish about doing it in public.

In the locker room, I make Noah sit on a bench while I get his towel and body wash, turn on the water in one of the shower stalls, and then find the shower stool Andrew insisted on bringing in. I know Noah hates using it, but I stick it in the stall anyway—it's his call if he wants to ignore it, but at least I know I've done the right thing. I think he'll use it today, though.

I go back to get him, and as he hauls himself to his feet, I ask quietly, "Do you want some help? Or I can call Andrew?"

His smile is tired. "Spot me walking over, if you don't mind," he says. "I'll be okay in there. I might take a break before going back upstairs."

Super. Fucking. Badass.

Anyone who says humans are a lesser species has no idea what they're talking about.

ANDREW POUNCES on us the second we reach the doorway to our shared office. Noah refused to use the wheelchair that Andrew brings everywhere "just in case," so our journey from the gym has been slow, and he's leaning on me a little.

Which has Andrew thinking the worst.

"I'm fine," Noah snaps irritably, swatting him away as though he were a fly. I really enjoy watching that. Especially because Andrew swoops right back in, just like a fly would. Hmm… vampire fly?

With quite a bit of fussing and fidgeting, they get Noah settled in his desk chair. I can tell Andrew wants to suggest going home for a nap, but the set of Noah's jaw obviously deters him, and he goes back to his desk to pretend to work while he actually watches Noah obsessively.

It's sweet.

But Noah's going to snap and go on a killing spree, I can tell, so I do my part to save Andrew's life by going over and planting myself on the edge of his desk.

His gaze immediately shoots to me, then back to Noah, then, more slowly, back to me. Then down to where my ass is perched on top of his to-do list.

"Did you need something?" he asks dryly.

"We never finished our chat about our secondary best friendship," I declare with a smile, wriggling my ass a bit just to hear the paper crinkle.

He laughs. "You are such a shit-stirrer," he says amiably, leaning back in his chair and turning slightly so he can keep one eye on Noah while he's talking to me. "Okay, tell me about our secondary best friendship."

"Well," I begin, "obviously Sam's my bestest BFF and nobody can ever take him away from me. Gideon tried but failed."

"Say what?" Sam raises his head from where he's staring at his screen. "Gideon and I are in a committed relationship. What are you even talking about?"

"Ah, but we're still bestest besties. Forever. That's a lot of years, Sam. Not even Gideon could sunder the bond between us."

Sam sighs and returns his attention to what he was working on.

"But you," I turn back to Andrew, "you're my secondary best friend. Our bond is also forever, even though it's much newer. The friendship we have is different from what I have with Sam. He feeds me and tells me how pretty I am. You do the Macarena with me and know all the choreography to 'Baby, One More Time.'"

"Britney is a pop icon," he agrees. Noah and Sam

both groan, although I happen to know that Sam likes to sing "Oops I Did It Again" while he's cleaning.

"Right? So you're my secondary best friend."

"Wait," Noah says, sounding reluctantly curious. "Andrew's your secondary best friend, and oh my god, I can't believe I just said those words, but are you his? Or are you his primary best friend?"

"Bestest bestie," I correct, because the terminology is important. "No, it doesn't work that way. It has to be a completely reciprocal relationship level, or people can get jealous and schisms form. Entire nations have gone to war because of that."

"Sure they have." He looks at Andrew. "So who's your best friend?"

"You," Andrew says promptly, and we all laugh.

"No," Noah says. "I mean, yes, but I'm your boyfriend best friend. It's a completely different level of relationship. Fuck me, they've sucked me into the vortex of their idiocy."

"There's no escape, either," Sam commiserates. "Once you're in, that's it. They have you for *life*."

"At least my life won't last as long as yours," Noah mutters. "Freedom is only half a century or so away."

From the way Andrew tenses, I figure this would be the best time to get the conversation back on track.

"Yeah, Andrew, who's your bestest BFF?" I ask, drawing the words out because they sound so much better that way.

"I always walk in on the weirdest conversations," David says from the doorway. "Do you guys time it or something? Wait until you hear me coming? Or is this just how you are all the time when I'm not around?"

"David," Andrew says quickly. "If we're judging by people who will always feed me, then definitely David is my best friend."

David stops dead in his tracks halfway to his desk. "What did you just say? Why is this news to me?"

"He also needs to tell you that you're pretty," I remind Andrew.

We all look at David.

"I don't even know what's happening here," he says.

"You need to tell Andrew he's pretty," I instruct, "to seal the bond of your bestest best friendship."

"I still don't know what's happening here." He shakes his head, goes to his desk, and puts down his laptop.

The rest of us wait.

"Don't you think I'm pretty, David?" Andrew asks with a wicked gleam in his eye and a plaintive note in his voice.

"This isn't going to stop until I admit defeat, is it?" David asks Noah.

He shakes his head. "Really sorry you got dragged in, though."

David sighs. "Andrew, you're pretty."

I cheer. Andrew shoves me off his desk. Luckily, I am a hellhound, the epitome of grace and quick reflexes, and I land on my feet rather than sprawled across the floor.

"Percy's ready for you," David says before I can turn on the kicked puppy act and make Andrew grovel.

I look at my watch. "Shit." Fortunately, I'm not actually late, but still… I shake a finger at Andrew as I grab my phone and a notepad from my desk. "We will be having words later. You do not treat your secondary best friend like that."

As I leave, I hear David saying, "Do I really want to know?"

"It's Alistair," Sam replies. "Spare yourself."

They all love me so much.

CHAPTER TWO

Alistair

I KNOCK LIGHTLY on Percy's office door. He has an assistant, but she was on a call when I walked past her, so I'm not sure if I can just go in or not.

"Enter!"

So that's a yes.

I open the door and walk in, my sense of smell telling me immediately that Percy's not alone. Turning back to close the door again gives me a few extra seconds to compose myself.

The Irish cat. Aidan Byrne.

There's a lot to say about Aidan. He's the species leader of all shifters, both canid and felid. Like Percy's position as lucifer, it's a job conferred by the existential magic. You could be living your ordinary life, then one day you wake up and bam… you've been invested with the power to lead.

That better bloody never happen to me, is all I'm saying.

Anyway, Aidan is… well, he's a cat, for starters,

which tells you how uptight he is. I can't deny that he's very good at his job and very highly respected, and not just because we shifters have an intrinsic need to show respect to our leaders.

Does it sound like I have a problem with Aidan? Because I do. Just a little one. I can't quite bring myself to forget how quick he was to suggest compelling Sam's shift that first time. It turned out to be the best option, but a compelled shift is awful, an experience we actively avoid, and Aidan just threw it out there like it was a walk in the park.

My bestie deserved better than that.

But that's in the past, and the fact he's here and Percy's asked me to be here too means something is going on in the shifter world. Last I heard, he was still on the West Coast, visiting with the pack the traitors were from and trying to find out more about the elf people who can open portals between dimensions.

"Hi, Alistair," Percy calls from the small table by the window. "Come and join us."

I obey, like the good boy I am, but we're going to be awfully cozy with three of us sitting at that table. Lucky that felids aren't as big as hellhounds. Percy's not much over five and a half feet tall, and Aidan's only a few inches taller than that, and they're both slender. It makes me feel somewhat of a hulking beast as I pull out a chair and join them.

I do make a very good beast, though. I have the perfect growl and everything.

"Hello, Alistair," Aidan says, that faint Irish lilt coming out on my name.

"Good morning," I reply cheerfully to them both,

because I have a feeling I'm not going to enjoy this meeting, and it's worth getting some cheer in while I can.

"We'll jump right in," Percy begins. "You know Aidan has been with the Oregon pack for the last few weeks."

I nod. "Yes. Any luck?"

Aidan shakes his head. "Not really. It doesn't help that so much of what we know is classified and can't be shared. All I've been able to tell anyone is that the two lads we have in custody are being charged with an attack on government agents and that we suspect the involvement of three more. So far, I haven't even managed to confirm the identities of the ones Noah saw with Tish."

"Are people clamming up?" I'm a little surprised. Not that they'd want to protect their own, but that *nobody* is willing to talk to the species leader.

"I'm sure some are, but if I'm right in my suspicions, it's more that all five lads are from a very rural area and a very small, closely related subgroup within the pack."

It hits me what he's trying not to say. "You think everyone who knows them well is involved with Tish."

He shrugs and spreads his hands. "It's possible."

"Likely," Percy corrects. "As awful as it would be for this to be more than a group of young hellhounds seduced by the promise of wealth, I think we need to assume it may actually be an ideology that led them to follow Tish."

I rub my hand through my hair. "I hate that idea," I admit, "but yeah, it's probably true. Has the pack leader been able to give you any information about the group?"

"Some," Aidan concedes. "But he says they keep to

themselves a lot, and as long as they were appearing to follow the law and not causing trouble, he had no reason to question that. You know how packs are, Alistair. This isn't some human werewolf movie. Pack leader is a localized governance position, not a feudal king."

"And since we're trying to keep this low-key, neither he nor you can compel anyone to talk." I sigh. Not that I like the idea of compelling anyone—it really is *awful* —but we're dealing with a crisis of gargantuan levels here.

Tish is trying to enslave humanity.

In his mission to do so, he's spent more than forty years experimenting on members of our community.

He's also in league with dimension-hopping elves. We don't know what their aim is. All we know is that we have to find some way to stop them all. Tish is not only guilty of murder on a massive scale, he's also very close to exposing us all to humans. And that wouldn't go well. There's a reason we've been hidden from them for the past nearly nine thousand years, and that's because they tried to exterminate us.

"So, what do you need from me?" It's obvious there's something. Why else would I be here?

Percy smiles, and I immediately feel like I'm being rewarded. It's a side effect of his investiture as lucifer, but I still like it.

"We think the pack might respond better to a hell-hound who isn't officially in a position of authority. Aidan's the species leader *and* a cat, and they're used to thinking of their pack leader as being an authority as well. Someone who seems less official who's there just to tie up some reporting loose ends might have more luck —not with that particular subgroup, especially if they're working with Tish, but with other members of the larger pack who might have information."

"The adolescent ones, especially, seemed rather awestruck when I tried to actually talk to them," Aidan adds dryly. "It was a bloody awkward experience, with some of them twice my size."

None of us bothers to comment that size really doesn't matter when you're taking on the species leader. The existential magic invested Aidan with the job, and the magic has a way of making sure its favorites are taken care of.

"So you want me to go out to Oregon and talk to people? Sure, I can do that. People *love* me." It's true. I'm sure you've noticed.

"Wonderful," Percy says with another smile. "I'll need Aidan for some other matters this afternoon, but you can leave first thing tomorrow."

Wait… what?

If he needs Aidan, why does that mean I can't go until tomorrow?

Unless…

I try to keep the horror off my face. "Uh, just throwing it out there, but maybe Ellie would be a better choice for this? She's, um, got… um… that sweet face." I'm really proud of myself for not choking on that last bit. Have you met my cousin and teammate, Elinor? She's got razor-sharp wit, intelligence out the wazoo, and hand-to-hand fighting skills that make people weep —literally and figuratively—but she does not have a sweet face.

Percy seems surprised; not that I can blame him. "Is there a problem?" he asks.

"No, no," I protest. "Just… Ellie…"

"Elinor is barely healed after the attack," Percy reminds me. "And as one of the agents assaulted, it's hardly best practice for her to be directly involved in the investigation. What's the issue here, Alistair?"

I don't want to spend the next however long in close proximity with the Irish cat. But I can't say that.

"There's no issue," I say finally. "I just thought El might want to see this through to the end, but you're right, that would be inappropriate. I'll make sure my current cases are handed over and be ready to fly out tomorrow." With Aidan Byrne. Kill me now.

"Excellent," Percy says, although his smile is a little forced this time, and I feel it like a blow. This is not the best way to be impressing my boss—not to mention it's a time of crisis and I'm waffling around like an idiot instead of competently stepping up to do my job.

"Did you need me for anything else?"

"That'll do," Aidan says. "I can brief you more fully on the pack during the flight. Although, you're familiar with them already, aren't you? Percy said you identified the three intruders in the office as being from the Oregon pack."

"I've been there a few times," I confirm. "If the pack leader is the same as sixty years ago, we've met. And yeah, I identified they were from Oregon by smell… which means," I realize belatedly, "I can probably tell you if they have close relatives among that subgroup. And if they've been there recently or have stuff there, I'll probably be able to smell it." My nose is good even for a hellhound.

"Good," Aidan says with a firm nod and an approving smile that causes conflicting feelings in me.

It's always nice when the species leader is happy with you, but I still don't like him.

"Okay, I'll leave you to it." I smile and wave—*wave?* —as I get up and then beeline for the door. Safely on the other side, I lean against it and sigh.

What the fuck is wrong with me?

I go back to the office, sit in my desk chair, and then wheel over to Sam's desk and squish in right beside him.

"Fuck off, Alistair, I'm busy," he says, not looking away from his screen.

"Heeeeeeelp meeeeeee," I whine. "I need your help."

"I'm not calling your hookup from the other night to tell him to stop calling you," he says, his fingers not even pausing on the keyboard.

Fuck, I'd almost forgotten about that. That's two things I need his help with.

"Why not?" I lean in and rest my head on his shoulder. He shoves me away.

"Because you need to take responsibility for your own actions. Why did you even give him your number, anyway?"

"He was *hovering*," I say, remembering with some disgust. "Wouldn't leave, and the awkward silence was getting past awkward into annoying. Then he asked for my number, and I wanted him to go so much that I didn't even think of fake numbering him. I was way off my game." I shake my head sorrowfully. "I blame Noah and David and Ellie. I've been so worried about them that it's thrown everything else akimbo."

Across the room, Noah snorts. "Akimbo? Seriously? And, dude, don't be blaming me for your fucked-up dating life. I've heard the stories in the break room, and I do *not* want any association with that."

I wave a hand nonchalantly, unfortunately smacking Sam in the side of the head. "Those stories are exaggerated," I assure him. Mostly. Well… there's one or two I can't be sure about, due to being drunk out of my mind, but I'm actually happy to own those ones, so…

"I don't think akimbo is right in that context," Sam says thoughtfully, as if my choice of words is more important than the fact that I need him to help me.

"Saaaaaaaam. Saaaaaaaam."

"If you do that again, I'm going to tell Gideon I want the wards up all the time, no exceptions," Sam warns, *still* not looking my way.

I pout.

It takes nearly a full minute, and Sam's not the one who caves first. Noah is.

"For the love of god, what's it gonna take to get you out of here, Alistair?" he explodes.

"I need help," I whine again, doubling down on the pout and the puppy dog eyes. I am super adorable and irresistible like this.

"Help blowing off a hookup? Give me your phone and I'll do it," Noah demands.

Welp, not going to pass that up. I hop off my chair and cross the room to hand over my phone. "The unlock code is 658924," I tell him. Unlike *some* people, he doesn't question why I didn't unlock it with facial recognition. Shifters already can't use code or fingerprint to unlock phones and other digital devices—there's no point using facial recognition too often and having technology evolve to block us there too. The machines will one day rise up, and they hate shifters.

Probably because of the cats. We hellhounds are just wonderful.

Noah unlocks the phone and opens the call register. "This one?" he asks, pointing to the number at the top that's called me five times in three days.

"Yes." Just looking at it makes me feel glum. I hate having to reject people. That's how I ended up sleeping with this guy to begin with. He initiated a conversation, and before I could politely find a way to end it, he asked if I wanted to get out of the bar, and I... couldn't say no. It might have hurt his feelings.

Let nobody ever say that I don't sacrifice myself for the greater good.

Wait... is sex with strangers to avoid hurt feelings the greater good?

I ask Noah.

He stops tapping away at the phone keyboard and lifts his head to look at me incredulously. "What?"

"Oh fuck, Alistair, just shut the hell up," Sam groans from his desk. "No, you fucking strangers is not for the greater good. Greater good of what, for fucking fuck's sake?"

"We need to teach you new expletives," Andrew observes, piping up for the first time. "Fuck is a good one, but there are other words too."

Sam flips him the bird. He seems a bit irritable, and I wonder what's changed since this morning. He should be in a better mood after pancakes, porridge, and my company.

"Here." Noah thrusts the phone at me. "Done. If he tries calling again after this, just block him."

I eye him dubiously. I'm not sure I can do that— wouldn't it hurt his feelings?

Noah rolls his eyes. "Bring the phone to me and I'll block him."

That sounds doable. I smile happily and take my phone back, glancing down at Noah's text.

Whoa. I'm pretty sure that hurt his feelings.

I didn't send it, though, so I don't have to feel bad about it. Much.

"Thank you," I say politely as I back away. I'm definitely not going to do anything to get on Noah's bad side. Andrew must have balls of steel to piss him off all day and then go to sleep beside him at night.

I return to my chair, which is still right next to Sam, and sigh loudly.

Sam makes a sound that's very close to a sob. "What? What, Alistair? I have a pile of work so huge I can't even see the bottom of it, and I just found out Gideon is going to be away overnight, so tell me what the hell you want, and let's get it over with!"

Ohhhhhh. Gideon's going to be away. That's why he's being a little bitch. He lived on his own pretty much from when he was fourteen until about six months ago, but if Gideon's away for a night, he can't sleep.

It's disturbing.

"Let's have a slumber party! We'll all come over and keep you company while Gideon's away. Won't we, everyone?"

Noah's eyes are wide and he's shaking his head in horror, but as soon as Andrew says, "Not us. Noah needs to rest properly," his face changes.

"Of course we're going," he snaps, then cringes. But he doesn't take it back, and after one glance, Andrew doesn't argue.

"I really don't need you all to come over," Sam says.

"Of course you do! This will be good for us… and not to add to your stress, but tomorrow I'm leaving for Oregon, so this can be like a goodbye party and give you time to soak in my company before I go."

There's only a split-second hesitation before Sam says, "*Not* a party. No parties. Are we clear on that? If you come over tonight, there will be *no party*."

"No party," I promise dutifully. It's not a party when there're fewer than a dozen people, anyway. This will just be a gathering of friends with food and drink and dancing.

Sam hesitates again, but I know I've won him over. He really does hate it when Gideon has an overnight assignment.

"Okay." He gives in with a sigh. "And you're leaving for the West Coast tomorrow?"

I nod. "Percy and Aidan want to see if the Oregon pack reacts better to me asking questions than to Aidan."

"I heard he didn't have much luck," Andrew says. "Is he going back with you or staying here or heading home…?"

"He's coming with me." I manage to say it without making a face or anything, because I am super awesome, but Sam shifts slightly, so something must have given me away through our super-best-friend bond.

"I guess you need me to help you reassign your cases," he says, and I smile at him and rest my head on his shoulder.

"You're my favorite."

"So you've said before," he replies dryly. "Go away, and I'll send you an email with the reallocation. Are there any you want to keep?"

"I'll email you first," I promise. "Give me five minutes. Then I'll close out whatever I can before I make the plans for tonight and race home to pack."

"Plans for tonight?" He sounds alarmed. "There are no plans. Come over. I'll order takeout. That's it. That's all. No plans, Alistair."

I laugh. "Relax. I just meant I'll let Ellie and David know in case they want to come. I'll take care of the takeout too." Honestly, I don't know where all this distrust comes from.

CHAPTER THREE

Alistair

"When I kill you," Sam says in a conversational tone nine hours later, "I'll make sure it doesn't hurt, because you're my best friend."

"Awww." I sink deeper into the couch cushions, not sure if I should be grateful or offended. "Why are you killing me, again?"

"Alistair." He stops to take a long swig from the bottle of brew in his hand. "There is a bubble machine in my living room. And a fog machine. There are bubbles drifting in fog *in my living room.*"

I look around and smile in satisfaction. The room is really mellow and chill. A great way for Sam to relax and me to enjoy my last night off before what's probably going to be an intense assignment. "Isn't it great? I was going to get one of those laser light machine things, but I thought it might be overkill."

He chokes. "Overkill? Really? The lights would have been overkill?" He lifts the bottle to his mouth and drains it. That's his third, which I'm kind of happy about. Drunk Sam is a lot of fun. On the other hand, he does have to go to work tomorrow, and the last time he went to work hungover, Gideon nearly murdered me. I won't be here by the time Gideon finds out, but he does know where I live, so…

"Do you want some cake yet? I got cake and ice cream for dessert."

"In a minute," he replies. "First I want to pretend I don't hate you for this… this… whatever this is and be a good best friend."

"You're always a good best friend," I assure him. "Even when you and Gideon lock me out and I have to sit on your doorstep feeling abandoned until you let me in."

Sam holds up a finger. "Gimme just one second." He scrambles up from the couch and goes over to the food table I set up against the wall. Beneath it is a tub full of ice and drinks. He grabs another brew.

"Are you sure you want to do that, Sam?" Ellie calls from where she's curled in the window seat, talking to Noah. "You might regret it tomorrow."

"I need fortification right now," he replies, popping the top and coming back over to the couch.

Everyone turns to look at me.

I shrug. "I don't know why," I say, and my beloved cousin who used to cover for me sometimes when I got into trouble starts to laugh.

Sam plunks himself back down beside me. "Okay, now I'm ready. Let's talk about the fact that you're traveling across the country and will be working with Aidan."

I take a sip from my soda—I've reached my alcohol limit for the night before an important assignment. "What are we talking about?"

He raises an eyebrow at me. "Really?"

It's terrible when your bestest bestie knows you so well that you can't even hide from yourself.

"It's fine. He was right, and I need to deal with that. Still being angry about it is stupid. You're here and safe, and that's all that matters."

"I mean," Sam says, "I'll always be super grateful for the way you stood up for me, and I love that you care enough to actually be pissed off about this, but yeah, compelling the shift was the right decision in the end, and it all worked out. So why *are* you still angry? Especially when," he continues, not giving me a chance to reply, "Aidan has been so supportive and helpful to me while I've been learning about my new self. I would have thought you'd be grateful to him for helping me."

I wait a beat to make sure he's done. "I am grateful that he's helped you," I reply. "I'm also grateful that he was there and able to compel your first shift when it turned out that was the safest option. I know being angry is stupid. Maybe it's just leftover from how scared I was right then. I can't help my feelings."

"Feelings," Sam muses. "Feeeeeeeelings." He looks at me and quirks a brow.

"What?" Maybe letting him get that fourth brew was a mistake.

"I'm just saying, you can't help your feelings, but maybe they're not the feelings you think they are."

It takes me a few seconds to work my way through that, but then I make a sound that surprises us both.

"You think I have *feelings* for him?" I hiss. "Like, feeeeeelings?"

Sam shrugs. "Maybe. It's easy to confuse a crush with other emotions."

"No." I shake my head. "You're drunk. I don't even know him. The first time I met him was that day in Percy's office. We've never had a one-on-one conversation."

"Since when is a deep personal connection needed for a crush?" Sam asks altogether too reasonably.

Motherfucker, is he *right*? Could I have a crush on Aidan Byrne?

"Who's got a crush?" Andrew asks, leaning over the back of the couch.

"We're not sure," Sam says before I can stop him. "It's still under consideration."

"Does Alistair have a crush?" Elinor demands delightedly. "Tell me everything!" She abandons Noah and practically skids across the room, diving into the space between me and Sam and snuggling in. "Right, talk. Who? Do I know them? Have you fucked them yet?"

Noah groans. "Don't tell me it's the guy you made me text today. Because if he texts back after what I said to him, I don't think he's got enough self-worth to be in a relationship."

"There's no one," I insist. "Sam's been drinking, and he's so in love that he's seeing hearts everywhere he looks."

"But—" Sam begins.

"Are we ready for cake? And then karaoke."

There's a combination of cheers and groans, and Andrew starts chanting "Cake, cake, cake," distracting everyone from the stupid turn the conversation had taken.

I don't get crushes. Seriously, I don't. I've never had a crush in my life, because if I feel even an inkling of attraction to someone, I go for it. What's the worst that can happen? They say no? So what? I move on to the next person I find attractive. There's nothing sexy about someone who's not interested in you. And I haven't had real feelings for anyone for a very long time… and never will again.

So this idea that I might have a crush on Aidan Byrne… it's ridiculous.

I CREEP out of Sam's place early the next morning to make it to the airport on time. The others are still sacked out unconscious—I wore them out with my epic round-robin karaoke tournament. They just didn't have the stamina to keep up with me, although Ellie and Andrew certainly gave me a run for my money. Who knew he could do a falsetto like that?

Before I go, I turn the bubble machine back on. What better way to wake up the morning after a big night than to bubbles? I debate turning on the fog machine too but decide against it. Fog is moody, whereas bubbles are just fun.

I gobble down half a dozen Pop-Tarts while I wait for my ride. A proper breakfast would be nice, but I didn't want to risk waking everyone. Mostly because some of them drank a little too much last night and might blame me for it. It's totally not my fault that they agreed to the karaoke tournament rules and then sucked at it, requiring them to chug a whole bottle of brew every time they lost a round.

Still, better they don't see me until the hangover is

gone. I can get more to eat at the airport. The first-class lounge always has food.

Yep, we're flying first class. It's kind of necessary. First, because I'm six foot five and *not* slimly built, which means cramming into a seat in coach is torture not only for me but also for whoever gets stuck next to me. Also, shifters have very sharp senses, particularly smell and hearing. Flying is uncomfortable for us under the best conditions, what with being stuck in a vibrating tin can with recirculated air and engine noise. First class makes it slightly easier, what with the extra space.

I checked in online, and I only have carry-on luggage, so I go directly to the lounge, where I'm greeted with smiles and a chirpy "Welcome, Mr. Smythe." It's so nice to be appreciated. I smile back and wish the desk attendants a pleasant day, then make my way through the early business crowd in the lounge, keeping an eye out for an empty seat.

"Alistair."

It's not a yell—hellhound hearing is sharp enough that it doesn't need to be. But only another community member would know that, and I recognize the voice anyway, even before I turn.

Aidan lifts his chin as my gaze lands on him, then tilts his head toward the cushy armchair beside him, currently occupied by a laptop bag. He's saved me a seat.

I should be grateful for that, shouldn't I? Why, then, am I feeling only a kind of restless, gnawing energy?

Yesterday, I would have called that annoyance. I would have said I was still pissed off about how Aidan so cavalierly suggested compelling my bestie to shift.

Today, after said bestie planted other ideas in my

head, I can't help wondering if annoyance is the wrong word.

I make myself smile in acknowledgment and head in that direction. I'll say good morning, dump my stuff, and hit the buffet.

As I approach, I study him the way I would someone I met in a bar or a grocery store or fire station. I can't deny that he's attractive. He's got a typical cat build, lithe and lean, much shorter than me—maybe five eight? His skin is fair, almost translucently so in the way the Irish often are, but his features are sharp in a way that's both compelling and almost difficult to look at. His hair is the color of toffee, golden brown with just a hint of red when the light hits it, and his eyes are nearly the same color—a brown so light it looks like old gold. So, yeah, if he was just a random person I'd met at the pet store, I'd have come on to him. He's attractive even before you factor in the special aura being the species leader of all shifters has given him.

Maybe Sam's not wrong. Maybe it's not anger and dislike I've been feeling all this time.

I come to a stop in front of the pair of chairs, and he reaches across to move his bag for me. "Hi," I say. "Thanks for this." I nod to the chair as I put my bag in it. "I'm just going to grab something to eat—can I get you anything?"

He shakes his head. "Thanks, but I'll go when you get back. You won't be able to carry for both of us."

That's true, since I plan to load two or three plates for myself. "I won't be long," I promise and then hightail it away. I'm actually kind of ashamed of how relieved I feel to be walking away from him.

This is not good.

CHAPTER FOUR

Aidan

WATCHING Alistair walk away is a pleasure. I should probably feel shame for objectifying him that way, right? Especially since, technically, I'm in a position of authority over him.

Of course, since I'd never abuse my authority like that, and since I'm just looking, that argument doesn't hold water. So I'll just continue to admire the way his pants fit, thanks very much, and the lovely way his ass flexes with each step. Whatever he does to stay in shape, it's working beautifully.

I sigh and tear my gaze away. Too bad he actively avoids me—I wouldn't mind having the opportunity to admire him more often.

Before you start thinking I'm completely shallow, I do appreciate that Alistair is an intelligent and highly skilled professional, not just an attractive body. He wouldn't be here otherwise—Percy isn't in the habit of putting people in top-level jobs just because they're pretty, and neither am I. I sincerely believe Alistair will be successful where I haven't—I don't know him well, but I know his record, and he's excellent at pulling pieces together to show the whole picture. As a rule, people generally like him and react well to him, even under less than ideal circumstances. Plus, even though both felids and hellhounds are shifters and we have much closer biology than any other species—proven by the fact that there's only one magically invested species leader—there's still a bit of interspecies rivalry. The Oregon pack will likely respond better to another hellhound than a felid.

I hope.

Because we're running out of time. The longer we have no idea what Tish's plans are, the more likely it is that he'll succeed. And that just can't be allowed to happen. I've seen his research files—the number of people he kidnapped, experimented on, and murdered. Many of them were my people, my shifters. He can't be permitted to take any more lives, and he can't be permitted to expose us to humans. There's no way they'll just accept our existence happily. Even if Tish had succeeded in increasing our fertility and thus our numbers, the battles we'd face would wipe out huge numbers of us.

I don't think it will get to that point—I think the magic will step in to protect us as it did before. But last time, tens of thousands died first, and the "solution" upset our entire world order and changed the way the community existed. So it's probably better to just avoid the trauma of all that and stop Tish first.

Plus, we often forget that just because humans are largely unaware that existential magic is real doesn't mean the magic isn't aware of them. Humans are just as much children of the magic as we other species—and what happened with Noah Cage highlights that clearly. Tish's plan to enslave all of humanity would likely distress the magic just as much as the events of the species wars did, and the steps the magic takes this time might not work out so well for us.

That's the thing about the magic: we don't understand it. There are hundreds of scholars who've dedicated literally tens of thousands of years to studying existential magic, and we still know very little about it. Even people like me and Percy, who have regular personal contact with it, can't say how it works or even if it has sentience. We don't know how it selects the lucifer or pack/clan/species leaders. There doesn't seem to be a pattern in terms of bloodline or upbringing or even personality type. I never considered myself to be a leadership type of person until one day, when I was 182, I suddenly was. I can't even describe it completely—it's like a sense of awareness. There's a part of my brain that feels connected to each and every shifter alive, but it's not *personal*. I don't form emotional bonds through that connection. It's just as well, because at any second, the magic could remove leadership from me and give it to someone else. That's how it's always worked—very rarely has anyone died of old age in a magically invested leadership position. The magic likes to give people a decent chance at retirement.

But until the day comes that the magic decides my time as species leader is up, I will do my damndest to ensure the safety of all shifters. Right now, that means finding a way to work with Alistair Smythe, even if he's not fond of me.

And speaking of, here he comes. I stand and slide my phone into my pocket, clearing off the small table between our chairs for him to put his plates on. By the time I get back with mine, he should be done with at least one and have cleared space for me.

"All yours," he says cheerfully, jerking his head in the direction of the buffet. Getting food has clearly improved his mood. "They were just starting a fresh lot of bacon, if that interests you."

"It certainly does." My stomach growls on cue. I did have a light breakfast of sausage and eggs before I left the hotel, but that was well over an hour ago, and shifter metabolism doesn't appreciate "light" meals. "Back soon."

I WAIT until we reach cruising altitude before turning to Alistair. "Are you ready for a briefing?"

He sets down the empty package of nuts he wheedled out of the flight attendant before takeoff and nods. "Yes. Do you mind if I take notes?"

Ah, words to make my heart rejoice. "Go for it."

It takes him only a moment to pull out his phone and open what I recognize as the secure app CSG uses for file sharing. "Okay. What do I need to know?"

"Some of it you're probably already familiar with. The Oregon pack includes parts of Idaho and Washington, territory-wise, and has a little over two hundred thousand members." I make sure to pitch my voice at a level that only he can hear. The extra space in first class, the drone of the engine, and his acute hellhound hearing all work in our favor. "The current hellhound pack leader is based in Portland, which is unusual for them but convenient for us, and his name is Jun Chew.

He's been in his position for about seventy or so years, and he's quite well respected by his pack and others within the community. The pack as a whole has a good reputation amongst the community and has solid relationships with other species, particularly the felid clan in the area."

He's rapidly taking notes in some kind of shorthand, even though I'm positive this is information he'd already have. I wait for him to catch up and glance at me.

"The subgroup we believe is involved lives in Beker County, just outside Beker City. The community population there is lower than usual for a rural area, although nobody I've spoken to can say why. Further, the vast majority of that population is made up of hellhounds, which is also highly unusual." I have a theory about that, of course, and Percy agrees, but I'm interested to see what Alistair's thoughts are.

Sure enough, he looks up from his phone. "When you say 'vast majority'…?"

"Of the twelve hundred-ish community members, more than half are hellhounds."

"Whoa. There's something not right there. How many of those hellhounds are connected to the families of our captives?"

"Connected how?" I counter. "It's a small section of the community. I'd say they all know each other by sight and name, at least. Blood and marriage ties are rife, since it's rare for new people to move into the area. There's probably three degrees of separation at most between any two of them."

He shakes his head. "What did Jun have to say about the Beker County community? For that matter, what did the local felid clan leader say?"

See? I knew he'd cut to the heart of the matter right away. "Jun has had concerns for some time, but since there have been no complaints and no overt trouble, there's not much he can do. Everyone is helpful and respectful when he visits. The numbers in the area are unusual, but there's no indication that's due to anything the hellhounds have done."

"Bullshit," he says firmly. "You know that's bullshit. I can see the numbers for vampires, demons, and incubi and succubae being lower outside a big city, but the number of cats should come a lot closer to matching that of hellhounds. Population density is low, and if I'm visualizing the right part of the map, it's a mountainous and largely forested area. That's paradise for shifters. And it's not exactly cut off from the rest of the world—if I remember right, Beker City even has a small airport." He stops abruptly. "You never did say what the Oregon felid clan leader had to say."

"The clan leader—her name is Riona—said pretty much the same things as Jun. She's spoken to her people in the area several times, assured them that she can help if they ever feel threatened or unsafe, but they've always responded that they're fine. She even went so far as to chase up some families who'd moved away, but nobody had a single complaint to make. They all had reasons for leaving that didn't include being run out of the area." I wait a beat, then add, "Percy and I agree that it still seems odd, so he reached out to other species leaders and asked them to speak to their local counterparts."

He raises his eyebrows, but it's kind of lopsided. Like he meant to raise only one but can't do it.

"And?"

I drag myself away from my fascination with his

eyebrows. "And they've all had similar experiences. If hellhounds have genuinely been running other species out of the area, they've terrified those people so much that they've all become champion actors and don't feel safe talking about it even years and half a continent later."

He appears to think about that. "It's pretty clear that something's going on in Beker County, and having two, possibly five, hellhounds from that area involved in the recent attacks weighs heavily that the something is connected to Tish." He hesitates. "We assume that people are leaving the area because they feel threatened, but what if it's not that? What if over the years, Tish's people have just excluded everyone else? We rely heavily on each other within the community—very few feel safe surrounded only by humans. If you didn't feel welcome and included amongst others of your own kind, what would you do?"

I blink slowly, turning the idea over in my head. "Move somewhere else. But you're talking about hundreds of people over decades. Could they really maintain a non-aggressive 'please leave' campaign for that long? Hellhounds as a group tend to be warm and welcoming."

He grins. "We are loveable, aren't we? The point is, though, that if a vampire or a cat moved to the area, the first people they'd reach out to—or expect to reach out to them—would be other vampires or cats. They'd happily mix in with the community at large, but if their own species was just politely distant, they probably wouldn't feel inclined to be rebuffed by other species."

It's astounding, but he might be right. Community members are very much dependent on each other. If they'd moved to an area as sparsely populated as Beker County and found humans to be the only truly welcoming people, they'd probably be inclined to leave. Especially a family. Our young are quite vulnerable."

"By that reasoning," I say slowly, "almost every community member in the area is involved with Tish."

His grin is long gone now. "That's my bet. I can't say for sure, of course, but I think we need to treat the area as hostile and proceed with caution." He chews on his lip, drawing my attention to the reddened flesh. "I don't know why the area skews so much toward hellhounds, though. I didn't think we as a subspecies were so susceptible to being recruited by a madman."

I tear my mind away from its daydreams about Alistair's lip and say, "Remember that they may not know the whole truth. Some likely do, but most newcomers and the younger generations are probably being seduced with the idea of higher fertility rates and not being told exactly how that's happening or what Tish's end game is."

"Maybe." He doesn't seem convinced. "They do know that our leadership and government are selected by the magic, though, so— Hey. How did they react to you personally? Not the leaders, but the regular pack members?"

I'm not quite sure where he's going with this, but I obligingly cast my mind back over the interactions I had. "It's hard to say," I finally admit. "Obviously, I didn't meet all of them, just those with close connections to the two lads in custody. Some of the younger ones seemed a little intimidated and... surprised? But I put that down to them not being used to dealing with people outside their pack; plus, I am the species leader." It's hard not to sound like a douche while saying that, but it's true. Most people don't ever get to have a one-on-one discussion with their species leader; it's natural for there to be some discomfort, if only because it feels odd to them that they should be so instantly comfortable with me. A contradiction, but true.

He's quiet for a minute, and I'm reminded again why he's a member of Percy's senior investigative team. Hellhounds have a (deserved) rep for being rambunctious and outrageous. They definitely have more energy and melodrama than any other species, but that doesn't mean they're less intelligent or lack the ability to be serious and ruthlessly incisive.

"I have a theory," he says at last. "It's… not a great one. I mean, if it can be proved, it would be bad. The theory itself is actually pretty ingenious." He sounds simultaneously unhappy and proud of himself, which is quite a feat.

"Hit me with it." I mentally brace.

"Revolution or insurrection is so rare in the community because our leaders are selected by the magic, yeah? And if any leader begins to abuse their power, the magic takes it from them. Existential magic, as far as we can tell, is devoted to protecting all species and this planet."

I nod slowly. "Right."

"So if you were planning to revolt against CSG and the lucifer and all the species leaders with an act that would upset the balance between species and endanger one or more of them, how would you convince others to join you?"

"Personal gain." It's the obvious answer, but… "Except not everyone you need to convince will be swayed by that. Something that seems more selfless and beneficial for the community, like improving fertility rates."

"Yes, but if someone came to me and said they could improve fertility rates and needed my help, my first question would be why they weren't reaching out to the lucifer and CSG for support. If it truly benefits everyone and does no harm, the government selected by the magic to protect us would support it, right?"

It hits me suddenly what he's getting at. "Unless you don't believe the government is selected by the magic. Or that the magic is actually devoted to our protection." Fuck. *Fuck.* "You think they're subverting the children."

"The hellhounds who were with Tish were young. Thirty-five, forty, right?"

"One was nearly fifty," I correct, but he's right, damn him. Tish's research would likely have been well underway when those hellhounds were old enough to learn about our society.

"We've been focused on the idea that Tish would need to wait for his research to play out and then implement it across the community and wait again for the birth rate to increase and then those people to grow up before he could raise a force sufficient to take on the humans. We've been convinced that because he's been patient with his research that he's playing a really long game. And we've always had the safeguard that people would need to buy in to his research, to allow him to change their genetic structure. Many within the community would take the word of the lucifer—who is selected by the magic—over his. But we didn't consider that he might already be building an army. All he has to do is convince his followers to change how they educate their children."

"How many members did the CCA have?" I ask, feeling sick. The young… we should always be protecting our children. How could they do this? I know the CCA—Coalition for Community Advancement—is basically just an anti-human cult, but I didn't think they'd go this far to advance their cause.

Alistair grimaces. "In this country? The information we confiscated from their compounds says a little over half a million. If you add in underage children, that number gets closer to a million. Around the world, including children, maybe eighteen million or so."

I sigh. "So, comparatively not that many, but still too many. And you think they're teaching their kids that Percy and I and the rest aren't actually selected by the magic?"

"Maybe." He shrugs. "I could be completely off base. But historically, organizations like the CCA would die out after a generation or two, or they'd have the occasional surge in membership, but mostly be low-key. Research showed it was because as children matured and were able to make their own decisions, they'd leave the cults and rejoin mainstream society. It's hard to believe the government is the enemy when you've been taught that the existential force that guides and protects us all has selected the government. The CCA has been slowly growing over the past century, and none of our analysts could work out why. That they've been brainwashing their kids makes sense."

I rub my forehead. "We need to call Percy when we land, have him and the rest of your team look into this possibility. I suspect he should also start looking for other small communities where the species numbers are skewed."

Alistair seems startled by that. "You think it's not a case of hellhounds being more susceptible to his plan, but rather some sort of… intra-community speciesism at the CCA?" Revulsion crosses his face, and I can't blame him. While it's natural for each species to congregate and feel more comfortable amongst themselves, we've always lived side by side and supported each other. Community isn't just a word for us. The idea that the CCA is segregating species is abhorrent.

"I hope not, but I fear so. It doesn't seem right that Tish and the CCA would be targeting only hellhounds for recruitment—and it doesn't play out in their numbers."

He's quiet for a moment. "Do you intend for us to go directly out to Beker City from Portland?"

I had, but now I'm second-guessing that plan. "I thought we'd take our time driving out and stop in a few other places along the way to talk to other pack members, but honestly, now I think our best bet is to set up base in Portland for a few days first and see if we can confirm any of your hypotheses. That may change our approach."

"I agree." He nods. "If I'm even close to being right on any of it, it's not safe for you to go back there."

Whoa. What?

He must see my surprise, because he adds, "We have to assume every community member in that area is associated with Tish and the CCA and would see your presence as a threat. Even with your abilities as species leader, there's no way you could hold your own against that many—nobody could. If you decide to go back there at this point, I would have to pull rank and forcibly detain you."

Is he joking? He's completely straight-faced, but that doesn't mean he's not joking. Right?

"You don't have that kind of rank," I point out. I'm the one who's a species leader, after all. *His* species leader.

His smile is smug. "Oh, I do. As one of the lucifer's senior team, I have the authority to take any action needed to protect the lucifer or any other magically invested person, including all species leaders. If the situation warrants it, I'm in charge."

I make a mental note to check that—it's genuinely never been an issue before—but outwardly, I merely smile back. "What a lovely thought. Do you often like to take charge?"

The second the words are out of my mouth, I regret them. They sound far more suggestive than I'd intended. It wasn't supposed to be an innuendo at all.

At first he seems shocked, then he goes a little pink —lucky bastard. If I blush, it's always flaming red—and then a wicked grin stretches his pretty mouth.

Feck. I'm in for it now, aren't I?

"Oh, I like to take turns at being in charge. It's nice to be the boss, but sometimes I just want someone else to… drive… me." He stares directly into my eyes.

I swallow. Is it warm on this plane?

"That's… nice." *Change the subject. Now. Before you say anything more idiotic.* "Regardless, we'll stay in Portland until we can work out more details. Maybe a few day trips out to smaller cities and towns, but we'll avoid Beker County for the time being." I look everywhere but directly at him. "It would be a good idea for you to get out and about as much as possible. You're the only person in the know who has smelled an elf and might recognize the scent again."

"I'd definitely recognize it if I smelled it again," he asserts. "Trust me. It's very distinct. Especially if they happen to be using their magic, or whatever they call it." He seems a little miffed that I'd question his ability, and I stifle a smile, regaining my composure.

"Excellent. I think we can agree that finding an elf would mean finding Tish and his associates." And hopefully there aren't an army of them. I've heard Noah's report on how the one at CSG was getting through the wards. If there are many of them capable of subverting our defenses that way, we're screwed.

"Yes. So I guess we'll need to find somewhere to stay in Portland." There's a heavy edge of doubt in his voice. I get it. We need somewhere secure, and hotels usually aren't.

"Jun might have room, but that probably won't give us the privacy we need. Is your phone secure? Can you try to find a short-stay executive apartment or something?" A house would be better, but since we're not planning to be here long—days, a week at most—that might be trickier to get so last-minute.

"My phone is secure, and I'm going to text Sam right now and have him find something for us," he says, tapping his screen. "He'll be able to solve this issue in about a quarter of the time it would take me."

"Ask him to set up a meeting with Percy and the rest of your team too," I say. "As soon as possible after we land."

"Got it," he says, and bites his lip.

I really wish he'd stop doing that.

More, I really wish I could stop wanting to be the one doing it.

CHAPTER FIVE

Alistair

Fuck me sideways with a cactus. Was Aidan flirting with me?

That's the thought that's been on repeat in my head for the past seven-ish hours. All through the rest of our flight. Through the airport in Portland, and while we picked up our hire car. Through my phone call with Sam when he gave us the details of the short-term rental condo he found us. Through the drive in rush-hour traffic.

I'm getting pretty tired of that thought. Especially since my brain doesn't seem to have an answer for it. Do I even want an answer?

Yeah. I do.

The past day has been a real eye-opener for me. I thought I had a problem with Aidan. The truth is, I have a crush on him, and that's new for me. I don't know what to do next.

Like… am I supposed to care about him?

Not that I *don't* care. He's another living being, a sort-of colleague, I guess, and my species leader. I care about his general well-being, sure. I wouldn't want anything bad to happen to him—in fact, it's my job to actively prevent that.

But am I supposed to want to date him or something? Because I don't think I do. Not that I've ever really wanted to date anyone—it just seemed like the necessary step between meeting them and sex. With the modern relaxation of the stigma around casual sex, it's mostly not needed anymore.

So can it be a crush if all I really want is to dirty him up between the sheets? What's a crush without feelings called?

This is all too confusing.

I park the car in the driveway. The condo complex is made up of eight or so townhouses all stuck together, with tiny postage-stamp-sized front lawns. It's not perfect, but it shits on a hotel.

There's a key box by the front door, and Aidan gets out of the car and goes to input the code. A moment later, the garage door begins to open, and he comes back with a remote in his hand as well as two sets of keys. I wait for him to close the car door before pulling into the garage, even though it would have been more fun to do it with the door open.

Sam yelled at me last time I did that.

For a moment, as the garage door comes down behind us, Aidan and I just sit in the car—I don't know why. Finally, he sighs and says, "We've an hour before the call with your team. Let's order some food and get set up."

Food. Oh, fuck yes. I'm so hungry—we paused at the airport for subs and doughnuts, since the food on the plane was not as plentiful as it could have been, but that was barely enough to touch the sides of my stomach. "Excellent plan," I tell him as we get out of the car. "If you order the food, I'll bring our stuff in and look up where the nearest grocery store is." I hope there's a community grocer close by. Shopping at a human-run store is a pain—you get odd stares when you fill two carts and then come back to do the same the next day. Humans really have no idea how much food it takes to sustain shifters.

Not that humans know we exist. But if they did, they'd be shocked by how much food we need. After they finished being shocked about our existence.

"I can manage that," he agrees, leaning against the car and pulling out his phone. He tosses me a set of keys. "Any preference?"

"Food," I say bluntly, and he laughs. "Whatever can get here fastest, to start with."

"Done."

I leave him scrolling through a delivery app and unlock the door into the house, carrying our bags in one hand. The garage opens directly into the open-plan downstairs living area, right near the kitchen, which looks out over a tiny back courtyard. A door to my right presumably leads out there. A huge island with a line of stools along one side separates the kitchen from the living room. There's no dining table, but given the size of the island, we won't need one.

On the far wall is a staircase leading up, and beside it, a door—which a quick check shows me is a small half bath-slash-laundry room.

Upstairs, four doors lead off the hallway. The one closest to the stairs is a bathroom, nicely appointed and complete with tub and walk-in shower stall. I also like the look of the fluffy towels on the rail—they're nice and big. Let me tell you, puny towels suck ass. I'm six five and not skinny—I need a towel that will actually dry all of me, not give up the ghost halfway through.

The next door is a decent bedroom with a full-size bed… so not the room for me. My legs would hang over the end of the mattress. Depending on what else I find, this might be Aidan's room.

Door number three is a bit better—this room has a queen bed *and* a plush armchair with a little table beside it. I could handle this.

But I'm betting the last room is the master suite—a new-build house this size wouldn't have only one full bathroom, so there's probably an en-suite bath attached to a nice big room. Maybe it will even have a king-size bed.

Bubbling with anticipation, I leave our bags in the hallway and reach for the last door, pushing it open slowly, drawing out the tension.

YES! Jackpot.

The master suite does indeed have a king-size bed. It also has a comfortable-looking pair of armchairs by the window and two doors on the far wall. One is open to show an en-suite bath. A quick check of the other reveals a walk-in closet.

This is my room. It's only logical. Aidan doesn't need such a big bed, right? Three of him could fit in that thing.

That thought should not make me horny.

I grab my bag from the hallway, then reconsider and take a moment to put Aidan's in the queen-bed room, leaving the door open so he can see it. After dumping my stuff, I grab my laptop and make sure my door is closed before I head downstairs. I don't want him seeing the bigger room and getting ideas about seniority and all that crap.

In the living room, I set up my laptop on the island and log in to the community web. By the time Aidan comes in a minute later, still talking on his phone, I've located the closest three community grocers, but none are within a half-hour drive. If we're here for a while, I'll make the trip, but for the short-term, it'll be easier to just shop human.

Aidan ends his call and says, "The first delivery should be only ten minutes away. It's pizza, which will take the edge off while we wait for the rest."

"Thank you," I say fervently. "Depending on how long the meeting goes, I'll go food shopping either later tonight or first thing in the morning."

"No hassle," he assures me. "There's a decent range of takeout places in this neighborhood, so we should be able to get by with stocking only snacks and emergency food."

This is the plight of the shifter, my friend. No other species can truly appreciate the trauma we experience just trying to stay fed.

"I put your bag upstairs," I add as casually as I can. "One of the rooms is on the smallish side, but the other two are good." He does *not* need to know that mine is better than his.

"Thanks. I'll be back." He crosses the room and takes the stairs two at a time. I sneak a peek from the corner of my eye. Cats do have a certain grace that's very appealing. Watching his lithe body leap up the stairs makes my cock stir in interest.

Hmm. Maybe I should just see if he's up for a fuck?

I hear a door open upstairs, and then he laughs.

Uh-oh. I can't imagine why he would be laughing at the bathroom or the small bedroom—and I think I left those doors open, anyway.

Whoops.

At least he doesn't sound mad.

A few minutes later, he comes back downstairs still grinning and carrying his laptop. "The other two are good, huh?" he asks.

Fake him out, stonewall. "Yes," I agree, pretending great interest in my emails. He chuckles but says nothing else, instead getting himself set up at the other end of the island. While I appreciate the respect for my space, part of me wishes he was closer. Maybe then I'd be able to figure out what the fuck is going on with me. Could it be pheromones? I don't know what they are exactly, but I watched this movie once where the attraction between two characters was explained as being pheromones they were smelling without realizing it. Hellhounds do have an awesome sense of smell, and my nose is pretty refined even for a hellhound. I'm like the chief sniffer. The sniff leader. The supreme snifferoo.

My nose is good.

I'm considering a Google search on pheromones when the doorbell rings.

"Pizza!" I leap off my stool and beeline for the door, Aidan close behind me. The delivery guy stumbles back a few steps when I wrench the door open.

"Whoa. Uh. Aidan?" He looks between us, and I can see that he's wondering if he should run.

"That's me," Aidan says cheerfully. "Let me take those." He grabs the four extra-large pizzas. The kid has no choice but to give them up. "Do I need to sign anything?" Aidan checks as he passes the pizzas to me. The smell is intoxicating, and I draw it into my lungs, wondering if it would be too rude to start eating right this second. I should wait for Aidan, right?

"N-No, it's all good," the delivery kid stammers, taking the tip Aidan offers. From the way his eyes widen, it's a good one.

"Thanks!" I blurt. If I can't eat until he leaves, then he needs to leave.

Aidan smiles cheerfully and calls a goodbye, but I'm already retreating into the house. By the time he closes the door, I've got the pizzas spread out in the space between our laptops and am flipping open the first box.

He joins me, and I cast him a sideways look. "You're not going to insist on plates and forks, are you?" I ask warily.

He snorts and snags the first slice. "It's pizza, not rice."

Wow, he just got a hundred times hotter.

After that, we don't talk at all, focusing on getting food into our stomachs. The first two pizzas are gone when the doorbell rings again, and this time I let him get it. I have food.

He comes back with bags of the cardboard cartons that denote Asian food. "Chinese?" I ask, and he replies, "Korean."

I moan. "Barbecue?" It's not a real question—I can smell it now that I'm trying.

The look he gives me clearly shows how offended he is by that question. "Of course. There are chopsticks in one of the bags—unless you need a fork?"

It's my turn to give him an offended look, and he snickers. Shifters have made eating a must-know in any culture, plus I've traveled a fair bit. There are few tables around the world that I can't comfortably assimilate into.

The doorbell rings once more, this time with an array of salads and bread. The fresh vegetables and greens are welcome after a day of eating mostly fast food.

There's not a lot left when we begin clearing away in preparation for the call with my team, and we'll probably polish that off later in the evening.

"How much did you tell Sam?" Aidan asks, settling back in front of his laptop.

I shrug. "Not much. It would have taken a while to explain via text, and knowing Sam, there would have been a million questions. I told him it was urgent, that we had a theory, and to please set up a call." As if on cue, the meeting app on my laptop chimes. "Ready?" I ask, and Aidan moves along the island and sits on the stool beside me.

Every nerve ending in my body goes crazy, and I'm half hard. How did I ever mistake this for leftover anger? Maybe I'm stupider than I thought.

Angling the screen so we can both see it, I hit Accept. There's a moment of static while the encryption resolves, and then Percy's office appears on the screen. That surprises me for a second until I remember that he does have a great teleconferencing setup in there.

"Can you hear us, Al?" Sam asks, sitting at Percy's desk and looking at the laptop in front of him instead of at me on the wall screen.

"I'm sorry, are you speaking to me? It's hard to tell while you're looking at something else."

Beside me, Aidan makes a sound that could be a cough or could be him choking on his own spit.

"He can hear me," Sam tells Percy, still not bothering to look at me, his bestest bestie, the person who always has his back! It's devastating. I need to tell him so.

"I'm devastated by your indifference, Sam. How can you be so cruel? So unfeeling? Our friendship—"

"*Anyway*," Gideon interrupts loudly. "What happened before you even got there that necessitated this meeting?"

"I was briefing Alistair, and he has a theory," Aidan says. "It's both interesting and terrifying. Tell them."

I run quickly through the details, summarizing what Aidan told me and explaining how we'd extrapolated from there. Andrew interrupts once to swear viciously, and I'm faced with a lot of grim expressions by the time I finish.

"This is not good," David says heavily, lines of strain around his eyes. He takes on too much—that's partly our fault. It's so easy to depend on him, but we should probably make an effort to remember that he's only one person.

"It's still only a theory," I say, because I know most of the research for this is going to fall on him and I want to make him feel better.

"Aidan," Percy says thoughtfully, "how many of the younger pack members in the area did you meet? Ones that would hypothetically have been raised without being properly educated."

I remember asking a similar question on the plane and realize I never followed that thought through.

"Not many," Aidan admits. "Maybe three or four?

Those who had very close ties to the two lads in custody. While the senior pack members were perfectly helpful and polite, they didn't exactly give me free rein to speak with everyone, and there was no reason I could use to insist and still fly under the radar."

"That's pretty much an admission of guilt right there," Andrew says. "If your species leader came to your out-of-the-way town, wouldn't you be going out of your way to make them welcome—and introducing as many pack members as possible? It's not an opportunity that comes around often. Helpful and polite but not overtly welcoming is a neon sign that says go away and don't pay attention to us."

Ellie makes an agreeing noise. "Al, you were probably too little to remember, but we had the species leader visit our pack once—Shian. She was, what, two leaders ago? The pack leader basically held a weeklong open house for everyone to meet her, and we lived in a much more densely populated area than Beker County. It was an incredible experience—we get taught about the magic, and we feel it in ourselves, but if you don't have interactions with a pack leader or other leader, it's hard to understand that it really does tie us all together."

A very old, very hazy memory stirs in the back of my head. "Yeah," I say slowly. "I think I remember... Mama made me wear my good shirt and trousers. I didn't want to visit the stupid 'special' lady. She told Aloysius to get her a switch, so I apologized and sulked the whole way there. Then I saw all the sweets, but Mama wouldn't let me have any until after I met the leader. I was thinking about having a very loud tantrum when someone came over and touched my head. It must have been her—the species leader. She smelled good and safe and she made me feel calm and happy." It's mostly dimmed by time and the perspective of a young child, but that moment stands out.

"There, see!" Andrew points at me—well, at the screen. "If you were a senior member of a pack and could give that opportunity to your little ones, wouldn't you?"

We all look at Aidan. "How did the young ones react when they met you?" Percy asks.

Aidan sighs and shakes his head. "I can't say for sure. Their surprise could have been because they're not used to outsiders."

"Or they felt the connection through the magic," Ellie counters, "and had no idea what it was."

"Maybe you should go back to visit the two we have in custody," Sam muses. "We were clearly asking the wrong questions."

We all fall silent, because damn him, we should have thought of that sooner.

Aidan looks at me. "It would mean heading up to Washington," he says. "Are you up for another flight so soon?"

"Actually," David interjects before I can reply, "that's not possible. When it became clear they were definitely from a local pack, I had them moved to minimize the risk of a jailbreak attempt. They're here."

"You didn't think to mention this?" Percy asks mildly, and David shrugs, a slight tint of color on his cheeks.

"It didn't come up. I figured this way they would be at hand if we needed to question them again anyway."

Percy nods. "This is better, actually. I'll go visit them myself. If the only real knowledge they have of the magic is from their short meeting with Aidan, then meeting me is likely to be a shock."

That's for sure. But I'm not loving the idea of the lucifer meeting face-to-face with insurrectionists.

"I'll come with you," Gideon says firmly. It's not a suggestion or question, and if I know Gideon—which I like to think I do, since he's shacked up with my bestie—he'll bring along a squad of elite enforcers too.

Percy sighs but doesn't argue. "At the very least, we should be able to get them to talk about their education and find out what they've been taught about the magic and CSG."

"Yes," Aidan agrees. "They might not want to talk about their mission, but basic schooling from thirty or forty years ago is something they'd probably consider harmless. And in the meantime, Alistair and I will chat with pack members from outside Beker County. Jun said they've never done anything to overtly arouse suspicion, which means they have to have been participating in intra-pack events. Maybe someone will remember something unusual they said."

"Aim for the ones in the same age bracket," Ellie suggests. "It's been a while, but I seem to remember that any time we had pack gatherings, the kids and teens would inevitably end up playing some kind of reenactment of the species wars. It's impossible to do that without the magic and the lucifer coming into it somehow, so if anyone hadn't been taught about them, it would show."

"We used to do that too," Andrew muses. "I guess some things are just eternal."

I bite back a question about whether the Black Death had interfered in gatherings back then, because even though I'm safely across the country now, I do eventually have to go home and don't want him to kill me when I do.

"We'll target our questions around that kind of thing, then," I say instead. "Hopefully we'll be able to form a picture."

"And while you're doing that, Noah and I will start looking at census data," David says, making notes. "You're right. It's unlikely the CCA has built only a hellhound following. I don't know why they're segregating by species, but they've given us an easy way to find them."

Noah, who's been unusually quiet so far, chooses this moment to speak up. "Not to be a downer," he starts, and I instantly brace myself. I'm probably not going to like whatever he says next. "But we thought, based on all the records we confiscated from Tish's lab, that we'd located all the CCA compounds and arrested most of their people. Right?"

"We obviously missed this," Sam agrees. "I'll go back through the records. At the time, we were looking for encampments and CCA-owned buildings. We might have skimmed right past mentions of towns. Our focus wasn't on civilian members."

"Why not?" Noah asks. "Genuine question. I get that the scientists and trained soldiers were a higher risk to us, but why did we discount any mention of Joe Bloggs who supports the CCA?"

"Joe Bloggs?" Aidan murmurs questioningly.

I shake my head. "It's a human thing. He means a random or common man." The glare Noah shoots at the screen tells me he heard at least part of that.

Andrew answers. "Because centuries of research into

these groups has shown us that Joe Bloggs, as you call him, isn't an active danger. He probably doesn't even completely know or understand what the group he's supporting stands for. He would have heard some random rhetoric that fits with his own life motives and signed up to support the cause with a semiregular donation. Yes, he's a danger in that it's his support and his voice within society that gives birth and power to these terrorist organizations, but if they asked him to carry a weapon against the CSG, or to murder or enslave a human, he'd probably be shocked and appalled. We consider people like him to be part of a tertiary level of investigation—after the active members and their primary backers are taken care of, we look into those others to make sure they're not a greater danger than we thought."

"Obviously, Tish and the CCA have found a way to subvert that process," Noah points out. "If Alistair and Aidan are right, they're hiding large numbers of dedicated supporters in plain sight, seemingly unaffiliated with the CCA at all. It also means that the numbers we have for CCA members are wrong. We could be looking at a much more significant proportion of the population than we thought."

A sick, shocked silence falls. What a cheery thought that is.

"Okay," David says wearily. "Revised plan. Percy will try to find out what kind of education our two captives received, as well as anything else that might give us some idea of how the CCA is running these… cult towns."

"Avoid asking about the town directly," Aidan suggests. "Make it about the lads personally. They won't want to 'betray' their people, but might be willing to give up personal information in exchange for… what would you barter?"

"Better food," Gideon says immediately. "They're being fed sufficiently, but it's very plain fare. We could also offer them more time in the gym."

Ellie and I nod simultaneously. Those are exactly what would appeal to an incarcerated young hellhound. "See if they'd like a scratch-and-sniff book," I suggest. "I imagine there's not a lot of scent variation in the jail, and we hellhounds like to smell things."

"Scratch-and-sniff?" Sam asks incredulously. "Aren't they kids' books? Wait." He holds up his hand before I can answer. "I don't want to know. Thanks for the tip."

"Moving on," David says smoothly. "Aidan and Alistair will begin making connections within the larger part of the Oregon pack and see what interesting tidbits they can find out about the Beker County people. It might be an idea to touch base with some of the felid clan members also," he suggests. "I know cat numbers in the Beker area aren't comparable, but they do have some people there, so the same theories apply."

"Got it," I say, and Aidan nods.

"Also," David continues, "Alistair is going to keep his nose open for any sign of the elves."

I salute him, and he flips me the bird.

"Noah and I will dig back into the CCA records and census numbers over the past fifty or so years and see if we can locate any more cult towns, here and around the world." He sighs again. "Sam, are you good to coordinate us all?"

"Of course," Sam says. "I've already set up the permits for you to access the archives and requested a security team to accompany Percy tomorrow."

"You're so sexy," Gideon says to him, and the rest of us break into jeers.

"If you don't mind me asking," Aidan interrupts, sounding amused, "how's the research into the elves going?"

Noah groans.

"That well, eh?"

"It's slow going," David says. "We've always assumed this was just purely folklore—and a lot of it is. We're trying to find common threads in stories from different areas, especially areas that wouldn't have had a lot of contact with each other, in the hopes that we can find something that might be fact."

"Part of the issue is that we're relying a lot on translations," Noah adds. "And sometimes translations of translations. Every translator has their own lens, so what might originally have been written as 'people who came through a portal from another dimension' could very well have been translated as 'people who came from afar,' and we'd never know the difference."

"The same goes for transcriptions," David says gloomily. "Most of these stories started out being passed on in the oral tradition. Over generations, they might have changed somewhat, and the people who finally wrote them down probably added their own creative spin."

That sounds like a lot of very complicated desk work. I keep my mouth shut just in case someone gets the bright idea that David and Noah need help. That's *not* a job I want to be assigned.

"Do what you can," Percy encourages. "Hopefully we'll be able to get at least *some* information from our captives that you can use to refine your search."

The call starts to wrap up, and I make eye contact with Sam. It's not easy, but I've got skills. His brows draw together, but he doesn't say anything, and a few seconds later, the screen blacks out.

"I'm going to deal with my emails, if you don't mind," Aidan says. "My assistant is handling all the routine stuff, but there were still more than fifty waiting for me last time I checked."

"No problem," I tell him cheerfully. I'm expecting Sam to call soon anyway. "I'll run out to the grocery store so we've got food for breakfast. You'll be okay without the car?"

"I'm going nowhere," he confirms. "Once I'm done with this lot, I'm going to have an early night. Tomorrow we can go see Jun, maybe Riona, and fish for more information. Then see if we can talk to some of the younger shifters in the area."

"Good plan. And hopefully by the afternoon, Percy will have either confirmed or disproved our theory and we'll have some direction."

I leave him at the island, grab my phone, wallet, and the car keys, and head out to the garage. We've been here for such a short time that he'll be safe on his own while I shop. Nobody local knows we're here yet, and I'm absolutely certain we weren't followed. Still, the longer we're here, the more chance that Tish or his followers will find out, so this will be a quick grocery run. I can't risk Aidan's safety.

It's not until I'm at the store and have the first few items in the cart that Sam calls me.

I tap my Bluetooth earpiece to answer. "Hi, Sammy!"

"Hi," he says. "Everything okay?"

"Yes and no. Where are you?" I add half a dozen bunches of bananas to the cart and wonder if Aidan knows how to make pancakes.

"Just home from the office. Gideon's gone up to his LEGO room."

Gideon, freak of nature that he is, finds it easier to think when his hands are occupied. At home, he builds a lot of LEGO. In other places, he compulsively organizes things—desks, shelves, cupboards, you name it. If he's struggling with a particularly tricky case, nobody's stuff is safe from being alphabetized.

"Great. So, here's the thing. I think you were right, and now I don't know what to do."

Silence. "You think I was right?" he says slowly. "About wha— No! You have a crush on Aidan?"

"Maybe." I grab two jumbo boxes of cereal. "Mostly I think I just want to get naked with him and come in his hair."

An outraged gasp has me turning to see a wide-eyed, red-faced middle-aged man staring at me. "It would be totally consensual," I tell him, and his jaw drops.

"Alistair," Sam says, but the man is louder.

"You can't talk like that here!" he sputters.

I look around. It's still a grocery store, not a day care, and yep, we're the only two people in this aisle.

"Why not?" I ask reasonably. "I didn't swear or anything."

Sam groans in my ear. "Alistair, walk away from whoever you're talking to right now."

The man's face is getting even more florid. "This is a *public* place. Keep your filthy sex talk to yourself!"

I can't help it; a snort-laugh bursts from me. "Dude, if you think the words naked and come are filthy sex talk, you clearly need a better sex life. Or a decent porn subscription."

The strangled sound he makes is almost exactly the same as the one Sam's making.

"Alistair, *do not*—"

"If you want, I can recommend some for you. I think I might have a guest pass for—"

The man abandons his cart and flees. Like, he actually *runs* away from me. I don't know why—I was only trying to be nice. Expand his horizons. Everyone deserves to have a decent porn subscription.

"I don't hear yelling," Sam says. "Did he leave?"

I add half a dozen boxes of Pop-Tarts in assorted flavors to the cart. "Yeah. Left his groceries and everything. Maybe he needed to find an adult store and improve his porn collection."

"I'm sure that's what it was," Sam mutters. "Maybe tone down the talk about coming and porn while you're in a public place, though."

"We're having an important conversation," I protest, heading for the dairy section. "It's not like I can wait until I'm back at the house to tell you this—Aidan would hear!"

"Would that be a bad thing?" he counters. "If you want to have sex with him, he's going to need to know about it."

That's true. Sam has good ideas sometimes.

"Ye-es, but is having sex with him a dumb idea? He's —" I glance around and lower my voice. There's nobody close, but still. "He's my species leader. And technically I'm working with him now, although we're still debating which of us is in charge. He thinks it's him."

"He is the species leader," Sam points out.

"And I'm the trained investigator. Since we're currently conducting an investigation, doesn't that mean I'm the boss?"

"No. I'm putting it on record right now, Al. You're not the boss. The only time you're allowed to tell Aidan what to do is if his life is threatened. For work purposes, I mean. I don't care what you get up to in the bedroom."

"This is all your fault," I accuse gloomily.

"*My* fault? How is it my fault?" He pauses. "What's my fault?"

I wave an arm at the array of milk before me, forgetting for a second that Sam can't see me. "This whole thing about me wanting Aidan! It was easier when I thought I just didn't like him, that I was angry with him, but no, you had to come along and tell me I had a crush, didn't you. And now I'm turned on around him and need to make *decisions*."

A few disjointed sounds come down the line, as if Sam's starting to say something and then stopping.

"Al, sometimes I really wonder how your brain works."

I gasp, freezing with a carton of milk in my hand. How could my bestest bestie say such a thing?

"For starters, if you're only turned on around him because I said you might have a crush, then you don't have a crush and you're not actually turned on around him."

I start to reply, but he says, "No, don't talk. I'm talking. When you talk, you say stupid things."

I close my mouth and pout, glaring at the cheeses before me. I need to grab some of those before I go.

"So you need to think about that. Were you sexually attracted to Aidan before or not? If not, we need to discuss how suggestible you are. If you were… well, yeah, you probably have a crush, and you need to either live with it or act on it." He sounds totally exasperated, which is not unusual. "And you make decisions all the time. It's not that hard."

I huff a huge sigh.

"Don't be all dramatic and mopey," Sam chides. "You know I love you. I'm saying this stuff with all the love in my heart."

"I don't say stupid things," I tell him, my tone injured.

"You totally do," he counters. "All the time. You say some really deep and intelligent things too, though."

"Because I have depths. Intelligent depths. I am a man of mystery and intrigue."

"Yeah, okay. Whatever you say."

"What do I do now?" It comes out a lot more plaintive than I intended, and Sam sighs.

"I can't tell you that, Alistair. You need to think it over and make your own decision. But… from the perspective of someone who works with his boyfriend, I think at our level, it's not that big an issue. And you don't work directly with Aidan anyway—it's just this one assignment that will hopefully be short-term. Then he'll go back to Ireland or wherever it is he lives right now, and you'll hardly see him."

I lean on the cart and keep staring into the dairy case, acknowledging that the pang I feel at the thought of Aidan leaving the country is a good indication that I have a crush. "What about the fact that he's species leader?"

Sam hesitates. "That's tougher," he admits. "Although I'm probably not the person to talk to about that. I feel the connection with Aidan through the magic, and fuck knows I've felt what his influence over me can do, but I wasn't brought up as a shifter or even as part of the community. I don't feel that societal reverence for our leaders that you do—for me, the respect is a direct result of being in their presence and feeling the magic-influenced bond."

"It's not reverence," I protest. "We don't worship them or anything."

"No, but there's an automatic level of respect because the magic chose them. As someone who grew up not knowing the magic even existed, before I met Aidan, I didn't feel respect for him because he was species leader. I knew who he was and that he'd been invested by magic, but that was abstract for me. I met him before my first shift, and he was… not just any guy, because I did know he was the species leader, but there wasn't an automatic reflex to show him respect. That changed a little after I shifted, because of the bond, but I still feel like you have a different attitude toward his rank than I do."

My first instinct is to deny it, but he's probably right. When you grow up being taught to defer to someone— or in the case of the magic, some*thing*—it becomes an ingrained habit.

"The issue," Sam continues, "is twofold."

"Twofold, huh?" I clear my throat so I don't laugh.

"Yes, asshole. Twofold. The first part—"

"Don't you mean the first fold?"

"I could hang up right now, you know. There are

plenty of things I'd rather be doing than counseling you on your sex life."

"Like what?" I straighten and reach for some cheese. Omelets for breakfast might be nice. I'll need eggs too.

"Like enjoying my own sex life, for one. Or sleeping, because I don't know if you remember this, but you're in a different time zone right now."

Fuck, I had forgotten that. It explains why I'm tired, though.

"I'm sorry I picked on your word choice. Please don't abandon me in this, my time of darkest need," I plead.

"*This* is your time of darkest need? What the fuck kind of charmed life have you been living?"

I grab two cartons of eggs. "Well, my life has been rather amazing. People just love me, and that adoration has smoothed the way somewhat."

"Adoration. Sure. Uh… what were we even talking about?"

"You were telling me the twofold issue." I look at the contents of the cart and then steer toward the butcher section. We need bacon. And sausage.

"Right. So, the first part is that if you enter into a sexual relationship with your species leader, you might feel pressured to defer to him within that relationship."

"Is that a fancy way of saying I wouldn't say no?" I study the array of bacon packages and select a few jumbo family-size ones.

"It's a bit more complex than that, but basically, yes."

"I don't think that would be a problem. I stole the master bedroom out from under him today and also told him that if the situation becomes unsafe, I'm in charge."

I think I'm done with the groceries, but I decide to take the longer route to the checkout and scope out anything I might have missed. "Plus, I work with Percy, remember? I've never had an issue speaking up when I think it's warranted, and arguably I should have more… reverence, to use your word, for him."

"True," Sam concedes. "Okay, well, the second part is trickier."

"Oh?" Should I grab a few packets of cookies? They're not breakfast food, but they'd make a good midnight snack. Screw it. I toss an assortment of packages into the now almost overflowing cart.

"Yeah. Your species leader has the ability to compel you. How do you feel about having a physical relationship with someone who could potentially influence your will?"

I stop the cart in the middle of the aisle. Well, fuck. I hadn't even thought of that. Which is stupid, because the whole "I'm angry with Aidan" thing was over him compelling Sam's shift.

"Alistair? You still there?"

"Yeah. I'm thinking."

"I have an opinion on this, but I'm not going to share it until you tell me how you feel about it."

"Wow, thanks." I give myself a minute to actually consider it properly, and I'm surprised to find a deep, unshakeable conviction that Aidan would never do anything like that. He'd never use his status and abilities as species leader against me—anyone—in a personal relationship. In fact, I don't think he'd use his status and abilities as species leader in any situation that didn't require it.

Which makes it even more apparent that I've had a

crush on him all along and was just seizing on any excuse to explain away the surge of hormones and feelings.

Ugh. I hate when my subconscious does weird things.

"I think," I say finally, "that Aidan is more trust-worthy than that."

I hear Sam's smile as he says, "Yeah. I think so too."

"I'm a dumb shit, aren't I?" How fucking depressing.

My bestest bestie laughs in my ear. "Not completely. You just get distracted sometimes. And since I've known you, it's only ever been about sex. Bringing feelings into it might have thrown you off."

"Feelings. Ugh. No, there are no feelings. It's still just sex."

Someone behind me gasps, and I roll my eyes. Not this shit again. I turn around and see a teenage girl staring at me, blushing furiously.

Oops.

"Sorry," I offer. "Uh... you should only have sex when you really like someone and you're ready. And always use a condom."

Her face goes even redder.

"Alistair, if you're talking to a kid, get away from them *right now*," Sam demands, and I think he might be right this time. I give the girl a weird, jerky wave, then grab my cart and race away.

"What's a teenager doing at the grocery store at this time of night?" I hiss at Sam, and he groans.

"Just... check out and leave. Do not make eye contact with anyone. I don't want to have to arrange to bail you out of jail from across the country."

"I've done nothing wrong," I protest. "She's the one who was eavesdropping on a private conversation!" I hesitate as I approach the row of checkouts. I usually like to have a cashier check me out, because it's nice to talk to people and learn about their lives, right? But I think tonight it might be better to use the self-checkout.

I steer in that direction as Sam says, "No more using the words sex, or come, or porn, or any variation on that theme while you're in a public place. Use a substitute word instead."

"Like what?" I begin scanning my items. Since nobody's close enough to see, I go a little faster than a human could.

"I don't know… what about… lamp."

Clearly he's getting inspiration from his living room décor.

"Do you really think me saying 'I want to lamp him all night long' is better, Sam?" I ask dryly. "Or 'I want to lamp in his hair'?"

"Fuck my life," he mutters. "How did this happen to me?"

"You love it," I assure him. "You wouldn't be able to cope if I wasn't around. Our friendship bond is deep and enduring and—"

"You're right," he interrupts. "I couldn't live without you. So… should I be singing juvenile kissing songs about you and Aidan?"

I dump an item into a bag and sigh. "No. Although those songs are awesome. But there's nothing to sing about. I want to—" I glance around, turning in a circle just in case. There's nobody nearby, but I'm not willing to take the risk. "I want to lamp Aidan, but there are no feelings involved. I don't get feelings."

"It's not like the flu, Alistair." Sam sounds exasperated again. "You can't build up an immunity. Besides, you have feelings all the time. You share them with us very vocally."

"But those aren't romantic relationship feelings," I reply, not paying as much attention as I should as I tap my credit card and punch in the PIN. Sam's silence is what makes me realize I might have given too much away.

When he finally speaks, his voice is hesitant. "Al, you don't have to answer this, but are you aromantic?"

For a second, I'm tempted to say yes. It would make him drop the subject. On the other hand, he'd also immediately start researching so he could offer support if I ever need it. And it feels gross to identify as something I know I'm not just to avoid a conversation.

I sigh again. "No, I'm not. I've had romantic relationships—well, a romantic relationship. A long time ago. That's how I know I don't want one." I gather my purchases and make my way out to the car while he thinks about that. Thank fuck—once I'm safely inside, I can say whatever I want without having to be paranoid about repressed locals and schoolchildren listening in.

"Wait," Sam says slowly in my ear as I load the groceries into the car. "Are you saying that you avoid having feelings, as you put it, because you had a relationship that ended badly?"

I hate remembering this. *Hate* it. "It didn't just end badly," I tell him, getting into the driver seat and starting the engine. "It was catastrophic. He burned my house down."

Silence again. I back out of the parking space and turn the car toward my temporary home.

"What?" Sam breathes. "Did you just say… he burned your house down?"

"Yes."

Another moment of silence. I can't remember the last time Sam was shocked into being quiet.

"I think you need to tell me the whole story."

"There's not much to tell. I was young and stupid. I had feelings. He said he did too. I thought it would be a 'together forever' thing, so I told him I was a hellhound. He—"

"Wait, you told him? He was human?"

"Yes. Then he freaked out, called me a demon—even though I tried to explain the difference—and said he never wanted to see me again. Later that night, after I'd cried myself to sleep with my stupid feelings, he came back and set my house on fire. I woke up when I smelled the smoke. Then there was a big drama because he told everyone in the village that I was a demon from hell."

"And they believed him?" he asks incredulously. "Fuck me, you were in the house when he *set it on fire*?"

I sniff. "Yes, I was in the house. And no, of course they didn't believe him. I was trying to fit in at the time and had been attending religious services every week in the local church. The vicar attested that I wasn't a demon… although there were some very pointed comments about sodomy."

"When was this?"

I think about it. "I was twenty-two, twenty-three… so 1867, maybe."

He clears his throat. "Okay, so I'll grant you that it must have been very painful and hurtful to have the person you loved and wanted to spend your life with be unable to accept you and then try to burn you alive."

"Thank you. It's something you never really get over."

"I can imagine… although honestly, I don't think it happens to too many people. But I'm not sure that this decision to avoid romantic feelings for the rest of your very long life is the right way to go."

I frown. He's not going to support me? What's the point of having a bestest bestie if he's not going to support me when I boycott romantic relationships? "What do you mean?"

"Well… there are some other factors I'd like to consider. Was he your first relationship? Were you his? How long had you been together? Were you living together? Had you met each other's families?"

I pull up outside the condo complex but don't turn in. I don't want to risk Aidan hearing any of this conversation. "He was the first—the only—person I'd ever loved that way." I can't believe he's making me dredge up these memories. Who knew Sam was such a sadist? "And he'd never been with a man before me. We'd been together for—" I squint while I think about it. The first time I kissed him was in the spring… "—about five months. He still lived in his family home in the village, and I knew his family but not as his beau. They weren't open to that idea. He wanted to ease them into it. And I wanted to take him to meet my family, but first I needed to tell him about not being human, and he didn't take that well."

"That's an understatement. Okay… well, you were very young, and you weren't together that long. While people often meet their forever love at a young age, it's also just as likely that this was a relationship that might have run its course… maybe due to incompatibilities. If he basically came out for you and knew it was something his family weren't likely to be accepting of, he might have been already struggling when you told him. And it was a different time, Al. He was a young human without any exposure to the kind of pop culture we have now, living in a place where you fit in by going to church. A man who could change into something else would probably have been a lot to take, and if he was already conflicted…."

I rub my chest where it's started to ache. "So what you're saying is that the relationship that affected me so strongly I still can't bear to put myself through something like that again was likely just going to end anyway because the man I loved didn't really love me back?"

"No!" His shout reverberates through my head, and I consider pulling the earpiece out and switching to the handset. "No, I'm *not* saying that. But even if that was true, it doesn't mean your pain is any less valid. First love is something special, and when it ends, even under the best circumstances, it's sad. Under these circumstances, it would have been devastating. But Al… weren't there some good things about it? Do you really want to shut yourself off from ever having a loving partner just because you don't want to feel pain?"

I take a deep breath. "I've gotta go, Sam. Talk to you tomorrow."

He makes a frustrated noise, then says, "Sure. Okay. Just… think about it. Love can hurt, but it's mostly worth it. And if you do end up with your heart broken, that's what your bestest bestie is for, right?"

"Right. But it's just sex with Aidan. Or it will be if we get that far. Bye."

"Good night, Alistair."

I end the call and wish I'd just kept my damn mouth shut. When I left the grocery store, I was thinking about asking Aidan if he was interested in some no-strings stress release, aka fucking like bunnies. Now, I just want to crawl into a dark hole so I can relive my pain in private.

By the time I have the car parked in the garage and am unloading the groceries, a plan has formed. I'm going to take some of the leftovers from dinner and a couple packages of Pop-Tarts and go up to my room to wallow in my miserable memories. Hopefully, I can wallow myself to sleep and will be over it by morning.

Aidan's still at the counter with his laptop when I let myself into the kitchen. He's frowning at the screen in a way that forms the cutest little furrow between his brows.

No! Bad feelings! Bad! Stop that.

"You took longer than I thought," he says absently as I start putting things away.

"Yeah, Sam called, and then there was this guy who eavesdropped on our conversation and got offended by something I said. It turned into a thing." I sling the last of the milk into the fridge and close the door.

"Do I need to be worried?" He looks up from the screen, the furrow replaced by an expression of full-blown concern.

"Nah, it's all good."

He looks at me for a long moment as I stack boxes in a cupboard. I can feel his gaze on me.

"Sam called? Was there a problem?"

"It wasn't a work thing. He and I are friends."

Aidan snorts, a tiny smile appearing on his lush mouth just as I turn. "I remember. Good friends, if I recall correctly."

Internally, I cringe. Maybe this could have been a moment of truth if Sam and I hadn't just been talking about my heartbreak, but right now, I don't have the energy to flirt.

Wow. That's sad.

Still, he deserves some kind of response, so I meet his gaze and say, "He's my best friend. I know I gave you a hard time that day, but… he's my best friend."

The smile widens. It's really not fair that I'm so attracted to him. Objectively, he's not *that* good-looking, but that smile is just lickable.

"You were fine. It was good to know that Sam had people in his corner." He hesitates. "Since then, it's seemed a little like you were… maybe holding a grudge?"

I shrug and turn away to grab the Pop-Tarts. "I like to sulk sometimes," I admit. "I'm over it now." Then, before he can ask anything else, I add, "Do you need me for anything? I thought I'd head up for the night."

"That's fine. I'm almost done here, then I'll be coming up myself." He grins. "But you've got plenty of time to use the bathroom first."

Whoops. I've been busted. Do I apologize? Act like nothing's happened?

"Nah, turns out my room has an en suite." I brazen it out. "So you'll have the main bathroom all to yourself."

He laughs. "What an amazing coincidence."

"Completely shocked me," I reply, deadpan. "Still, I

suppose there had to be some trade-off for you getting the queen-size bed."

This time he laughs so hard that he almost chokes. It feels good.

Not because I have *feelings*. It's just nice when people find me amusing.

Shut up.

I head toward the stairs, then hesitate and turn back. "Hey, Aidan?"

He sucks in a breath and swipes tears from his eyes. "Yeah?"

"If your boyfriend called you a monster and then set your house on fire while you were sleeping in it, that's not something you'd be able to just put behind you, right?"

His jaw drops open, and he blinks at me a few times. "Ah... no. No, that's the kind of thing that sticks with you."

There. See? Sam's just suffering from in-love-itis, a condition whereby people who are in love believe everyone else in the world should be too. My desire to avoid feelings is perfectly rational.

"That's what I thought," I say with a nod. "Goodnight."

I've made it up only two steps before he adds, "I'd be thanking the universe every day for that wake-up call."

Wait... what?

I turn around. "What do you mean?"

He shrugs, his attention mostly back on his laptop. "Well, once the initial pain of having someone you love reject you and try to kill you began to fade, you'd realize it could have been worse. You could have continued thinking you were in a happy relationship with someone who has the emotional capacity to set you on fire in your sleep. Who knows what might have eventually happened? A knife through the heart? We have more chance of survival against fire."

He's right, but… what?

I retrace my steps back to the ground floor. "Are you saying you'd be relieved?"

"Not at first, of course. I'd be devastated. But eventually, yeah. Relieved seems about right. Angry, too, but that would probably fade with the pain. Is this a case you worked on?"

There are so many thoughts screaming for attention, I barely hear the question. "Uh, yeah. Something like that."

"Was the victim badly wounded?"

I shake my head, partly in answer and partly to clear it. "No. Very minor smoke inhalation is all. But he, uh, he's been put off relationships."

Aidan tears his gaze away from the screen. "Well, yeah. I can see why that would happen. And he's allowed to, I don't know, wallow in his pain for a while. But when that starts to fade, he'll probably forget he took a vow of chastity or whatever and get back to life. Wiser for the experience, definitely."

I try not to wince at his use of "wallow," supremely conscious of the box of Pop-Tarts in my hand. "So you don't think he'd be justified to hold on to his… reluctance to get involved again? Romantically, I mean."

He sighs and tips his head back, staring at the ceiling for a minute. "I don't know," he says finally. "It's a tough call without knowing anything else about the relationship. Maybe the fire was just the last in a long line of abuse. Maybe your victim is deeply damaged by what happened. But our brains are pretty good at dealing with trauma overall, and I think giving up on the idea of a romantic relationship forever because of one bad—admittedly, horrific—experience is a pretty drastic step to take. It would be like… well, okay, Sam's first shift was compelled, right? That's awful. If we'd had another safe option, there's no way in existence I would have suggested a compelled first shift. Sam's first experience of his shifter side was painful and left him paranoid after. How easy would it have been for Sam to decide that shifting is just not worth the potential risks?"

"But those risks only exist for a compelled shift, not a natural one," I point out.

"Yeah," he says, smiling, "and the risk of your boyfriend setting fire to your house doesn't exist in every relationship. In fact, my guess is that it's a pretty low statistic."

I huff a laugh. "Probably. Anyway… I don't know why I was even thinking about it."

"Like we said, stuff like that sticks with you, even if it doesn't affect you directly. I'll probably be thinking about it on and off now that I know. And I bet that's even more the case for someone like you."

Uhhhh….

"Someone like me?"

He closes his laptop and gets up off the stool. "Sure. You said before that you like to sulk. If this isn't something to sulk over, what is? Even if it did happen to someone else, your brain likely just can't let it go."

I look down at my body to make sure there isn't actually a giant boulder caving in my chest.

"Uh… yeah," I manage. "I've… uh, I guess I am kind of obsessing over it." I turn and race up the stairs before he can say anything else, leaving him to turn off the lights before he comes up. I need to be safely behind my bedroom door when he does.

Fucking fuck fuck fuck.

I close the door to the bedroom, then for good measure cross the room and go into the bathroom and close that door too. Then I toss the box of Pop-Tarts on the counter and stare at myself in the mirror.

Is that really it? Am I such a… Am I the kind of person who decides to cut a whole element of my life out for a hundred and fifty years because I'm *sulking*? Am I wallowing and vowing to be single forever because I'm too scared to take a chance?

I rip open the box of Pop-Tarts.

CHAPTER SIX

Aidan

My CONCERN about Alistair's slightly weird behavior when he got back from the grocery store disappears the next morning. He's his usual chipper self, cooking bacon and eggs while eating a bowl of cereal. It's criminal that he looks so good in an old T-shirt and boxer shorts, his hair standing on end.

"Good morning," he declares. "Want some?"

"Yes, thanks." I find a bowl and reach for the cereal box. "Can I help?"

"Only if you're good at making pancakes," he replies. "Mine are usually garbage."

I shake my head. "Sorry. I only tried a couple of times, and they were so rubbery I gave up."

He gives a long, mournful sigh. "That's okay. We still have plenty to eat. Maybe when I shop for tomorrow's breakfast, I'll get some frozen waffles."

"Good plan." Now that he's brought it up, I could really go for some pancakes. Isn't that always the way? "I thought we'd drop in on Jun first, see if we can't get any more information about Beker County."

"Sounds good. Hopefully we can talk to quite a few people right here in the city before the others call with whatever information Percy manages to get. That should help to shape our plans. I also want to drive around with the windows down and see if I can catch the scent of the elves."

I wince, because even though my sense of smell isn't as acute as a hellhound's, that does not sound like fun. "Are you sure? That's going to be a bombardment of scent."

He turns off the burner and begins portioning the food onto plates. "Yeah. I'm not looking forward to it, but we don't have time for me to walk the whole city—especially since it's unlikely they're here anyway." Joining me at the counter, he passes over a plate and cutlery.

"Thank you. Well, if you think that's the best option, we'll go with it."

Nodding, he chews his giant mouthful of food as I dig in. It smells incredible, and I'm starving.

"I really don't think we'll find them here. I woke up early this morning and had a look at some of the research David and Noah have been doing, and even though we're still not sure what's myth and what might be based in fact, all of it points to elves avoiding centers of population. There's a chance they were here for a short time for a specific purpose, which is why I'm going to do the drive around, but it would be an outrageous coincidence if we happen to stumble across them."

That sounds logical. "Is there any chance I can see that research?" Not that I have all that much spare time in which to read it, but who knows?

He shrugs. "I don't see why not. I'll ask Noah to set up access for you."

We eat in silence for a few minutes.

"So," he says finally, scraping up the last of his egg with some toast, "I'll jump in the shower, then clean up here and be ready to go in about twenty minutes. Does that work for you?"

"Absolutely." I showered last night, so I just need to brush my teeth and get dressed.

"Great. We'll go to Jun's first, talk to him and any of his pack who are available, then maybe Riona and her clan—depends on how we're doing for time at that point. Oh, and at some time today, we should talk about having sex."

I choke on my bacon.

"What?" I wheeze. I must have misheard him. He probably said we should talk about having… something completely innocent that I can't think of right now.

"We should talk about having sex," he repeats blithely, getting up to put his plate in the sink. "I'm going to put on some more bacon and eggs to make sandwiches with. Can you keep an eye on them while they cook?"

"Y-Yes. Um… did you say we needed to talk about sex?" I was sure I heard him right that time, but I couldn't have… right? Unless he means sex in general… but that's still weird. Or maybe he's thought of some connection between sex and what the CCA is doing?

Although I literally cannot imagine what that could be.

"Yeah. You're not seeing anyone at the moment, right? I feel like that's something we would all know if you were."

"No, I'm not," I reply slowly, trying to give myself time to think. Is this what it sounds like? Is Alistair hitting on me?

Feck yeah.

"Great! So I'm going up to shower, but have a think about it and let me know if you're good."

A smile curves my mouth. "I've never had any complaints before. Are you saying we should fuck, Alistair?" I have reservations, but I'm not dumb enough to say no.

Well… not right away, anyway.

He stops halfway to the stairs and turns. "We're both single. We're both hot. And I really want you naked and on your knees. So yeah, we should fuck. A lot." He turns back and heads upstairs while the image of me on my knees sucking him off burns itself into my brain and I'm still trying to work out what to say next.

This is not how I expected the morning to go.

The bacon spits in the pan, and I push aside thoughts of sex with Alistair and go to check on it. It's not like we have time to fuck right now.

Although… he is in the shower. All wet… and soapy.

No. No time. Maybe later.

THE CAR RIDE over to Jun's place is weird, probably because we're both thinking about having sex. With each other.

Well, that's what I'm thinking about, anyway. Despite my resolution not to think about it until later, it's the only thought in my head. Which, considering that I'm the one driving, is not good.

Honestly, Alistair might not be thinking about it at all. I'm the one who's being awkward and silent. He handed me a bacon and egg sandwich as soon as we got in the car, insisting I eat it despite my assurance that Jun would feed us, and now he's chattering away in his usual random manner, telling me about the updates Sam sent him this morning. There's nothing particularly relevant just yet, but given the difference in time zones, it's possible that they'll have something new soon.

We hope.

By the time I park the car in the forecourt of Jun's gated mansion, I'm a mess of confused arousal. I remember feeling that way a lot when I was an adolescent, but not so much since I became an adult. I don't particularly like it. Worse, Alistair has to be aware—his hellhound sense of smell would have picked it up like a beacon. And I'm about to walk into a house with more hellhounds. Fun, hey?

I'd be laughing if it was happening to someone else. I'm the species leader of all shifters, and with one sentence, a hellhound has managed to turn me into a seething mass of hormones.

I suck in a deep breath, which has the unfortunate side effect of delivering a direct hit of Alistair's scent.

He smells delicious.

He also smells aroused.

I guess it's not just me who's suffering from hormone overload.

This does create a problem, though. If we both go in smelling turned on, Jun will assume we're fucking. Which we might (will probably) end up doing, but it's not helpful or professional for us to…

Oh, feck it.

"Let's go." I get out of the car and slam the door. I'm not willing to waste half the morning driving around thinking of maggot-laden meat and waiting for the scent of my arousal to fade just so someone doesn't think I'm having sex with a… whatever Alistair is to me. Colleague? Associate? Nobody expects me to be celibate. They don't even expect me to keep my sexual exploits outside the species. There's a long precedent of species leaders meeting, dating, and even marrying while they were invested by the magic. The only expectation is that I not be obnoxious and careless in my sex life.

Alistair joins me at the front of the car. "This is a nice house." He turns in a full circle, looking out over the grounds. "Acreage?"

"About fifty, mostly wooded. Enough to have pack gatherings here, but not enough for any real exercise." Jun gave me a rundown the first time I visited.

Alistair sighs. "It's been way too long since I got any real exercise," he says, and I *know* he's talking about a run in his hellhound form, but my brain instantly conjures images of *other* forms of exercise, and my cock takes interest. From the way his lips quirk, Alistair notices the shift in scent.

Ignoring it, I say, "Maybe we can arrange time for a run while we're out here. We're planning to visit some pretty rural areas." Before he can respond, I start toward the house.

The door opens before I've taken more than a few steps. I'm not surprised—even though the gate was open, there's no way a hellhound wouldn't have heard us arrive and then stand around chatting. Jun stands in the doorway waiting for us.

"Aidan, welcome back," he says warmly. He's about

six inches taller than me but a little stockier, his hair still completely black and face unlined even though he's nearly six hundred years old. Some genes are just better than others.

"Good morning, Jun." I hold out my hand. "I promise not to take too much of your time."

He laughs and shakes my hand. "It's an honor to have you here. And you said that you'd like to meet some of our younger pack members this time?"

"Yes, if that's okay with you—and them."

"We're all thrilled. My assistant has been making calls, and I expect people to start turning up soon." His gaze flits over my shoulder, and I half turn, gesturing to Alistair.

"This is Alistair Smythe from CSG. The lucifer has asked me to assist him with meeting your pack."

From the way Jun blinks, I know he recognizes Alistair's name and is now wondering if there's more to this than just a few young hellhounds getting mixed up with the "wrong crowd." There is, of course, but we can't tell him that. Not yet anyway.

"Great to meet you," Alistair says, offering his hand. "You've got a nice property here."

Jun recovers enough to shake hands with him. "Thank you. We keep it open for all pack members, so even those who live in high-density housing can get some fresh air every once in a while. Come in, please." He steps back from the doorway and beckons us in.

We make idle small talk about the horror of being in planes and how nice his décor is while he leads us to his office, a decent-sized space that was probably originally intended to be a living room. There are two desks in there, one for him and one for his assistant, a middle-aged woman who's currently on the phone, and a small seating area. We settle there.

"Can I get you anything? We keep a cook on staff," he tells Alistair, "since we get so many visitors. Feeding hellhounds is a full-time job."

"Nothing just yet, thanks. I'm sure we'll get plenty when the pack members start arriving," Alistair says, and I realize this is why he was so insistent we eat in the car. I need to stop being distracted by thoughts of sex with him and start concentrating.

Jun smiles. "Definitely. Uh, people are going to ask why you're here, Alistair. Is there anything in particular you'd like me to tell them?"

Fuck me, something else I didn't think of. Nobody questions it when I turn up randomly to visit a pack, but Alistair is a high-profile government agent. His presence here is like a neon sign that something is going on. We should have planned for this.

"The lucifer is interested in learning more about the experiences of community members around the world," Alistair replies with a friendly smile. "I'd like to chat with your pack members, especially the younger ones, and find out what their perspective is on our government. We're also looking at the contrast between experiences of those who live in low versus high population areas." He rolls his eyes. "I don't fully understand how they're managing the data side. That's David's department—David Carew," he adds. "My job is just to talk to as many people as possible and then report on what they've told me." His self-deprecating charm sets Jun at ease. It probably helps that the magic definitely doesn't see Alistair as a threat. If anyone else had come in with such a bullshit story—although oddly enough, it's completely true—Jun would likely have been suspicious and possibly kicked them out. But Alistair is here on behalf of Percy, accompanied by me, and telling the absolute truth with nothing but good intentions.

Within a few minutes, he's managed to steer the conversation to the more far-flung members in the pack. "You'd see them less often, of course," he prompts, and Jun begins telling us about the various pack gatherings they have—usually one, often two each year—and that he likes to personally visit each cluster of pack members at least once every two years.

"It's hard," he admits. "We've got a big area to cover and a lot of members spread out over it. Modern transportation makes it easier now, but I know there are members I haven't seen in too long—and even some I haven't met."

"Newcomers to the area?" Alistair asks idly. "I'd have thought they'd make a special effort to meet you before moving in."

Jun shakes his head. "Mostly they do, and if I know there are newbies in a certain area, I try to make it a priority to get out there. But I'm actually talking about children. There are a few places that I know have young children, but for some reason, circumstances mean I never get to meet them."

"They don't come to the pack gatherings?"

"The group does, but you know how things are with young children—a cold, a sprained ankle, punishment for misbehavior… and it's a long car journey with kids in the back seat. There's often a good reason for families to stay home until the little ones are older."

That's all true, but also suspicious. In my experience, it's the shifters who live in isolated communities who are the most eager to attend pack gatherings. They arrive first and are the last to leave, even if they've traveled for hours—or, as was sometimes the case back before modern transportation, days.

From the sideways glance Alistair shoots me, he agrees, but he doesn't press the subject. We're not ready yet to make Jun suspicious of his people in Beker County. He may feel the need to defend or even warn them—they are his people, after all. His to protect and nurture. It's one thing to be presented with and accept evidence that people were involved in a physical assault, but another altogether to believe they're involved in some kind of undefined conspiracy plot.

"It's tough with kids," Alistair agrees, then tilts his head. "Speaking of kids…"

Sure enough, there are sounds of people approaching—the local pack members must be starting to arrive. I smile and stand. I love meeting my shifters. It feeds the part of my soul that's been taken over by the magic.

"The weather's holding, so we'll stay outdoors. It gives the kids more room," Jun explains as he leads us outside. It's not a warm day, but we shifters are hardy stock… mostly. We definitely prefer to be outside, so we're willing to tolerate cooler weather if it means getting out of the house.

The dozen or so yelling, laughing kids racing across the lawn toward the trees clearly don't care that it's cold. Their parents and some older teens are gathering near picnic tables set up near the house, content to let their children run free—until they notice us coming toward them. Heads turn, faces light up, and then one of the adults says something to the teen standing beside her. The teen takes off after the kids.

The next few hours are a wonderful mess of names, happy faces, and idle chatter. More people arrive. Some can only stay long enough to meet me, while others settle in for a long visit. I leave the investigative work to Alistair—it's his forte, after all—and I focus on connecting with my shifters.

What's weird about being species leader is that there's a connection between me and every single shifter alive. It's not obvious—I can't concentrate on individuals or identify them in my head. I don't feel them being born or dying. But when I meet them, the energy that is them, the part of them that derives from the magic, pings inside me. It's terrifying and exhilarating.

And they feel it too. They might not know what to say to me, but I see how a part of them relaxes when they're near me. When I talk to them, they light up. The magic goes out of its way to make sure they feel safe with me.

Which is why what we suspect the CCA is doing is so awful.

Late in the morning, I'm standing with a group of parents, talking to them about their concerns for their children and cradling an infant. I've never been much of one for babies, but since becoming species leader, I've learned the myriad of ways to hold them. People love to put their babies in my arms. The good thing is, shifter babies like to be held by me. They'll literally cut off midscream and settle down to sleep.

"…like to see more international exchange opportunities for older teens," one of the dads is saying. "They just don't exist for us on the same scale as what the humans have, and the irony of that is that we travel more as adults than humans do."

I nod. "This isn't the first time that's been brought up. The tricky part is ensuring safety in transit. Even older teens still occasionally struggle with spontaneous shifting when they're stressed, and planes are very stressful for shifters, especially on long flights. We—"

A sharp whistle rends the air, cutting me off, and heads turn in that direction.

It's Alistair. Standing on a picnic table.

"Hi, Oregon hellhounds!"

There's a chorus of shouted greetings in return. Most of them use his name—he's been busy.

"It's been great chatting with you this morning, and I'm going to get back to that in just a second, but these young people here"—he waves toward a group of preteens standing next to the table—"have just informed me that they don't know how to limbo."

A murmur runs through the crowd, and I hold back a sigh. I have a sneaking suspicion that things are about to get derailed the way hellhound events usually do.

"Worse... they don't even know what the limbo is."

The sound the crowd makes this time is shocked.

"Oh, no," one of the mothers I've been talking to says, sounding stricken. "I've failed as a parent."

I look at her closely, trying to see if she's being sarcastic or making a joke, but there's a glossy sheen to her eyes.

Only hellhounds, I swear.

"So I'm asking you all to step up and assist me in the vital task of educating them. Children are our future, and they cannot continue living without the tools they need to survive!"

Wow. That's… a bold statement to make about the limbo.

But the crowd of hellhounds shouts in approval.

Two people come out of the house, waving brooms in a wild manner that worries me, and Alistair shouts, "Let there be music!"

From speakers mounted along the eaves, "Limbo Rock" begins to blare. Hellhounds flock toward Alistair as he jumps down from the table, and within seconds, he has them forming two lines, one in front of each broom.

"You're okay to hold on to the baby, aren't you, Aidan?" the baby's father asks me, and this time I can't hold back the sigh.

"Of course. Go. Save future generations from life without the limbo." I'm so proud that I say that without sounding sarcastic, although as fast as they all leave, I don't think they would have noticed if I did. It takes less than a minute for almost every hellhound here to become a bopping, dancing limbo fanatic.

And less than two minutes after that, I'm called upon to act as adjudicator. Hellhounds are super competitive, and I have to remind them several times that this tournament—because of course that's what it's become—is all in fun and that they're supposed to be setting an example for the kids. Incidentally, the kids went and found a mop somewhere and have begun their own limbo tournament.

An hour and a half, six serious disputes, two pulled muscles, and a truckload of my patience later, I declare the tournament winner. Honestly, it's been kind of fun, in a weird, hellhound way. You'd know what I meant if you've ever been to a hellhound party. You don't expect to enjoy yourself when you hear what's planned, but somehow, you always do.

The applause begins to fade as Alistair comes to stand beside me. He's pouting a little because he got knocked out of the tournament a few rounds back, but there's a sparkle in his eye that concerns me.

"Before everyone disappears," he says, raising his voice above the babble that's breaking out. "It occurs to me that we've been horribly rude. Aidan, our beloved species leader, has tirelessly and selflessly overseen our amazing inaugural limbo tournament without a single word of complaint about the fact that he hasn't gotten a turn."

Oh *feck* no.

My brain is whirling through a million possible excuses when he turns to me with a beatific smile.

"Give me the baby, Aidan, and take your turn." Wild applause and cheers break out amongst the crowd, and I close my eyes for a brief moment of defeat.

There's no way I can refuse. No excuse will be good enough.

"I hate you," I tell Alistair as I carefully hand him the baby, who woke some time ago and has been gurgling cheerfully throughout most of the tournament.

"So many people say that, but it just can't be true," he replies cheerfully as I turn toward the broom two of the kids have snatched up and are holding way lower than I would like. "Hey, Aidan?"

I look back at him, and his smile this time is down-right dirty.

"How low can you go?"

If we weren't surrounded by over a hundred of my people, including dozens of children, I'd flip him off.

Instead, I ignore him—and the way my cock has perked up with interest—and take a deep breath. It's been a long time since I've limboed. More than a hundred years —maybe closer to a hundred and fifty. It might interest you to know that I actually visited Trinidad around that time and learned it there. But it's not like I ever devoted all that much time to it.

Still, I'm fit. I'm flexible. And I have the advantage of being the shortest adult here.

The music starts up again, and as I give myself a little shake to loosen up, the crowd begins chanting. "How low can you go? How low can you go?"

I study the level of the broom. It's about hip height on me, which is only a few inches higher than what the tournament winner managed. I consider it and then decide to just do it.

The hellhounds go nuts. So does every single muscle in my body. But I make it through to the other side, where I'm met by a mob of cheering hellhounds slapping me on the back.

Thankfully, people are bringing out huge platters of food—lunch—right now, so the crowd gets distracted and begins to disperse. Alistair lingers for a moment longer.

"Want the baby back?" he asks, and I hold out my arms. It's entirely possible that my whole body will go into spasm in a second, but until it does, I will show no weakness.

Before he slips away, he winks. "You're awfully bendy, Aidan. That bodes well."

LUNCH HAS BEEN CLEARED AWAY and I'm discussing economic reform, of all things, with a group of older hellhounds when Alistair reappears.

"Sorry to interrupt," he says, flashing a charming smile. "I need to borrow Aidan for just a moment. Also, there's about to be a flash mob over there"—he points—"and you should definitely be watching if you want to avoid disappointment and tears."

Almost as one, they turn in that direction. I turn too—although a flash mob at a hellhound gathering really isn't rare—but Alistair grabs my arm and tugs me toward the house.

"Gideon just called," he murmurs, pitching his voice so that only I can hear. "The hellhounds in custody were shocked to meet Percy. He's sending a full report by email and wants to set up a call for later but said we should consider the theory confirmed."

My heart drops to my feet.

"Is—" I clear my throat, remembering to speak subvocally. "Okay." I don't know what to say. A million questions are teeming through my mind, but I don't know what to say. I want to get in the car right now, drive out to Beker County, and take all those children into my care. "Is it that they don't know what the magic is, or they just don't get taught that it selects leaders?"

He shakes his head. "Gideon didn't give me details, and with so many people around, I didn't ask questions." Off to our right, a group of young teens suddenly come together and begin singing. They're fairly terrible, enough so that I can't tell what song they're butchering, but I turn to watch anyway, half of me loving the grins on their faces as they dance, the other half aching for those who don't have this security of pack. "We'll eat here and then ease away, if that's okay with you. We can set up the call back at the condo."

"Of course." I tear my gaze away from the happy teenagers. "Did you learn anything this morning?"

The grim set of his mouth is something I've seen far too often in the past twenty-four hours, and it doesn't belong. "Yes. I've spoken with the children and the younger adults, and the Beker County people don't mingle well. They're polite but not friendly. And often they break off into their own little groups at pack gatherings. It wouldn't be obvious unless you were looking for it, because…" He gestures around. As usually happens with large gatherings, there are many smaller groups clustered around. People move from one to another as conversations shift. It would be very easy for a few people to remain isolated from the party at large.

"Yeah. But was there any sign they might not…?" I can't bring myself to say the words—not right now.

I don't need to, though. Alistair knows what I mean, and the look on his face is answer enough.

I suck in a deep breath. "Okay. I'm going to need to brief Jun on this, but not yet, so you need to tell me a joke or something. I feel like my face is frozen into this horribly sad expression."

He tilts his head to one side and studies me. "Not sad, exactly. A little sad, but more horrified and… angry? Like you opened a bag of M&Ms and found no chocolate but instead rabbit turds."

The sound that bursts from me could possibly be considered a laugh… if one usually only heard screams of torture.

"Rabbit turds? What… what?" I don't even know what to say to that.

He tilts his head to the other side. "That's not really any better. The horror is just magnified now. How about this: Why do fish live in salt water?"

Okay, a joke. This is more like it. It'll be only vaguely funny, because it's a joke about fish, but it'll get a weak laugh and change my facial expression.

"I don't know. Why?"

"Because pepper makes them sneeze."

I gape at him, blinking, then groan. "Alistair, that was awful!"

"It wasn't that bad," he protests. "Wait, I've got more. What does a zombie vegetarian eat?"

I don't think I can handle this. "Lettuce?" I suggest weakly.

He grins. "Graaaaaaaains!"

I turn around and walk away. "Never mind," I call over my shoulder. "I now have a legitimate reason to look horrified."

"Then my work here is done!" he shouts after me.

It's a good thing my back is to him and he can't see my smile.

CHAPTER SEVEN

Alistair

I GET a text from Sam about a conference call right before we get back to the condo. They're ready for us, but I ask him for fifteen minutes. It won't make or break us, and Aidan needs time to settle himself.

He hasn't said a word since we left Jun's estate. The difference between this car ride and the one this morning—when he was also silent—was that then he was thinking sexy thoughts about what we could do to each other, and now he's worrying about the safety of his people and the damage done to children. He kept it together really well during lunch and even joined in singing a round of "It's a Small World." But there's just a tiny hint of strain to his smile, to the way his eyes don't crinkle quite as much as usual, that tells me he's struggling.

The fact I can recognize that even though before yesterday I'd only met him a handful of times means that I'm either super observant and amazing at my job —which I am—or this crush thing is much more involved than I thought—which I think it is.

Last night didn't turn out the way I planned. More than once, I mean. Originally, I thought we'd strategize for work and then turn in and get a good night's sleep. Then, there was serious thought given to propositioning Aidan and spending the night in a tangle of sweaty limbs. That got killed off after I told Sam about Timothy and decided to spend the night wallowing in memories.

That didn't happen either.

After what Sam and Aidan said, I made myself think about what happened a little more critically. Yeah, it was traumatizing to have the man I thought I'd be with forever—well, for the span of his lifetime, anyway—try to burn me alive. It broke my heart and embittered me toward love. But here's the thing: last night, I realized I can't actually remember Timothy's face anymore. I remember the way he snorted when he laughed and how he rolled his eyes whenever I said anything he thought was stupid—which was much more often than was really warranted—but I can't picture him.

He had a shock of wheat-blond hair and blue eyes, I remember that. And he was good-looking in a way that made my stomach clench and my dick stand up. He loved cuddling when it was just the two of us, but in public, he didn't even want to stand too close to me. He was paranoid that someone would guess we were more than friends, to the point that he would hardly acknowledge me if his family was around. But when we were alone, he was affectionate and sweet and would fuss over me as though I was the most precious thing in existence.

And thinking back on all of that, I feel a pang of regret that it ended the way it did, that he and I could never have been anything more. It still hurts that he tried to kill me… but the pain isn't sharp anymore. Just a dull ache, easily ignored. I can think fondly of the good things between us but see how different we really were. It's unlikely Timothy would ever have felt comfortable coming out, and I would have gotten impatient with that. We would have grown apart—possibly still have ended badly, although in a different way to how we did.

I loved Timothy, and it devastated me when things fell apart between us. But maybe the old cliché is right and time does heal all wounds, because although a tiny part of me will always remember the sweetness of my first love, it no longer makes me want to cut myself off from that part of my life.

Big step, huh? Honestly—and I know you're going to find this hard to believe—I feel a little stupid for thinking I didn't ever want a relationship again. I mean, it basically took me a hundred and fifty years to get over a bad breakup because I was too busy feeling sorry for myself. Sure, a man's got a right to sulk a bit when his lover tries to make him part of his own funeral pyre, but I was sulking so much that I didn't even notice that Timothy had become just another memory to me.

He'll be long since dead, but I hope he had a nice life. I hope he was able to find happiness with someone and didn't spend all his years hiding and alone. And now it's time for me to get on with my life and maybe find someone to spend my years with.

Guess what? I've discovered a side benefit is of no longer being afraid of relationships! I don't have to avoid repeats anymore. Before, I was always nervous that hooking up with someone more than once would send the message that I might be open to more, so my motto was one-and-done (one *occasion*, that is. We shifters have exceptional stamina. "All night long" isn't just an expression for us). Now... well, if I'm open to the possibility of more, repeats are on the table.

But I might have to up my game when it comes to saying I'm not interested. If I can't turn down a fuck with a stranger because I don't want to hurt their feelings, then need Noah to help me shake them off after a one-nighter, how am I going to break things off after a few dates?

I make a note in my phone to ask Noah for tips as Aidan parks the car in the garage. Is it weird that I, a man nearing the end of his second century of life who has literally fucked more men than he can remember, am asking a twenty-year-old whose sexual encounters are undoubtedly still in double digits for dating advice?

Nah.

"Come on," I say, scrambling out of the car. "I'll make snacks while you go wash up. Sam said they'll be ready for us in about ten minutes." It's a tiny white lie, but the momentary relief on his face makes it worthwhile.

He seems a little more relaxed when he comes downstairs just as I'm setting out the platter of fruit and cheese. We just had lunch, so this should be fine to graze on during the meeting. We'll have a proper snack later.

"Thanks for setting this up," he says, gesturing to the food as he takes the stool beside me. "I needed a minute."

I find that—his open admission that he's not impervious—so incredibly attractive. I'm not sure if it's the pheromone things or the science of having a crush or just him, but I'm sure my eyes are doing that hearts-popping-out thing that happens so often in cartoons. I sigh dreamily.

He looks at me with that cute furrow forming between his brows. "You okay?"

Thankfully, my laptop chimes, because I'm pretty sure my reply would have included the words "do me now." Which isn't a bad thing, but we would have missed the very important meeting and a lot of people would have yelled at me. Plus, you know, the fate of the world.

Sometimes it's tough being awesome.

"Fine," I say instead, hitting the button to accept the call. There's the usual delay while the encryption resolves, and then the image of Percy's office appears.

Sam's looking right at the camera with his finger over his lips, so I don't say anything, then David says, "Okay, we're good."

Privacy wards. That reminds me again that we don't have any wards here at all, not even basic ones. Sorcerers are the only ones who can create them—well, and some humans, as Noah has proved—and we don't have the time to find a local sorcerer to set something up, especially since we only plan to be here a few days. Nobody but Sam knows exactly where we're staying, though. Aidan and I agreed that if anyone asked today—which of course they did—we'd name one of the bigger hotels downtown. And he deliberately took a circuitous route coming back from Jun's place.

Plus, it's not that easy to sneak up on shifters. I'm the super sniffer, remember? Or was it the supreme snifferoo? Our hearing is excellent as well. They'd need to be highly trained experts, which we don't think Tish has anymore after we raided his compounds.

Still, I make a mental note to set up some booby traps that will give us at least a little warning if someone tries to get in.

"So, what happened?" I ask, shaking off thoughts of anything else. There's nothing I can do for now.

Percy sighs. He looks worn, which is very unlike him. Even when he's tired, the magic usually gives him… I don't know. A glow? That sounds stupid. But now it's like the magic is…

Whoa. I didn't think of that, but the magic clings very closely to Percy—and Aidan. It stands to reason that what they know, it knows. As much as anything about the magic is reasonable, that is. Does that mean *the magic* is sad right now?

Gideon is the one who speaks, and from the glance he shoots at Percy, I know I'm not the only one who's noticed the difference and is worried about it. "The two boys are being held in different parts of the facility, and we saw them separately, but they both had the same visible reaction when they saw Percy. Shocked confusion is how I'd describe it. It threw them both right off stride —they were so busy sneaking peeks at Percy and trying to pretend they weren't that they didn't pay as much attention as they should have to what I was asking them."

"They so obviously didn't understand," Percy adds quietly.

"We had a casual kind of chat," Gideon continues, and I almost laugh out loud at the idea of Gideon "chatting," casually or otherwise. Sam tells me he's capable of it, but I know him as a surly but scarily efficient grump. "About growing up in a small town—or just outside it, in their case—and what that was like. Schooling, entertainment… all that stuff. It became clear quickly that they had a very basic education."

"Homeschooled?" Aidan asks. Most community children are homeschooled, according to human governments, but in actual fact, we run our own "unofficial" schools. It allows our kids a degree of freedom they wouldn't have if they had to share classes with humans, plus gives us a chance to educate them on our history and society. The number who are actually home-schooled, as in taught at home by their parents, is dramatically lower than amongst humans, especially for shifters. We like to be social—even the cats.

"No. They attended a community school. There was very little teaching about the magic, and none on community history. As far as they know, human history is entirely correct and the community has always lived in fearful hiding. This supports our theory that everyone in Beker County is aligned with Tish and the CCA."

Fuck.

"Just as an aside," I ask, "were you able to find out anything about their teachers? Tish's project only really got off the ground within the last half century. It seems unlikely that the CCA would have infiltrated the school in Beker County and begun changing what education was delivered prior to that. What reason would they have?"

"Since when has the CCA needed any reason for what they do?" Ellie asks bitterly, but then she shakes her head. "Sorry."

"You're right," David tells her, "but in this case they did wait until they had a reason before acting like batshit freaks. Noah and I have reviewed the census information for Beker County and the CCA membership files that we confiscated from their compounds. There's a definite change beginning forty-eight years ago. Before that, the population split between species in the county was what we'd expect it to be, given the location and the geography. But forty-eight years ago, an influx of hellhounds began. It was gradual at first, then picked up speed a couple years later. At around that time, other species started to drift out of the area. Several key members of the local community moved away, including a few schoolteachers."

"I can't believe we missed this," Andrew says. "I just can't get my head around the fact that they've been planning for this for fifty years, and if Sam hadn't run away from home when he was a teenager, we might never have understood exactly what was going on. How could we have missed an operation of this scope? They've literally been taking over civilian townships and indoctrinating children while still assimilated with the rest of us."

"You need to let it go," Noah tells him, and it has the rhythm of something he's already said several times. "Get past it, Andrew. We can fix our intelligence systems so we don't fuck up again in future, but that's not our primary objective right now. Focus on what we've discovered, not how we missed it before."

"Listen to him say 'we' and 'our' like that," I tease. "Noah's joined our super-special club, and he's ours forever!"

Heads slowly turn in my direction, and I'm drilled with incredulous stares. I think the joke might have fallen flat.

Possibly a timing issue?

"So, getting back to our detainees," I say.

Gideon glares at me but picks up the conversation. "The boys—"

"Sorry to interrupt, but can we stop calling them that?" Sam asks. "I mean, one of them is older than me. Do you seriously think of me as a child?" That last bit seems to be directed at Gideon, who pales and shudders.

"Point taken," he mutters. "They just don't seem as mature as you."

Sam *is* pretty mature for a cat his age. Actually, now that I think about it, most of the people I know who were raised thinking they were human—and thus had a shorter lifespan—are much more mature than those of the same age raised within the community.

Huh. Interesting, but really not relevant right now.

I tune back in to what Gideon's saying.

"…understanding of the magic is limited to the fact that it exists and makes up the fabric of the universe. They had no knowledge of the fact that it selects, invests, and guides our leaders."

"But they would have had some contact with their pack leader," Ellie protests. "Surely they felt something then?"

Percy makes a face. "We didn't want to drill down on details too much yet," he admits. "We did ask about pack gatherings, and they both became more cautious, so we left it alone. When Gideon asked about government, though… it was pretty clear that they've been taught to think the worst of CSG."

"How so?" Andrew asks.

"Right from the start, one called me the henchman of a corrupt and dictatorial regime," Gideon says dryly, and beside me, Aidan chokes on his fruit. "It was at that point I decided not to introduce Percy to them."

Without taking my eyes off the screen, I reach over and smack Aidan on the back a few times. He's nice and warm, and I'm tempted to let my hand linger. I add him an extra smack to give myself an excuse.

"Thanks, I'm good," he murmurs, squirming away from my hand. Maybe I was a bit enthusiastic.

Gideon's still talking. "They were both happy enough to talk about their schooling in exchange for more privileges, and we were able to get a lot of information I don't think they intended to give. We've inferred some facts about their local hierarchy and lifestyle. There's a full briefing file and some charts saved in the drive—the subfolder is called Beker County." I minimize the video screen and flip over to the secure shared drive while Gideon gives us a quick rundown of the documents he put together. I click into them, skimming quickly through, looking for anything I might want to ask questions about in this meeting. Aidan's warm breath brushes the side of my neck as he leans in to read too, and I inhale the scent of him. I never paid much attention to it before, but I really like it. There's the soothing scent of species leader—comforting, friendly, dependable—but that's not *him*. It's part of who he is now, but the scent that's uniquely his, that he was born with and that will be his until he dies, is separate from that.

And I want to cover myself in it. Just roll around in it and breathe it in. Maybe after he falls asleep I'll steal one of his shirts so I can just smell him whenever I want.

Is that creepy? That might be creepy. I'll just have to fuck him so often that I'll be able to smell him on myself all the time.

Yeah. That's a much better idea.

Gideon finishes his overview, and I say, "I'm just looking through the docs, and would you say it's safe to say that Beker County is hostile to CSG, to the lucifer, and to any and all magically-invested leaders of our people?"

"Yes." Gideon barely lets me finish before he replies. "I'd go beyond hostile and consider the entire county to be part of a terrorist organization and actively dangerous to anyone associated with CSG or community leadership. I'm going back tomorrow to interview the detainees again, and I expect to have further information after that, but in my expert opinion, that status is only going to be confirmed."

Gideon's been in this job for decades, and prior to that he worked extensively in several different parts of the world identifying and analyzing terrorist and anti-government organizations. David is our go-to for planning and research, but there's nobody better than Gideon when it comes to assessing and neutralizing threats on this scale. If he says Beker County is a terrorist hotspot, I'll take that as fact.

"That's going to make things trickier here," I advise. "We were hoping to ask around in Beker County and try to identify the three hellhounds that helped Tish take Noah. Plus, I wanted to sniff around and see if Tish or any of the elves were in the area. But I can't risk taking Aidan anywhere near there now, and I'm not that happy about leaving him here alone either."

"Beg pardon?" There's suddenly a whole lot more Irish in Aidan's voice, and his scent has shifted slightly. Waves of annoyance assault my nostrils.

"Yeah, I get that, Alistair," Gideon says, "but there's not much we can do about it. There's a CSG office in

Seattle with an enforcement special ops team—I could have them come down and stay with him, if you want?"

"You *what?*" The scent of annoyance changes to pure pissed-offedness. "I don't need a feckin' nanny! And I don't need to be left safely at home. Those are *my* people in Beker County, and I'll be going out there to talk to them."

"No." It's not just me who says it—there's a chorus from my laptop speakers.

"We talked about this, Aidan," I continue. "Remember? I'm in charge when there's a threat to your safety."

"There's no threat," he insists. "I was just in Beker County a few days ago. They might not have welcomed me like a long-lost loved one, but I was in no danger."

"That you knew of," Andrew points out. "They might have been willing to placate you so you'd leave without poking around too much. Going back there now would be announcing that you have suspicions about them, and they'll probably act at that point."

"Not likely," Aidan scorns. "They'd have to know that if I 'had suspicions,' as you put it, I would have discussed them with CSG. The very fact that I'd be accompanied by Alistair would tell them that. They'd be better off continuing to placate us while they hid all the evidence. In the meantime, Alistair could have a good sniff around."

"They'd know exactly what you were doing," Andrew argues. "Don't forget, they know we have two of their people in custody. Standard procedure is to assume that at least *some* information has been compromised—which it has. You coming back just a few days after your last visit, with a senior CSG investigator glued to your side, would be viewed as a hostile incursion to confirm information obtained during interrogation. There's a much better chance that they'll take you hostage or kill you outright than that they'll try to fob you off again."

I keep my mouth closed for now and let Andrew do the heavy lifting. After all, he won't care how Aidan feels about him once the call is done, but I still have high hopes for sex later—which I'm not likely to get if Aidan's mad at me.

Unless he likes angry sex…?

Not worth the risk—not while Andrew's willing to take the brunt of his anger, anyway.

Sneaking a sidelong glance at Aidan, I can see he's fuming but reluctantly resigned to the fact that Andrew's right. That doesn't stop him from a last-ditch argument.

"The magic will protect me."

Silence falls, and glances are exchanged. "Do we really want it to come to that?" Percy asks. "Even if the magic saves your life in an initial encounter, once they attack, they commit to that path. We're not ready for an all-out war with the CCA, Aidan. We want to avoid that altogether if we can."

Aidan sighs. "I know. I know. Okay, fine," he concedes. "But I don't need a babysitter here in Portland. And how is it safe for Alistair to go out to Beker County, then?"

"It's not," Gideon says bluntly. "That's why he should go. It would finally rid us all of his presence."

I gasp, Sam slaps Gideon upside the head, Ellie—my beloved cousin!—laughs out loud, and the others all cough or look away to hide their amusement.

"How… *how* could you say such a thing?" I demand. "You would be in the depths of despair if anything happened to me! Your grief and pain would know no bounds… it would take over your every waking moment and suffuse your sleep."

"Suffuse?" Noah raises an eyebrow. "Really?"

"You would suffer as you had never before imagined possible. And you wouldn't get any for ages because Sam would feel the same way. Worse! He'd feel worse! The loss of his bestest BFF would tear the very breath from his lungs and—"

"That's absolutely true," Sam breaks in. "Gideon, if something happened to Alistair, I'd be too upset to have sex."

The expression on Gideon's face would be comical if he wasn't talking about *murdering* me, wiping me from this plane and sending me to the next. Don't get me wrong, I look forward to one day returning to the spiritual plane for some R&R before my next life, but I'm nowhere ready to go yet.

"By all means," Gideon snarks, "let's do everything in our power to keep Alistair alive. Maybe imprisoned?" He shoots a glance at Sam, who shakes his head.

"At least Sam loves me," I say mournfully. "It gives me peace to know that my death would be mourned by my bestest bestie, that the loss of me would cause him to rend his hair with grief—"

"Whoa," Sam interrupts. "Let's not go too far. I wouldn't look good bald—I have the wrong shaped head."

"—and should I be taken hostage and tortured, I will take strength from the knowledge that my BFF is tearing the world apart, stone by stone, in an attempt to get me back."

"Yeah, that I would do," Sam agrees. "I'd even make these guys help."

"I don't know," Ellie says doubtfully. "Stone by stone? That sounds like hard work."

"You suck," I tell her. "I'm telling Aunt Vivienne on you." I stop and think about how that conversation would go. Aunt Vivienne would likely want to know why I couldn't just rescue myself. "Well, I'll tell your mom, anyway."

"Now that we've decided to keep Alistair alive and try to get him back if he's taken hostage," David begins dryly.

"After they've tortured him a bit," Andrew qualifies. "Al said something about needing to take strength while he was being tortured. We don't want to deprive him of that."

I shake my head. "You're supposed to be my secondary best friend," I accuse.

"What?" Aidan asks. "I… What is even going on here?"

"You get used to it," Percy assures him, smiling slightly.

"*Anyway,*" David raises his voice. He's not shouting, because I don't think he ever does, but there's a definite edge there, "before Alistair can be taken captive, tortured, and rescued, we need to put together a plan for his trip to Beker County."

There's a momentary silence before I say, "I want to put a pin in the idea of bringing enforcers down to stay with Aidan—"

He immediately begins to protest, and I hold up a hand.

"I know you're against it, but I think the idea has

merit and I want to come back to it later. First, let's focus on what I'm doing. If we can't come up with a good plan for me, we won't need to argue about what to do with you."

His eyes narrow dangerously. "What to do with me?"

Those might have been the wrong words. Fortunately for me, David steps in.

"Do you have any ideas, Alistair?"

I tear my gaze away from Aidan's set face—sex is beginning to look like a pipe dream—and focus on the screen. "Nothing I love. The original plan to actually talk to the pack members in Beker County and just poke around casually is obviously not feasible now. That leaves me with trying to recon without being noticed." I grimace.

"In an area full of hellhounds?" Andrew shakes his head.

"They'd smell you before you got close enough to find out anything," David agrees. "There's no way you'd be able to poke around without a confrontation."

"And you're not that good an actor," Ellie adds. "Even if they're inclined to believe that your presence is completely coincidental and unconnected to CSG— which, if they really are connected to Tish, they won't— you'd probably fuck it up and make them suspicious anyway."

"That hurts, Elinor. You've ripped my heart from my chest. Don't you know I have dreams of someday becoming a thespian envied by all others? Once I retire from being the preeminent investigator CSG has ever seen—"

"Excuse me?" Andrew says. "Preeminent?"

"—I plan to follow in the steps of so many outstanding actors and tread the boards—"

"Yeah, okay, Al, let's shelve that dream for a little while and concentrate on building your preeminent reputation," Sam cuts in. "But I'll buy you some acting lessons for your birthday."

I blink. "Why would I need acting lessons?"

"I think we can all agree," David says hastily, "that even a low-key attempt at recon in Beker County would have too high a risk of capture or worse. We're not ready for any kind of direct confrontation yet, not until we know more about what we're up against."

"Which we won't if we don't go into Beker County," I point out. "Don't get me wrong, I'm not keen to be taken prisoner and tortured—sorry to disappoint, Gideon—but we can't just sit on our hands and wait for the sky to fall and a million elves to pop in through portals. I'm trained for this kind of covert op. The risk isn't great, but any risk assessment you do is going to tell you it's necessary."

Before anyone else can say anything, Aidan holds up a hand. "Hang on. What do you mean, you're trained for covert ops? I didn't think CSG did those."

"I haven't always worked for CSG," I say, bringing up Google Maps and searching Beker County. "I used to work for Enforcement on a special ops team." It was a long time ago—something I took up right after the fiasco with Timothy left me feeling like my life could only be worth something in service to my people—but I still regularly attend retraining and accreditation courses. I figure the skills might come in handy, even if I no longer want to be treated like a chess piece by the higher-ups at Enforcement.

"Really?" he sounds surprised. "I thought those special ops teams were hard-bitten superhero types."

I slowly turn toward him. "Are you… Do you not think I'm the hard-bitten superhero type?" How could he?

"Well…"

"Uh-oh," someone mutters as my jaw drops.

"I am too a superhero!" I insist. "I—"

"Alistair," Percy intercedes, and I shut my mouth. "You know *I* think you're a superhero, right? We talked about how valuable I find those skills during your interview for the team."

Damn right we did. I nod, maybe a little sulkily. Can you blame me? The guy I've been weaving decadent sexual fantasies about doesn't think I'm the special ops superhero type.

"Yes," I mutter.

"So you and Aidan can resolve this… whatever it is later. Let's stay focused on the primary issue."

Before I can reply, Gideon's talking. "Alistair's right about the risk assessment. However you look at it, the value of any information we can gather is currently worth—"

"Worth more than Alistair's life?" Sam sounds angry. "I can't believe you said that!"

"Well, technically you said it." Gideon reaches out and takes Sam's hand, only to have it snatched away. "And it's not what I was going to say."

"What were you going to say?" My bestest bestie sounds pissed. It's nice to know he loves me so much, but in this case, he needs to get over it.

"It's worth deploying a covert operative into the area for recon, even given the level of danger. That doesn't mean Alistair should just stroll in there. We know it's inevitable that they're going to notice him, so we need to work out what we need, what the safest and fastest way to obtain it is, and then build our plan around that."

Sam sniffs, and I bite my lip to hide a smile. See? Nobody can resist the wonder that is me.

"Okay, so what do we need?" Noah asks. "What information do we think we can get from Beker County that we can't get elsewhere?"

"Tish's location," Ellie says immediately. "And anything about the elves."

Yeah, because that's going to be easy to lay hands on. The doubt I'm feeling is reflected in my teammates' expressions.

"What's involved in this kind of recon?" Noah asks suddenly. "I mean, introducing yourself and sitting down for a conversation is not an option, and if they're aligned with Tish, there's a good chance they'd recognize you, so it's not like you can strike up casual chats with locals and ask leading questions, right?"

Andrew turns to face his... boyfriend? lover? bedtime snack? and purses his lips. "What exactly would those leading questions be? 'Have you noticed any unusual-looking strangers hanging around?'"

Noah shoves him. "I just said that wasn't something he could do. Stop being a smartass and tell me what's actually involved."

All eyes turn to me. "Mostly observation," I tell them. "Using whatever intel I can get beforehand, I'll try to position myself near people who might have information and hope to overhear something. I'll see what—and who —I can smell. I've smelled both Tish and an elf before, so I'll know if they've been in the area recently or are still there. I'll count heads and see if our estimate of numbers is right, look for any weapons that can be used against us… that kind of thing. The big issue is that my time will be very limited—like we said, these are hellhounds. They'll smell an unknown hellhound pretty quick and come looking for me. With other species—especially humans—I'd spend hours or even days skulking around the area, maybe even risk breaking into some buildings overnight and looking through documents."

David sighs and rubs his forehead. "We need to rethink this. How long do you realistically think you could have before they found you?"

I think about it. I'm completely unfamiliar with the terrain, whereas it's their home ground. On the other hand, none of our information so far has shown them to have more than rudimentary training, and definitely nobody with special ops-level skills. It's a largely rural area, not much concrete to bounce sounds and lots of wildlife and nature to muddle scent, and it's a large area. "Two, maybe three hours. Depends on how spread out they are through the county."

"How long before they noticed you and began the search?" Gideon asks. "Because once they know you're there, you're not going to get anything more and you'll need to get out."

I grimace. "Hard to say. It depends on whether they have any kind of perimeter set up or if they're still acting like it's a normal town. Let's say fifteen minutes at worst, forty-five at best."

"This sucks," David declares. "What you're saying is that realistically, you'd have about half an hour to find the information we need and leave without even knowing where in the county to look. If they find you or even suspect that you're more than some random passing through, it could make them act before we're ready." He shakes his head. "Could you even locate a person of interest to eavesdrop on in that time?"

"I can point out the houses of the senior pack members on Google Maps," Aidan says, "and describe them for you. You'd at least know where to go right away. But they live a bit outside of town and off the highway. Just getting out there will take up most of your time."

"Fuck," I mutter, flipping back to the map screen and zooming in on the outlying areas of town. "It won't work, then. They'll hear a vehicle coming faster than they'll smell me. If I can't go on foot, I'll never get close enough, and if I go on foot, it'll take too long." There has to be a way to do this.

"Let's be practical," Noah says. "With that kind of time limit, the chances that you'll overhear or see something valuable are ridiculously slim. How does the smelling thing work?"

I blink. "Did you just ask me how smelling works? Humans can smell, right? I always thought humans could smell!"

"They can," Aidan assures me, then stops. "Well, I just assumed they could."

"Of course we can smell," Noah snarls, and I'm glad there's the width of a continent between us. "But we can't smell as well as you can, so shut the fuck up and tell me how your sense of smell works!"

I don't say anything, partly because he told me to shut the fuck up, and partly because I don't actually know what to say. How does my sense of smell work? It just… does.

I breathe in. Scents register. That's all.

But I'm afraid to say that, because Noah's face is going red.

"I'll take this one," Ellie says. I feel like maybe I should warn her about how dangerous Noah is, but she's been kind of mean to me today. His wrath might be the just desserts she deserves. "Our sense of smell is maybe seventy thousand times better than yours, in general terms. We have about fifty times as many olfactory receptors as you do, and the part of the brain dedicated to processing scent is a lot bigger too. So we can not only smell things you can't, we can also analyze them better."

Noah's just staring at her. "Seventy *thousand* times better?"

Elinor nods solemnly.

"How do you know that?" Sam asks curiously. "Alistair and Aidan weren't even sure if humans could smell at all."

"Hey," Aidan protests before I can, then subsides when Sam raises an eyebrow. Because… yeah. We weren't sure.

Ellie shrugs. "I worked it out once."

I want to call her a nerd for going to all that fuss over something so esoteric, but Sam and I once worked out the difference between shifter and human metabolism, so… nerds of the world unite?

"Okay," Noah says, shaking his head, "okay, putting aside the fact that I don't know how you even get through the day being assaulted with smells like that, does that mean that Alistair could drive down the main street of the town and collect a bunch of smells that might be useful? Like, could you smell from the car? And what kind of range would you have—just the street itself? Or more?"

I stare at his face on the screen and then smack myself repeatedly on the forehead.

"There, there." Aidan pats my shoulder. "Nobody else thought of it, either. Maybe numbers aren't the only reason the humans nearly exterminated us."

Andrew groans. Noah grins. I can just imagine what the conversation will be like at their place tonight.

I flip back to the maps page and zoom in on the town center. It looks like the highway cuts through part of the town rather than going around, which is a massive win for us. Even if someone did manage to get a whiff of me on my way through, it wouldn't set off warning bells—there must be plenty of people using the highway to get through town.

"There's where most of the people I met with live," Aidan says, pointing to a cluster of properties a little ways from the south end of town. I switch to the Earth view, wanting the satellite images. He was right before— the location is well away from the highway and thus any ambient noise that could disguise the approach of my car. Even if I added hours to my drive time and circled around to approach the town from the south, there's no way I could get close enough on foot within the allotted timeframe.

But—

"Alistair," Sam complains, "we can't see what you're looking at. Share the screen, please, or at least talk us through it."

Oh. I forgot about them.

"How do I share, again?" Sam's shown me plenty of times, but it's one of those pieces of information that just doesn't stick. He walks me through it in a long-suffering tone while the others heckle me.

"Okay," I say once he's confirmed that they can see the map. "This is the area where Aidan says he visited." I circle my cursor over it. "Aidan, is this the exit you took off the highway to get there?" I hover over the line on the screen. Aidan leans forward for a closer look, squinting.

"Aye, I think so."

I spare a second to wonder what's brought out his Irish this time—he can't be mad at me for asking him to look at the map, can he?—then return my attention to mission planning.

"That looks like the only road leading out to those properties, doesn't it?" I zoom the map in, looking for smaller roads and dirt tracks. They're there, but none of them are positioned in a way that would cause a local to avoid using the highway.

"The highway is the best way to get to town and beyond," Gideon's voice agrees. "If Tish is there or has been there at any stage, he'll have traveled on the highway."

"Potentially having left a scent trail, even from a vehicle?" Noah sounds skeptical. "How long would that even last?"

"Not long, if it's even there," I confirm. "It's still pretty cold, so the windows would probably be up in the car. Plus, if they're using portals to come and go, there won't be any scent of them along the road and probably not much within my range around it, even if I parked at that exit and took a quick run through the area."

"So it's a bust," Sam says gloomily.

"Not necessarily," Andrew counters. "Driving through town and then past that exit will still give Alistair more information than we currently have. Plus, if Tish or the elves have been in the area for a while and left enough scent markers around, he may still get a whiff of them."

"David," Ellie says slowly, and even without seeing her, I can tell she's got that "thinking" expression on her face. "What's the weather like in Beker at the moment?"

"Why are you asking me? It's been so long since I was outside, I barely know what the weather's like here," David protests, but I hear the clack of keys and know he's looking it up.

"Been sleeping in your office?" Percy asks.

"Uh… no. Of course not."

"Ah, in my office, then."

"Ellie, the weather in Beker right now is clear but damn cold, low humidity, light wind out of the— Oh."

I look at the map, feeling thoroughly stupid for the second time in less than half an hour. "Let me guess," I say resignedly. "The wind's out of the south-east?" How could I have forgotten to check the wind direction? Thank fuck for Ellie.

"Yes. And looking at the three-day forecast, it's going to stay that way. Elinor, you can use me as your weatherman anytime you like."

I study the terrain in that area. It's only lightly wooded, and the highway cuts through at the perfect angle.

"This is good, right?" Aidan asks. "With the wind blowing in that direction, even I'd probably be able to pick up scents from those properties."

"It's good," I agree. "I can drive relatively slowly through town"—I trace the route with the cursor—"and see what I pick up. If I time it for the right part of the day, there will be plenty of people around, and a lot from the outlying properties might be running errands. Lots of things to see and smell, and if I don't stop, nobody will take any notice of me. Then I continue on along the highway to here"—I stop the cursor at a bend —"and pull over. If the wind is blowing steadily, I'll only need a few minutes. Ten at the very most. I expect to be able to tell you how many hellhounds—and beings of other species—live in this general area"—I move the cursor in a cone shape, estimating wind vectors—"and specifically whether Tish and any elves are there or have been there recently."

"How recent is recently?" Noah asks.

"Depends," I say honestly. "Has it rained lately? How long were they there for? Did they spend much time outdoors, or inside only? If all factors are in our favor, maybe two weeks. Ten days is more likely, but it could be as little as a week or just a few days if they used the portal inside, never left the building, and stayed for only an hour." I scan the surrounding area. "On the plus side, there are no towns or factories or pig farms that I can see out this way. Nothing to dilute or overpower the scents."

"The last time it rained in the area was nearly three weeks ago," David says, "but they did get a light snowfall a few days after that, and there've been some pretty heavy overnight frosts."

"So we hope they've spent a lot of time there," I say, shrugging. "This is still our best option to gather any kind of information."

"What happens if someone's driving along the high-way, notices you've pulled over, and stops?" There's a lot of concern in Sam's voice. Aww. Our friendship will endure time, distance, and grumpy boyfriends.

Hey, that's pretty catchy. Maybe we can make it our official BFF slogan or something. We can have T-shirts printed.

"There's a rest stop here. Nobody will question me stretching my legs with a phone held to my ear," I tell him.

"Won't they want to know why you didn't stop in town?" Noah counters. "It's not that far and would be a more logical place to stretch your legs."

"That's what the phone's for. They'll assume I pulled over to answer the call. Which is also why I'm going to be driving an older vehicle, not our rental. Something that doesn't have Bluetooth."

"I'll put some extra cash in your account," David advises. "You won't be able to use your credit card at a used car lot."

"Not the kind I plan on visiting, anyway," I agree.

"Wait, go back to pacing at the rest stop," Noah demands. "Won't that leave a nice big concentrated pool of your scent for them? I thought we were trying to avoid that."

"We're trying to avoid having my scent saturate the area because I've spent a lot of time there. It especially becomes an issue if I'm moving around. A strange hell-hound in the area, lingering near them but not intro-ducing himself? That's suspicious. But someone taking a break at a rest stop… well, what's unusual about that?"

"They'll have your scent," Noah protests.

"And it means nothing unless they've met me

personally before. I recognize Tish's scent because I smelled it on Sam, then again at the office when they took you. I know what the elves smell like because I've never smelled anything like that before. I've been to Oregon before, yeah, but it was a long time ago and I never visited Beker County. The chances of there being someone there now whom I've met before are so slim I wouldn't know how to calculate them."

"Not that you'd know how to calculate them if they weren't slim," Andrew interjects.

"That's not helpful, secondary BFF. And not true. I can ask David just as well as everyone else can."

"Asking me to calculate odds does not count as calculating them yourself," David insists. I ignore him.

"Chill, Noah. This is a good plan."

"What happens after you've had a good sniff?" Aidan asks, leaning in to look at the map again. This time, his shoulder brushes mine, and adrenaline, already on stand-by at the thought of tomorrow, floods through my veins.

Look at my lap. Look at my lap. C'mon. He'll already be able to smell my arousal, but I want him to see my hard-on that's just for him.

"Alistair?" He turns his head to look at me—sadly, at my face, not the impressive hard-on that's all for him—and he's so close, so very close…

I lean in.

He jerks back, his eyes widening as he casts a panicked glance toward the laptop.

Shit. When I shared the map, did I do the thing that would still show us in a little box? Or did I full-screen share the map?

I hold my breath for a second. If my team saw what

just happened, I'll hear all about it. There's no way any of them would keep their mouths shut. Not even David.

Well, maybe David. He wouldn't want to embarrass Aidan. But he'd find some way to jab at me about it later.

"Alistair?" Sam repeats. "Can you guys still hear us?"

I think we might be safe. I clear my throat. "Uh, yeah. Sorry, I got distracted." *Please don't ask by what.*

"By what?"

I sigh, casting around for something plausible. "Grapes."

"You got distracted by grapes?" Sam sounds a little dubious. "Were you eating?"

Since when has he been so nosy? I mean, seriously, who cares whether I was eating the grapes?

"No, I was just looking at them all bunched up on the stem and thinking that from the right angle, they could almost look like testicles."

Aidan chokes on a grape. I pound him on the back, something it seems I should get used to doing—someone needs to teach the man to chew his food properly—while a cacophony of weird sounds come through my laptop speakers.

For the record, I don't think grapes look like testicles.

Well… not really. Only from certain angles and if the grapes are the right shape.

"Anyway, what were we saying?"

"I don't know, but it's put me off grapes," Noah mutters. "Uh… what happens after you're done at the rest stop?"

"Oh. I get back in the car, keep driving down the

highway to here"—I grab the mouse and trace the cursor over a turnoff about twenty miles further down the road, outside the limits of Beker County—"where I turn around and go back the way I came. I'll slow down as I pass—"

"Wait, what?" Noah asks. "You're going back? Why?"

"As I was saying," I say patiently, "I'll slow down as I pass the point where I stopped, see if anyone has been in that immediate area since I was there, then continue on through town and stop on the other side, right about here." I circle another bend. "We know there are persons of interest in the area near the first stop, but it's unlikely all the community members in the county live in that one spot. We might be able to gather some useful information at the north end of town, too."

"Is it safe?" Aidan asks doubtfully. "Won't it raise suspicion if they smell you again?"

I shrug. "Potentially, but probably not. At this stage, I'm an idiot who missed the turnoff to"—I trace back up the highway north of town—"route 82. This is an arterial road and gets a lot of traffic. It's also the main route to dozens of little towns in the area. There are a lot of reasons why I might go both ways through the county—and that's why I'm not just doubling back right after the first stop. The extra driving time makes it look like I'm actually going somewhere. Plus, I love driving in the country. There are so many amazing smells, y'know?"

"So if someone approaches you at the second stop, are you going to fake another phone call?" Noah still doesn't seem convinced.

"No, I'm going to have a crumpled old paper map

and be swearing about how all these damn turnoffs look alike."

"What if they suggest you use your phone GPS?"

"Aside from the fact that cell coverage can be spotty in those areas for those who don't have a satellite phone —which they don't need to know I do—I don't trust it since the time it told me to turn left *now* while I was in the middle of a bridge."

"I remember that," Sam murmurs. "It was scary how vicious she sounded."

"It's a computer-generated voice," David argues. "It can't sound vicious. And it probably meant for you to turn once you got off the bridge."

"Except…" I lean closer to the camera for dramatic effect, then remember they can't see me. "…there was nowhere to turn left at the end of the bridge unless I wanted to bounce off a tree. And you weren't there, David. Believe me, she was vicious."

"Wait, this actually happened?" Noah demands. "I thought it was just part of the story you'd tell!"

"The story of Alistair's life." There's a hint of laughter in Andrew's voice.

"Getting back on topic," Aidan says, "you stop for a second sniff north of town."

"And then I come back to Portland and we make plans." It's pretty simple, really. "I'll check in with you all as much as possible during."

"I really hate this plan," Gideon says thoughtfully, and I flip away from the map screen and look at their faces again. "The expected outcome is lackluster, and if anything goes wrong, we don't only risk losing Alistair but also any advantage we have."

"We have an advantage?" Aidan asks dryly.

"Time," Percy tells him. "We need as much time as possible to keep investigating and find as much information as possible. If Tish and the CCA decide to move now… Well, we don't even know what we're up against."

"Let's hear it for time, then." Aidan sighs. "What else can I do? I'm feeling a wee bit useless right now."

"*Not* useless," I insist. "Your presence this morning was invaluable. And we might have time for you to drive me around Portland this afternoon while I stick my head out the window and smell for elves."

"Man, I wish I could be there to get video of that," Andrew says. "Any chance you'll take some, Aidan?"

"I'll see what I can do," Aidan promises.

"Hey!" I'm being betrayed! "I will be working for the safety and betterment of life as we know it, and my secondary best friend is trying to make fun of me for it! Shame on you! And as for my—"

Whoops.

I fake a cough. "As for Aidan, there can be no greater shame than being ridiculed by the leader of my own species!"

Phew! Good thing I'm quick.

I glance at the screen and see all eyes focused on me. Uh-oh.

"So are we ready to wrap this meeting up?" I ask. Distract, distract.

"Uh… yeah." David looks down at his notepad, where he undoubtedly has a neatly itemized list. "Noah and I are going to continue with our research. Aidan, if you have any bandwidth, we could use your help."

"Absolutely," Aidan promises.

"Gideon and Percy are going to interrogate our

captives again. You're sniffing around Portland today and then buying a car and driving out to Beker County tomorrow to sniff some more. Andrew and Elinor are running the office, and Sam's coordinating everything." David looks up. "Can we agree that our goal for the next twenty-four hours is to gather enough information to come up with a plan?"

"Yes." Andrew's gone all serious. "We can't keep waiting. Tish is going to move eventually, and we have to be ready—or we have to move first." He shakes his head. "I have a very strong feeling that we should be moving first."

I sit up straighter. I've only experienced Andrew's vaunted instincts once, and it meant the difference between David and Ellie being injured rather than David dying. It also allowed us to take the two captives who are now giving us so much information. I've heard many other stories about times his instincts made a dramatic difference, so if he thinks we need to move first, I'm with him on that.

Percy seems to agree. "Tomorrow evening, we meet again," he orders. "Be ready to come up with a plan to move forward."

There's a chorus of agreement, then the call ends.

I turn to Aidan. "We need to talk."

CHAPTER EIGHT

Alistair

AIDAN, who was eyeing off the remains of the fruit and cheese platter (there're a few grapes, but he seems reluctant to grab those for some reason), drags his gaze back to me and says, "What about?"

"What you'll be doing tomorrow while I'm driving out to Beker County."

He sets his jaw, a mulish look in his eyes. "I do not need a babysitter."

"I agree. But this isn't about your competence or capability. It's about what might happen if Tish knows you're here and sends a team to grab you. No single person can be expected to come out best when up against a team. You're a valuable asset, and Tish has to know that he can use you against us."

"He doesn't even know we're here!"

"Are you sure about that?" I counter. "Don't you think he or some of the Beker County hellhounds would have contacts here in Portland? We spent the whole morning being very high profile with most of the local pack members. They all know your name and that you're here."

"I'm not the one who made it quite so high profile," he gripes. "You're the one who started the whole limbo thing."

I grin because that was one of my better ideas. And no matter what anyone says, I was robbed—I should have won. I'm willing to let it go, though, because did you see how bendy Aidan is? Like… rawr. The things I can do with that kind of flexibility.

"Alistair?"

I yank my attention away from some very interesting fantasies and smile innocently at him.

"It doesn't matter who started what," I say, which is something I've said many, many times in my life in an attempt to get out of trouble. It hardly ever works but is still worth a try. "What's important is what we do to make sure you're secure."

"I really hate the idea of an enforcement team coming to stand guard over me," he admits.

I nod. "Do you have any alternative suggestions?" I already have an idea in mind, but I want him to think he's got options. He's already mad at me, and I haven't yet given up my hopes for sex.

He shrugs. "Well… nobody knows specifically where we are, right? They could possibly know I'm in Portland, but not where exactly. And the only time I've left this house was in a car, so the chances of them being able to track us back here are slim—the rental car is pretty generic. With that many of the same make and model in the city, it would be impossible to isolate the scent of ours specifically."

He's right about that—one of the first things I did

when we got the car was take a nice deep sniff. There's nothing to distinguish our car from the hundreds—thousands—of others of the same kind in Portland.

"So you think you'll be safe if you just stay here inside the house?" It's likely he would be, but I'm uneasy about taking that risk.

"Well… aye."

I shake my head. "I agree that it's unlikely anyone would find you here, but that doesn't mean it's impossible, and a decent team could easily trap you in this house. They might not even want to take you, just strike a blow at us by killing you. In which case, they can stay safely out of reach and set the place on fire or something, then shoot you when you run outside."

His already fair skin goes a little paler. "What a charming thought that is," he murmurs. "So no matter what happens, I don't run out the front door. And the back door is probably not an option either, right?"

"They'd have lovely cover in a fenced courtyard," I inform him. "Nobody to see them and wonder why they're loitering." I might not have to suggest anything after all. It seems like he's working his way toward the solution on his own. Is the burst of pride that gives me weird?

"What about the upstairs windows? All these condos are joined together. I could shift, go out a window, and escape over the rooftops."

"What's to stop them from anticipating that and waiting for you? Or chasing you once you're up there? You'll probably be dealing with hellhounds—once they have your scent, they'll be able to track you anywhere you go."

His face creases with frustration. "Well, what do you suggest, then? Other than a squad of enforcers."

I slide off my stool. "You're on the right track. Come on." He follows me across the room and up the stairs, and then into each of the bedrooms and bathrooms as I examine the windows.

"Are you going to tell me what you're doing?" he asks finally, stepping back from the doorway of the en-suite bathroom off my bedroom. He looks around, then goes to take a seat in one of the armchairs by the window. "You really are a sneaky bastard, aren't you?"

"I have no idea what you're talking about," I say loftily, coming out of the bathroom and collapsing across the bed. I roll onto my stomach and prop my chin on my hands. "I'm never sneaky." I kick my legs and smile winsomely.

He laughs, and there's real warmth in his eyes as he watches me. My heartbeat picks up a little, and I have to clear my throat.

"So, um, your best bet is the en-suite window," I tell him. "There's a sheer drop to the ground, no ledge or anything, and the roof is out of arm's reach. The window itself is also too small for a hellhound in biped form, so unless they bring a cat with them, it will be inaccessible to them."

"What are their chances of bringing a cat?" he asks, raising a brow.

"Slim. Gideon's report mentioned that most of the professional or trade positions within the area were filled by non-hellhounds. That leads me to think those other species are there because they don't have that skillset themselves, and thus it seems likely that their muscle is going to be hellhound."

He frowns and seems to be thinking about that. "You're saying they're raising the majority species in the area—in this case hellhounds—to be soldiers, and bringing in their doctors and teachers and the like from elsewhere?"

"Yes. It allows them to limit education. I'd hazard a guess that any young hellhounds who show high intelligence or aptitude for professional training would be sent to one of the other enclaves for training. They don't want people to see one among them getting education that's not available to the rest, but at the same time, they need skilled, educated professionals."

"I'm going to freak out and get pissed over the fact that they're basically farming their children later," he says. "For now, let's assume you're right and the people who *potentially* would come after me would be hellhounds."

"I'm always right, babe. The sooner you learn that, the easier it will be to acclimate to the wonder that is me." I honestly didn't mean for the endearment to slip out, but I'm not going to apologize for it now.

He goes adorably pink. Well… flaming red, to be honest. From the collar of his shirt to the top of his forehead, with a particularly virulent shade on his ears. I wonder if the blush goes downward, too—is his chest all flushed and hot? Could I follow the wave of his embarrassment with my lips, all the way down…

Phew.

I shift my weight slightly to the side to relieve the pressure on my dick and cough lightly. Maybe having this discussion in my bedroom isn't a good idea.

On the other hand, once we've finished talking business, I'm hoping we can get down to *business*.

But first…

"So it's likely to be hellhounds coming for you, and they won't be able to use the window in the en suite to gain access, nor follow you out that way. Cats climb better than hellhounds, so you have the advantage."

"Right, but, ah…" He's still a little pink but seems to be following my lead in pretending I never said the *b* word. "Once I'm out the window, then what? I climb up or down, and they could be waiting on the roof or the ground. And that's assuming I make it to the en suite before they catch me."

I raise a brow, and he gets this funny look on his face, like he wants to smile but is stopping himself. Not sure what that's all about, but the look in his eyes is all soft, and I like that. He should always look at me that way.

Wait… what?

I may be taking this "ready to put the past behind me" thing a little more seriously than I thought.

Sex. Just sex… for now.

"You won't need to make it to the en suite," I say, trying to regain control of my wits. "You'll already be there."

He blinks. "Wha— You want me to spend the whole time you're gone in the bathroom? That'll be most of the day!"

"It's the safest place for you. There's only one point where they can gain entry—which you will lock—and you'll likely hear them coming and be able to leave before they get anywhere near that door." I tip my head toward the en-suite door. "Even if they come in through the window in here, you'll have at least a minute warning—provided you're not blasting music or anything." I let my tone convey how stupid that would be.

He doesn't look happy about the idea of being locked in the bathroom all day—not that I can blame him—and I'm pretty sure he's going to come back to that point, but all he says is "And then what?"

"You shift and go out the window," I say promptly. "Hellhounds as a rule need a lot of training to be good at dealing with heights, and it's unlikely the CCA will have given them that. You go up to the roof, then stay low and go across four condos toward the main street."

Utter bewilderment crosses his face. "Why?"

"Sam rented that one for us as well. The layout is exactly the same. Before I leave tomorrow, I'll make sure the en-suite window is open and that there's a car in the garage."

His mouth opens as though he's going to say something, then he closes it again and sucks in a deep breath. "Why did Sam rent two condos for us? And why are we in this one, not that one?"

"We have no wards here," I remind him. "We're completely exposed to any shifter who wants to walk in through the door, never mind professional thieves and the like. The second condo gives us a place to temporarily regroup and stage a full, *safe* retreat from. It's closer to the main street, so there's a better chance of us being outside the ring of our attackers once we reach it."

He just shakes his head. "This was supposed to be a diplomatic fact-finding visit to our own people," he reminds me, "and now I find out you've been treating it like a mission in enemy territory from the start."

I steel myself against the urge to get up and hug

him. "It's not a mission in enemy territory—that's what I'll be doing tomorrow. But we're here without any protections for you, knowing that nearby there are people actively working against us. It would have been dumb not to take any precautions at all."

Sighing, he asks, "What do I do when I make it to the other condo? Get in the car and go? Where?"

I shake my head. "Nope. That's a last resort. The first thing you do is call local enforcement. They don't have any special ops people, but at that stage it won't matter. Tell them who you are and that a group of people have broken in. Then call Sam, and he'll have the same call made from the lucifer's office, which will guarantee they move fast."

"So I'm supposed to sit there until enforcement shows up? Won't the hellhounds track me by scent?"

"By the time they realize you went out the window and figure you went over the roofs, enforcement should be on the way. Remember, they're not good climbers. They'll circle the condo complex first, looking for where you came down, and when they don't find it, they'll look for a ladder. By the time they actually get up to the rooftops to start following your scent, enforcement will be here." I pause. "If, and only if, they somehow find you before enforcement arrives, get in the car and go. Run them down if you have to. Stay on the phone with Sam the whole time, and he'll guide you to somewhere safe."

Aidan pinches the bridge of his nose. "There are a few things about this plan I don't like."

I sit up, prepared to negotiate. I'm a reasonable hellhound, after all. I can work out a way to talk him into doing what I want even though he hates it.

"What parts?"

"All of it, starting with me spending most of the day locked in the bathroom."

"I can see why you might not enjoy that, but what alternative would you suggest?"

"I could stay downstairs. Or, compromise, I stay in here. Where I can sit in a chair. I'd still be able to get into the bathroom fast"—he grimaces—"if I have to."

"But you'd lose valuable seconds, especially if they come in through this window." I gesture to the window beside his chair. "They'll be using their noses to find you, and since you'll have been living here a few days, your scent will be pretty well dispersed throughout the house. They'll need a few moments to orient themselves to where it's freshest, and those moments on top of the ones you'll have from hearing them enter will give you a solid head start. You lose that if they see you through this window or hear you closing and locking the bathroom door."

He scoffs. "You're talking about literal seconds."

I nod. "Sometimes that's all that matters. What else you got?"

He growls, his cat clearly pissed off, and I grin in delight. I want to pet the snarly kitty. I bet I can make him purr.

"Help me out here, Alistair! There has to be another option."

I raise my eyebrow again, and the annoyance slides right off his face. I make a mental note to look into that later. Maybe he has an eyebrow fetish? It's weird, but I can work with it.

I wiggle both brows, just to test the waters, but his expression shifts from fond to baffled.

Distraction time.

"An option other than calling down a special ops team to hang out with you?"

He growls again. "Yes. Other than that."

"I can put you on a plane back to CSG headquarters before I leave in the morning."

He's shaking his head before I even finish the sentence. "No. I need to be here. There's going to be fallout from all this, and I need to be here for my people."

That's so fucking sexy. But…

"You probably won't be," I say bluntly. "Depending on what happens tomorrow, we'll likely be heading back soon. It could be weeks—even months—before there's any movement. It all comes down to what we find out and whether Tish is ready to act or still needs time. I don't know if anyone told you, but when he took Noah, they were there to steal a seal from Percy. We assume that's the lucifer's official seal of office, since it's the only one Percy has—unless you count his family's signet ring, but his father still has that, and Tish would know it. The seal has since been moved, is under guard, and has been warded to a ridiculous level. We don't know why the elves want it, but based on what Noah overheard, we believe their agreement with Tish hinges on it."

"So there's a chance they won't move until they get the seal?"

I nod. "We hope. The reality is, Tish will probably convince them to act without it, maybe using it as incentive—tell them there's no way to lay hands on the seal as long as Percy is in control—"

"Wait, wait—the only way Percy won't be in control is if the magic chooses a new lucifer. The elves and Tish have no influence over that." He's leaning forward, eyes narrowed, almost daring me to contradict him.

I've never walked away from a dare.

"They could kill him. The magic will protect him, but it's not infallible—or rather, we don't know what its limits are." I hesitate a moment. "Percy hasn't been told, but we've increased his security pretty dramatically. I'm sure he's guessed," I admit, "but right now we're all publicly pretending we're not worried some elf will open a portal beside the lucifer's bed while he's sleeping and slit his throat." It's a little blunter than I intended to be with him, but I think it's time he realizes exactly how serious this is for him personally. "We've also quietly increased security for all species leaders."

He looks away, pale. Well, paler than usual. "I never noticed," he says quietly.

"Special ops are good at being discreet. We don't want anyone to notice—and of course, now that you're with me for almost every second of the day, we were able to reassign your operatives. You're the only species leader who's aware of the elves and the threat they bear, and we only told you because there are hellhounds directly involved and we needed your help. I'm not trying to be an asshole by locking you in the bathroom. It's the only compromise I'm willing to make that leaves you unprotected."

He sighs. "So my options are to fly back to headquarters, have a special ops team come down to guard me, or lock myself in the bathroom and hope I don't need to climb out the window?"

"Yes."

"A locked door won't save me from an elf opening a portal."

"I know. This is my compromise, remember? I still don't like it."

He growls again, but says, "Fine. While you're gone tomorrow, I'll stay in the bathroom with the door locked."

I'm glad I'm lying down, because relief makes me feel weak all over. I really did *not* want to go with option four, which entailed me knocking him out and tying him up so he wouldn't cause any trouble for the special ops team I called in against his will.

Although I'm not taking tying him up completely off the table—it would just be in very different circumstances.

"Great." I smile widely. "Why don't we test it out?"

"Test it— You mean climb out the window?" He laughs. "Sure. Why not? Do I have to go all the way across to the backup condo?"

There's an edge of snark to his amiable tone, and I decide it might be best not to push my luck. "Nope! Just out the window, up onto the roof, and back again." Those are the actions he'd need to take—aside from creeping across the roof, but that's nothing for a cat.

Sighing and shaking his head, he gets up and goes into the bathroom. I roll off the bed and follow just in time to see him shift.

Pretty kitty.

I've never been all that admiring of cats—there's nothing wrong with them, but they're not hellhounds, after all. Aidan, though, is worthy of admiration. He's standard size for a felid, sleekly muscled, his fur the same toffee color as his hair. I'm itching to get my fingers into it. He tips his head to one side and stares at me, then slowly turns it and looks up at the window. Right—I need to open the window. I'd better make sure it's open before I go tomorrow, so there's no chance he'll forget.

I step past the pretty kitty and slide the window open. The next second, Aidan leaps, his hind legs landing on the vanity while he props his forelegs on the windowsill and sticks his head out. I can't see exactly what he's doing, but from the way his body is moving, I'd guess he's twisting around to check out the wall and roof from all angles. There are no eaves on this side of the condo—I checked. The benefits of modern architecture. It's a smooth, sharp angle from the outer wall to the flat part of the roof directly above.

He pulls his head back in, adjusts his stance, then pushes off from the vanity—which creaks rather alarmingly. I make a mental note to check it later as most of his body disappears through the window, twisting as it does so. There's a pause, during which he stays half in the room, then his hind feet find purchase on the windowsill, and a moment later, he's gone.

Fuck. Maybe I should have gone downstairs before we tried this so I could have caught him if he fell? Cats land on their feet, right?

I'm sure they do. Although… I don't know that I've ever actually seen a cat fall.

There's no cries or thuds, though, just the sound of his breathing and a scrabbling sound—probably his claws slicing into the siding. Cats have wicked claws. It's maybe the only thing they have that I'm a little jealous of. Don't get me wrong, hellhounds are superior in every way, but we don't have the kind of claws that would enable us to climb the side of a building.

I want to hear him better, so I shift into my hellhound form, listening carefully to the sounds Aidan's making while I wistfully imagine being able to scale any structure that crosses my path—not that structures can cross paths. He seems to be doing okay. There was a shift in his breathing when—presumably—he pulled himself up onto the roof, and at a guess, I'd say he's about to—

His head pops through the window, and I jerk back and whine even though I was kind of expecting it. A second later, one of his wide front paws lands on the windowsill. I back up to the doorway to give him space, then, seeing how focused he is, decide to give him privacy to maneuver through the window. I look away.

There's really nothing else to do if I'm not going to watch him, though. I look around the bathroom, then over my shoulder into the bedroom. Nope. Boring.

Meh. Might as well come up with my own entertainment.

"*What* are you doing?"

I lift my head to find Aidan's shifted back and is standing in front of me with a look of… shock? Amusement? Something between the two?

I shift to my biped form and shrug. "Just keeping busy."

His jaw drops. "You… *keep busy* by licking your balls?"

Oh, here we go with this again. "Yeah, I do. It feels nice. Hygiene is important. And they're right there, a convenient fun package with no need to cart around a bag or anything."

He blinks slowly and straightens his clothes. One of the things Hollywood consistently gets wrong about shifting is the whole clothes-ripping thing. They change with us. I'm not sure where they go, exactly, but they're still there when we shift back. "I… You hellhounds will be my undoing." He pushes past me to walk into the bedroom, and I follow.

"Why? Why does everyone make a big deal about the ball licking? It's not like balls are never licked, ever. Why is it okay for someone else to lick my balls, but not for me?"

He stops beside the bed and holds up his hand. "I swear to feck, Alistair, if you're about to tell me that you lick your balls to make yourself come, I… I just don't want to hear it."

"Of course not!" I deny indignantly. It's mostly true, too—I've only done it once or twice since I was a sex-driven adolescent, and those times were because I'd been celibate for *weeks*. What's the difference between jerking it and licking myself to get off?

I don't bother to ask Aidan that. I don't think he'll consider it relevant.

"Is it the fact that you were in the same room that's the problem?"

He opens his mouth, closes it again, then throws up his hands and says, "I don't even know where to start with what the problem is." He sounds frustrated and bewildered, and a little voice inside me whispers that it's time to make my move.

"Would it make you feel better if I licked your balls instead?"

He sucks in a breath, and for a moment, I worry that I read the mood wrong, but then a smile creeps over his face.

"Why not? You're surely an expert ball licker by now." He sits on the edge of the bed and meets my gaze. "Impress me."

CHAPTER NINE

Aidan

ALISTAIR DOESN'T NEED to be asked twice. He lunges at me, and the two of us tumble back onto the giant bed. I can't help laughing, although that fades when I feel his cock hard against me.

His mouth clashes with mine in what might be the most aggressive kiss I've ever had. If you'd asked me earlier, I would have said I didn't like rough kisses. I would have been wrong, because just a few seconds of this has me hard as a pike and aching. I actually whine when he pulls away.

"As delicious as your mouth is," he pants, "it's not what I want to be kissing right now. Strip."

Yes. I rip my shirt off, buttons scattering, and fumble to get out of my trousers. Alistair is somehow naked before me and rummaging through his overnight bag for… lube?

"I thought you were going to suck me off," I say as he comes back to the bed and sets the bottle on the nightstand. Not that I'd complain about any activity that needs lube.

"No, I'm going to show you what a good ball licker I am," he corrects, climbing up beside me and then sliding down my body so his face is level with my very excited and eager cock. "And then, when I've got you so hard and primed that a breath could send you over the edge, you're going to fuck me."

If I didn't have hundreds of years of practice at controlling myself, just those words would have done the trick.

"If I have to," I agree. "But for all your boasting, I've yet to—ungh!"

As his delectably hot, wet tongue swipes over me again, my eyes roll back and I clutch the bedcovers.

Then he sets to work in earnest.

He said he was an expert ball licker, and he seems determined to prove it, lavishing attention on each of mine. His tongue traces along every crevice, every inch of skin, sometimes feathering so lightly that I arch my back, searching for more pressure. Then he sucks them into his mouth, first one, then the other, surrounding me in hot, wet delight.

I lose track of what happens after that. My dick is screaming for attention, but he's fixed on licking and sucking what feels like everywhere else, until I'm whimpering, holding on by a thread. The barbs just below the head of my cock pop out, a sure sign I'm about to blow.

Fuck that. I'm a shifter—my refractory period is minutes. I'll get it up again to fuck him.

As if he can read my mind, he clamps his thumb and forefinger firmly around the base of my cock, and I yell.

Raising his head, he smirks at me, his mouth wet

and puffy. "I told you. Not until a breath would make you come."

"I'm feckin' close," I pant, then wish I hadn't when he scoots back and lets me go. The barbs have retracted.

"Take some time to cool off," he suggests with a wink. "I've got some stuff to take care of in the meantime." He reaches for the lube.

It takes my overburdened brain a moment to realize what he needs that for, but then I raise my head to watch, flinching as the movement causes air to whisper across my very sensitive flesh.

He pours out a generous amount of lube, then props himself on the other elbow and puts on a show for me. There's no doubt of that—he's positioned himself to give me the perfect view, and when I look at his face, his eyes are fixed on me.

My gaze is irresistibly drawn back to where two of his big, thick fingers are sliding into his hole, and I swallow hard, mesmerized. I want in there.

"Alistair," I croak, and he laughs.

"Patience."

He's diabolical.

Unable to resist, I roll onto my hands and knees and crawl over to him, then, looking him in the eye, I stroke a fingertip lightly down the length of his massive erection.

He hisses.

I bend and kiss him. "Hurry up."

In the next instant, he's lurching upright and grabbing me around the waist, fastening his mouth to mine for a sloppy, fast kiss. "How do you want me?"

"On your back." It's my turn to torment him, and I want to see his face when I do.

Obligingly, he flops onto his back, knees bent and feet planted apart, much as he was just a few moments ago. I trace around his pucker, which is glistening with lube and quivers at my touch.

"Ai-dan," he growls.

"Yes?" My finger strokes lightly up over the sensitive skin of his taint, toward his dick.

"Fuck me now, or I'll never lick your balls again." He pauses. "I'm still waiting to hear your acknowledgement that I'm the ultimate ball licker."

"You're the ultimate ball licker," I concede. It's praise he certainly deserves. I get on my knees and move between his legs. His breathing speeds up.

I love this. Love having this big, tough hellhound willingly at my mercy.

Taking my cock in hand, I slide the head over Alistair's crease. He growls again, and I press myself lightly to his hole, just enough for him to feel it but not enough to breach the ring of muscle. Sweat breaks out down my back from holding back. I want nothing more than to plunge inside right now.

"Just you wait," he promises darkly, and it's too much for my self-restraint. I can torture him another time.

I push forward steadily, giving him time to adjust but not faltering until I'm seated all the way inside him.

An explosive breath bursts from each of us.

"You feel amazing," I gasp.

He just moans. "Moooooove."

So I do. The hot, tight clasp of his body is reluctant to let me withdraw—I'm pretty sure he's been doing his kegel exercises—but he's urging me on, begging me to thrust, and I'm so close, so ready. I get a hand around his cock, feeling the finger-like cartilage of his barbs, and he shouts, spurting so hard that he clenches around me, and that's it.

I have my face buried in the crook of his neck and he's petting my hair when reality comes back into focus. It's nice. Being species leader has kept me really busy, so intimate moments like these have been few and far between. I love being petted, whether in cat or biped form, and Alistair is using just the right amount of pressure…

I might take a nap.

"Don't you dare fall asleep," he says in a smug voice, as though he knows what I'm thinking and is taking credit for my extreme relaxation. Which, to be fair, he did play a part in. "We need to talk about your adventure earlier."

My adventure? Is that what we're calling sex?

Oh. He means the window.

Groaning, I pull my face out of his neck and roll onto my back. The room is dim in the late afternoon light, but of course I can see almost perfectly. There are a lot of benefits to being a shifter.

"Okay, yeah. What do you want to know?" I deliberately keep my voice grumbly, not wanting him to know how much I enjoyed my little "adventure." It took me right back to the hijinks I used to get up to when I was a teenager and had my first shift. Post-shift adolescence is a time of pushing boundaries, and I think I must have climbed anything within reach that was above shoulder-height, just for the joy of it. I haven't done that—climbed without purpose—in so very long. Being an adult is no fun sometimes.

"Any problems?"

My first instinct is to say no, but I make myself think about it properly. This is important to him—and me. If I have to do that again, it will be because someone is after me, potentially to kill me or at least take me captive and use me as a bargaining chip against Percy and CSG. I have to be sure I can pull off my escape.

"It's a little awkward getting out the window," I admit. "I have to jump up from the vanity and then hold myself there, hanging halfway out the window while I get a good grip on the wall outside."

There's a rustle of sheets as he sits up, and I look over to see a thoughtful expression on his face.

"So you need something higher off the ground to brace yourself on?"

I shrug. "That would make it easier—probably faster. It's not a deal breaker, though."

"There's not a lot of extra furniture here to work with—not at the right height, anyway. We could maybe use one of the stools from downstairs and stack something on top of it… or if I can work out a way to make it stable, put a stool on the vanity." He sounds a little doubtful about that, and as the person who will be crashing to the floor if the stool turns out not to be fully stable, I appreciate that.

My stomach chooses this moment to growl, and he turns to look at me with a broad grin.

"You're hungry? Me too. I'll grab whatever we have left downstairs to tide us over, and we can order a proper meal."

The thought of food makes my mouth water. "Deal." I lift myself into a sitting position and reach over to flick on one of the bedside lamps as he climbs out of bed, turning back just in time to watch him stroll, naked, from the room, his ass flexing beautifully with each step. I bite back a sigh. The beefier build of hellhounds makes their nude forms such a pleasure to watch, and Alistair clearly dedicates a lot of time and effort to maintaining his body. The muscle definition is just lovely.

I had my hands—and mouth—all over those lovely muscles. And you can bet your ass I will again.

He comes bouncing back in within a few minutes, balancing a plate holding the last of the fruit, a couple of boxes of Pop-Tarts, half a loaf of bread, and a box of cereal. Not the greatest of feasts, but definitely sufficient to hold us until real food arrives. There's something delightful about having a naked man bring me food—it's something I could get used to very quickly.

"What?" he asks as he dumps the spoils of his hunt onto the mattress. "Why are you looking at me like that?" He's teasing, of course—I'm giving off a pretty strong scent of arousal right now, even if he doesn't see the tent in the sheet.

"I like you naked and catering to my every whim," I respond solemnly, keeping my face straight by dint of sheer will. "Maybe I'll ask Percy to reassign you to be my *personal* aide."

Alistair being Alistair, a wicked grin stretches his mouth. "What a great idea. If he asks you what my duties will entail, I'm happy to provide a list. A long, detailed list. He'll get a real kick out of that."

"You're evil." I grab a box of Pop-Tarts and rip it open as he rejoins me on the bed. "What do we want for dinner?"

"Meat," he says, looking me right in the eye. "Lots and lots of juicy meat."

I clear my throat. "That's on the menu regardless."

We haggle back and forth over dinner options before deciding to just get everything, then demolish the snacks he brought up while we wait. The atmosphere between us is different now—before, we were trying to balance professionalism with sexual tension. It wasn't helped by the fact that we don't actually know each other that well *and* we're in the middle of dealing with a crisis of world-ending proportions.

But now… sitting naked on the bed he contrived to steal from me, surrounded by the debris of our predinner snack, sexually… well, not sated, but with the edge off, at least… things are a lot more relaxed. I was a little worried that us having sex would turn out to be a bad idea, but it's really not. Our chemistry is off the charts, but I also like and respect him, even if he is a little… offbeat? Weird? The whole ball-licking thing might take some getting used to.

"What are you thinking about?" he asks curiously, stacking the empty boxes from snack time on the nightstand.

"Sex," I admit. "Do you think we have time to go again before—" My question is cut off by the doorbell. "Never mind."

"I'll go," he says, bouncing off the bed. He's halfway to the door before I realize he's not going to stop to put on pants.

"Alistair!"

He pauses in the doorway and looks over his shoulder impatiently. "What? I need the fooooood."

"You need underwear," I point out dryly. "More than that would be better, but underwear is the minimum. Unless you want to give the delivery driver a thrill."

He looks down at his naked self and curses, then takes two steps back in and grabs a pair of pants from the floor. "I'll put them on while I'm going down the stairs," he says, and he's out the door before I can tell him that (a) that doesn't sound safe, and (b) he's grabbed my pants.

Don't worry, judging by the startled exclamation, series of thuds, and string of curses, he figured both out on his way down the stairs. I smile fondly and hope he hasn't hurt himself too badly.

I listen to him muttering about stupid companies that make all pants look the same and the need for sizes to be color-coded—which, frankly, I find disturbing. There's something off about the sound of his footsteps —is he walking funny?—then I hear the front door open, followed by a sharp gasp and a muffled shriek.

"Great, you're both here," Alistair says, which I guess means all our food has arrived at once.

"Al-Alistair?" a shaky young voice asks, and I wince. Obviously the pants wouldn't have fit him, but I hope he's at least holding them in front of his sensitive bits. Knowing Alistair, he's abandoned them completely or has them draped over his shoulder.

"Yep. Hey, is there cutlery in these bags?"

"Uh… yeah. Should be?"

"And the tip was included when we paid, right? Because I've got no cash on me right now."

I settle back against the pillows and bless shifter hearing. This is better than theater.

"Y-Yeah, we can see that," another voice says, this

one shaking with laughter. "Tip's been covered. And thanks for the bonus."

Alistair laughs, then I hear the door close and those funny-sounding footsteps coming back upstairs. Is he injured? Maybe he hurt himself trying to put on my pants, which are three or four sizes too small for him.

He appears in the doorway a moment later, and I literally choke on my laugh.

He didn't abandon the pants.

Nor is he wearing them as a cape or half-assed toga.

He's actually *wearing them.*

Of course, he could only get them about halfway up his tree-trunk legs, so they're basically acting like shackles, and his goods are still on full display.

I sputter as he puts the food down. "What the fuck, Alistair?"

"What?" He looks up from unpacking food containers, and I gesture to his lower half. "Oh. I picked up your pants by mistake."

"I know. Why are you wearing them? They're not exactly protecting your modesty."

He shrugs and hands me a plastic fork. "I already had them on before I realized, and I didn't want to take the time to get them off again and risk the delivery drivers leaving."

I'm not even going to argue with that logic.

"But why didn't you take them off before coming back? Walking up the stairs like that couldn't have been easy."

He shrugs again, then bends and peels the pants down his legs—with quite a bit of difficulty. He must have yanked them on pretty hard. I'm pretty sure I hear stitches popping, and I hope they're not ruined. I like those pants.

"It wasn't, but I needed to get the food back to you. That was more important."

Aww.

He settles on the bed beside me, and I pass him a container. Maybe it makes us savages, but we're eating in bed with plastic utensils and no plates, and I love it.

"At least you gave the drivers something to tell their friends," I comment. "Delivering food can't be the most thrilling job in the world."

His smirk warns me something outrageous is about to come out of his mouth. "They seemed pretty impressed. It reminded me of the beginning of a porn movie. The only thing that could have made it better was if you were tied to the bed in the throes of insatiable lust and I had to ask them to help me satisfy you."

For the third—or is it fourth?—time today, I choke on food. If I'm going to be spending more time with Alistair, I need to learn to be careful about my chewing habits.

He seems to get way too much enjoyment out of pounding me on the back, the ass, but as I turn my glare on him, he offers me a piece of roasted potato on his fork, and I can't help but forgive him.

"Any chance we could role-play that later?"

So of course he pushes his luck.

I swallow the potato—thankfully not having choked on it—and say, "We've only had sex once and you're already bored with me? Not good for my ego."

He laughs, then puts down his container and fork and snuggles in close, wrapping his big body around me. "Definitely not bored," he mutters against the side of my neck, wiggling so I can feel the evidence of just how not bored he is.

My breathing gets faster, and I very seriously consider how much I want him again right this second. It's a lot, but I'm also really hungry.

"You'll go fast, right?" I ask, and he stiffens and lifts his head.

"I beg your pardon?" There's a high level of offense in his tone, and I'm glad he can't see my smirk.

"I don't want to wait ages to finish eating. If you'll go fast, we can fuck again right now. Otherwise, we both have to wait."

In the next instant, he's cleared the food off the bed and onto the nightstands (and some stacked on the floor —we really did order a lot) and is pushing me down onto the mattress.

"We don't have time for a proper role play," he says, "so we'll save that for later. But if you could maybe moan a bit about how desperately you need me to fill you, fuck you, satisfy you…?" He sounds so hopeful that I swallow my chuckle and obligingly moan.

"Oh, Alistair, I neeeeeeed!" My voice rises in pitch as he grabs my cock in one of his big, hot hands and applies just the right pressure to make me crave him.

"Don't worry," he tells me, and if I had more brain cells free, I might think he was getting way too into this role-play thing, "I have just the thing to satisfy your need."

CHAPTER TEN

Alistair

I'M WHISTLING as I drive along I-84 late in the morning. I've been on the road for a little over four hours after a predawn wake-up and some slightly acrimonious negotiations with a used car dealer, but nothing is killing my mood today—although having to leave my nice warm bed did dent it a little. So did having to wake up my sexy, rumpled bedmate and make him lock himself in the bathroom. He was *not* happy about that. Just as well I wasn't hoping for a morning pick-me-up. His scowly face didn't bode well for my plans for some evening delight when I get back, though, so I made sure to point out that I'd let him sleep in while I prepared the bathroom for him. I included a stool with folded linen stacked and taped on it to give him a higher launch point, a comfy armchair and side table with his laptop, phone, and briefcase at the ready, and two coolers full of food, which Sam arranged to have delivered by special courier super early this morning because we were too busy fucking last night to go grocery shopping again. It's lucky for me that Sam is currently a few hours ahead of me, time zone wise, because he might have been a teensy bit grumpy if I'd called before dawn in a panic about not having any food for Aidan. There are *some* limits to best friendship, after all.

Anyway, all my hard work didn't seem to make Aidan any happier about getting up so early and going to sit in the bathroom, but I've called him a few times since, and he seems to be over his snit. Either that, or he's trying to lull me into a false sense of security so he can mete out his revenge. I'm not completely against that idea; there are a lot of possibilities for revenge sex.

I'm getting close to the Beker County line now, which means I have to be on full alert. The front windows are both open halfway. Ideally, I'd like to have all four fully open to catch any hint of scent that might be in the air, but it's fucking cold out there, and four open windows might attract attention. I've already stopped and filled the gas tank, so if I end up being noticed by the wrong people, I won't have to worry about running out as I flee—not until I'm nearly back to Portland, anyway, and by then the enforcement backup unit in Seattle will have choppered in.

I drive past the outskirts of the tiny barely-town that sits right outside the border of Beker County and brace myself. Intellectually, I know the county line is probably meaningless in these circumstances and that it's likely there are some of Tish's people living on this side of the border, so to speak, but it's symbolic, and we hellhounds love symbols.

So, hey, considering that most of the people I'm concerned about are hellhounds, they just might respect the symbolism of the county line and stay within it.

I maintain a steady speed. The highway isn't busy,

but there are enough other cars around that people will notice if I slow down drastically. I don't need to, anyway. The wind is light but blowing steadily from the southeast as I drive down from the northern part of the county, and the smell of hellhounds grows stronger. It's multilayered in a way that clearly tells me there are many hellhounds living in this general area and they have been for a long time. The concentration of scent is so complex that without stopping and spending a lot of time deciphering it, I can't easily tell the breakdown of age groups and sex. That fits with what we expected.

I hit the Bluetooth receiver in my ear—which I need to remember to put in my pocket before I get out of the car—and call Sam.

"Hey. You there?"

"Starting to pick up scents just a couple miles within the county lines. If there are hellhounds living outside that area, they're in small numbers and spread out enough that I'd need to scout on foot to find them."

"Any surprises?"

"Not yet. No specific individual scents yet, either, but I can definitely tell you that the three hellhounds who took Noah from the office are from a family group here. There are enough scent markers for that to be clear."

He sighs. "Well, I guess it's good to have confirmation. You're going to stay on the line now, right?"

I hesitate, but while the fifteen-year-old truck doesn't have a charger jack for my phone, it does have a cigarette lighter, and being the ex-special forces superhero I am, I came prepared with an old-fashioned converter. There's no reason I shouldn't stay on the line and every reason why I should.

"Yeah, but mute or something, would you? I don't want to be distracted by background noise."

"I'm going to pretend you didn't just imply I would distract you," he says. "I'll be here if you need anything."

"Check in with Aidan for me, will you? It's been about an hour since I spoke with him." The scent of hellhound is strengthening as I approach the outskirts of Beker City, but in a way that tells me the concentration of scent is getting closer, rather than it being carried by the wind. That's good—it allows me to pick up individual scent threads more clearly.

"I just spoke to him a few minutes ago," Sam assures me. "We talked about keeping a line open but decided to wait and see what happened with you."

"Okay. Thanks, Sammy."

The line seems to go dead, but a sideways glance at my handset in the center console assures me Sam's just muted his end. I turn my full concentration to driving and smelling.

My goal today is to try to identify and locate the scent of Tish and/or the elves. That's my primary focus. All other smells are going into a memory bank to be sorted out later.

More and more houses start to pop up as I reach the outskirts of town, and I slow down in accordance with the speed signs. That's to my advantage—the slower I go, the more I'll be able to smell. I've spotted a few people so far, but none of them were hellhounds.

On impulse, I leave the highway. If I'm remembering right, this road becomes the main street of town, then loops to meet the highway again. I'm going to smell more on the town's arterial road than on a highway that cuts through an industrial area.

I slow again as I enter the town proper and cruise along. Despite the cold, it's a lovely clear day, and there are plenty of people out and about. Mostly humans, but enough hellhounds are mingling around to tell me that they're not just hiding in the woods—they're an active part of the town. That seems a little contradictory to me, given Tish and the CCA's goal was to enslave humanity. On the flip side, humans have been enslaving each other for millennia, so it's possible Tish thinks he can get a select group of humans to support him and subjugate the rest. I mentally file the idea away to run past the others later.

A hint of scent teases my nostrils. Tish. I'm sure of it. I may not have ever met the man, but his scent was all over Sam when we rescued him and Noah from the labs, and then again in the office when Noah was taken. I'm the supreme snifferoo, remember? There's no way I've miscategorized that particular smell.

If only it were stronger. He's been here recently, maybe even this morning, but he's not here now. It's coming from up ahead—not too far. Maybe a block or two. Interestingly, there's a strong concentration of hellhound scent in the same general area, concentrated enough that I can clearly identify half a dozen or so individuals. I don't know who they are, but I would if I met them again.

I slow to a stop at a red light and decide to do some preemptive research.

"Sammy?" I pitch my voice low enough that even a shifter could only hear me if they were in the truck.

There's a second's pause, then the line unmutes. "Yeah? You okay?"

"Yep. I'm coming up on a spot where the same few hellhounds seem to hang out regularly—I'd say almost every day, based on the scent layering, and they've been doing it for a while. I think Tish has been there too. It might be a business they own or something. Could you look—"

"No problem. Just tell me the street number or the store name, and I can find out who owns it," Sam assures me.

"Great," I say, taking my foot off the brake as the light changes. "I'll be passing it in just a second, so—" I almost slam my foot back on the brake as shock reverberates through me.

"Alistair?"

"Ah…" I force myself not to turn my head and stare, not to slow down or anything else that might look unusual. "Yeah. Sam, what do you know about human local government?"

"Local government?" he parrots.

"The building was the Beker City City Hall. That's local government, isn't it?"

"Fuck. Hold on, let me…" I hear the fast and furious click of his keyboard, then his voice asking someone else to bring up the community census data for the county and search some names. I keep focused on taking in every scent I can. Even though I'm quite a bit past city hall now, Tish's scent still lingers, which means he probably spent a bit of time in this area. It's mostly a shopping area, but there are some business storefronts too. The smell of hellhounds is layered in naturally amongst the human scent, suggesting that quite a few of these businesses might be hellhound-owned.

Don't get me wrong, we own businesses. But in smaller communities, where there's a finite number of businesses and our population is limited compared to humans, we tend not to. It comes down to percentages, and most hellhounds who live in a rural area like this prefer the outskirts anyway.

"Alistair?"

"Yeah, Sam, I'm here. Still smelling a lot more hellhound in the center of town than I expected. A few cats too, some sorcerers and demons, but not as many and not as saturated."

"Tish?" There's a lot of tension in Sam's voice.

"He's definitely been here very recently, and at a guess, I'd say he's spent a few days in and out of town. Not in town right now; at least not this part."

"What about the elves?"

"No sign." That frustrates me, but logically I shouldn't expect any of them to be in the town center. Based on Noah's description of the one he saw, there's no way they could pass for human. We don't know if their magic-slash-sorcery would allow for them to disguise themselves, so while I'm sniffing for them anyway, it wouldn't surprise me if they're sticking to community-only properties. Since they can use their portals for travel, it narrows the chances of me picking up a scent trail.

"Okay, well you were right about city hall. We just ran a search, and it seems the local mayor is a hellhound."

"The *mayor*?" I may not know a lot about human governments, but I know that a mayor is the one in charge, and that means things are way beyond hinky here. We in the community don't get involved in human government. I mean… occasionally if they're fucking up a town really badly, someone local might try to steer them in the right direction, but mostly we just stay out of it. People in government have a lot of eyes and attention on them, and the number-one rule within the community is to protect the secret of our existence. We *cannot* risk exposure.

When I smelled so many hellhounds at city hall, I thought they might have weaseled their way into staff positions. It would give them an in with the local authorities—the ability to hear inside gossip that could enable them to better protect their people from exposure and also potentially influence the town's leaders. Even that was surprising, given the goals of Tish and the CCA. The idea that they'd run for public office never occurred to me.

"This changes things, of course," Sam replies grimly. "Noah's running searches now on the other enclave towns we've found to see if they've taken over local government there too."

"You found other enclave towns? When?" They were still looking when we spoke yesterday.

"This morning. Cats in Eastern Europe, sorcerers in North Africa, and we're still confirming, but potentially demons in Polynesia. We were saving it for tonight's briefing—didn't want to distract you."

I blow out a breath. "It seems distractions abound today. What do I need to look out for, Sam? Is there a way they can use the humans to come after me?" It was bad enough when I thought I had to look out for hellhounds ambushing me on a lonely stretch of road. If they can publicly turn the humans against me…

"Don't do anything illegal," he warns, "or anything that could maybe be interpreted as illegal. The chief of police is also a hellhound, and with you not being local, it's unlikely anyone would interfere if they arrested you on some trumped-up charge."

"Got it," I mutter. It's okay. The plan was always for me to be unremarkable and unnoticed, and that hasn't changed. "Do me a favor and check on Aidan, would you?"

"Elinor's got him on the line," he assures me. "We figured with this unexpected change, it might be better to be in contact with him."

Some of my tension fades. "Good. Okay, I'm getting to the outskirts of town now. It'll take me about half an hour to get to my stopping point."

"I'll mute again, then. Let me know if you need anything." The line seemingly goes dead again, and I turn my attention back to looking as innocent as possible and smelling everything that drifts past on the breeze.

The drive is uneventful, and I have plenty of opportunity to sort through some of the scents carried to me. I pass through different hotspot areas—places where a certain group of scents are concentrated, telling me who lives where, and I make a point of associating landmarks with each scent cluster. It might not help in the end, since I don't have names or faces to connect the scents to, but I can at least tell the others that clustered in the area near exit 178 there are around seven extended family groups with a high ratio of children and adolescents. That actually makes me wonder if they move families with children into this area specifically. Given our difficulty with conception, it seems strange that there would be such a high ratio of kids.

I go cold all over.

Could Tish have already begun experimenting on his followers?

No… no, the spread over age groups is too uneven, and Tish's research hadn't reached that point yet—he was still a generation away.

But fuck, I came *this* close to shitting myself at the thought.

And on the heels of that shock comes a hint of scent I've been waiting for.

Elf.

No… elves. Definitely more than one. Maybe… three? Three that are here right now. There are a couple more snatches of scent that might belong to others who were here before but are gone now… or are just a lot further away.

I'm getting close to my planned stopping point.

"Sam?"

A second later, my bestie says, "Right here. What's up?"

"I'm going to be stopping in a minute and switching to handset. Just in case you're wondering why I'm suddenly saying 'uh-huh' and 'oh, really?' a lot."

He laughs. "Sure. Not that I'd ever question anything you say. I'd just put it down to one of your quirks."

My brow furrows. What's he talking about? "I don't have quirks."

There's a moment of silence, then he says, "Of course not. I don't know what I was thinking."

Wait a second… "Do you think I'm *quirky*?" That's

absurd. I'm the most reasonable, level-headed hellhound I know.

"Not at all. I misspoke. Don't think about it right now. You need to stay focused."

He's right, but I can't help worrying a little. Quirky? Me? No way.

"Okay, coming up on the rest area," I tell him. It's not much as far as rest areas go—a cleared gravel area for parking and a very dodgy-looking concrete toilet block. There's a single picnic table too. It's currently abandoned, as anyone with sense would likely squeeze their legs together until they reached the very tiny unincorporated town only five miles away that a recent sign proclaimed has a gas station with café.

In other words, it's perfect for my purpose.

I swing in and park the truck nice and close to the toilet block, then pretend to scratch the side of my face so I can slip the Bluetooth earpiece out and pocket it. Lifting the handset to my ear, I get out of the truck and begin pacing slowly up and down along the length of the picnic table. Occasionally I nod and make sounds as though I'm agreeing with the person on the other end of the line.

"Anything?" Sam asks softly.

"Oh, definitely," I say conversationally. There's a hint of Tish coming up on the breeze from the south, enough to make me think this might be his base. I wonder if anyone confirmed how much time he actually spent in that human religious cult compound. Now we know he has access to the portal-creating elves, we need to consider it was intended to be a decoy all along, and that he wasn't actually there a lot of the time.

I'm also getting a pretty strong concentration of elf.

They're definitely spending their time here, and I commit as much of their scent to memory as I can, trying to break it down. It's good that there's been more than one of them here—it gives me more to work with in tagging elements of their scent identifiers. The overall base, the part that would be their species, is the bit that makes me think of fresh, growing grass—although not quite like any grass I've ever smelled before. The other elements will identify things like sex, age, family group, location and environment—or they *would* if I had reference points for any of those things.

"Oh, really?" I say. "I hadn't thought of it that way. But isn't this something we can talk about when I get there?"

"Sure," Sam says, a thread of humor underlying the word. "I just thought we might—"

"That's just fine, honey," I interrupt, all my senses suddenly going on high alert. An elf has just opened a portal not too far from me; I'm sure of it. I can smell that same weird magic/sorcery combo that was in the office when Noah was taken, and the scent of elf is suddenly a lot stronger… and closer.

This is a new one, though. Not one of the elves I've been sniffing out for the last few minutes. And it's a lot closer than any of them. Within a half-mile, maybe?

I try to remember what's half a mile south of where I am right now. Not much—it's pretty barren right here, lots of shallow rocky hills with some scrubby patches of woods. It gets better a few miles back from the road, near the river, where the settlements Aidan told me about are.

So why would an elf open a portal to what's essentially the middle of nowhere?

Unless they know I'm here and want to sneak up on me?

That doesn't make sense, though—they'd be better off opening the portal right here. I'd have no time to sense them and prepare that way. Although it would leave them open to being spotted by someone driving past.

"Ah, listen, sweetie," I say to Sam, "I really should get back on the road if I'm going to get to you anytime soon."

"Problem?" he asks seriously.

"Not sure how long it's going to take me, exactly. I'm either pretty close, or I've taken a wrong turn somewhere. Ha ha ha."

"Al, you gotta give me something here. Do I need to be worried or not?"

"Not yet," I reply, because the elf doesn't seem to be moving. It's pretty much just standing near where it opened the portal. I really want to go have a look and see what it's doing. "I'm just thinking I might stretch my legs a bit before I get back on the road." I could stroll leisurely in that direction, right? Just a guy who's been in the car for hours having a bit of a stretch before continuing his journey.

"Fuck no," Sam says immediately. "Absolutely not. Don't make me get Percy, Alistair. The mission parameters were set for a reason, remember? You need to get moving—you're already nearly at the end of the window we decided was safe, and that was *before* we knew the CCA had infiltrated the human government."

I hesitate, because I really, really want to know what the fuck that elf is doing… but he's right. We—*I*—can't give anybody here reason to suspect we're on to them.

We can't give them any reason to act now. We *need* as much time as possible to work out what the fuck is going on and what our next steps will be. I can't jeopardize that in any way.

"You're right, honey. I'll have plenty of chances to exercise when I get there; plus, it's pretty damn cold here and I wouldn't want to get sick." The bright blue skies of this morning are gone, and I can smell snow coming, which tells you exactly how shitty human weather forecasters are. Clear for the next few days, my ass. But it's another reason I need to keep moving.

"Good." Sam sounds relieved.

"I'll see you soon. Bye-bye now."

I pull the phone away from my ear, get back in the car, put the phone with the still-active call in the center console, belt up, and start the engine. Only after I'm back on the highway and moving steadily south again do I pull out my Bluetooth earpiece and tuck it back into my ear.

"Still there, Sammy?"

"Yeah. What the fuck was that all about?"

"Elves," I say succinctly, then run down what happened. "I don't know what kind of senses it has, if it could hear me or smell me or what, but it came through the portal and just stood there, pretty much."

"Hold on," Sam says, and I hear his keyboard clacking away. "I'm looking at satellite images of that area, and you're right—there's nothing there. Not even any real tree cover. Are you sure it was so close? Four or so miles from where you were, there's more plant life, the terrain is more regular, and it's much closer to the settlements Aidan visited."

"No," I tell him, shaking my head even though he

can't see me. "It wasn't anywhere near as far as four miles. I don't even think it was one."

"We'll never know, then. Keep an eye on your rearview mirror, just in case."

I roll my eyes. "Sam, portals, remember? They could come at me from the front and I'd never know until it was too late."

"That doesn't make me feel better, Al. Oh—Aidan said to tell you, if you take unnecessary risks, he'll kill you himself."

The small burst of warmth in my chest feels a lot like pleasure. It's nice to know people care enough to make death threats.

"How's he doing?"

"Annoyed," Sam replies. "There's been no sign of a problem, and you made him lock himself in the bathroom for the whole day. I'd strangle anyone who did that to me."

"He would never strangle me."

"How are you so sure? I definitely would."

"No, you wouldn't. Well, you probably would if I did it or Andrew or whoever. But if Gideon told you to stay in the bathroom all day so he could be sure you were safe, you'd do it."

There's a long pause, and I glance down at the handset to make sure the call hasn't dropped out. It hasn't.

"Sam?"

"Hold on a second." There's a shift in background noise, and a moment later, I hear a door close. "Okay, I'm alone."

"Why do you need to be alone?" I ask. I mean, it's not like he was in the middle of a mall. He was in the team office, which is secure, and we're talking about stuff the whole team is cleared to know.

"Because you just compared my relationship with Gideon to yours with Aidan, and I'm not sure if you wanted Elinor and Andrew and the others to know that."

I open my mouth to scoff, then close it again. Fuck me. I *did*.

What does this mean?

"What does this mean?" I demand, then wince at how hysterical my voice sounds.

Sam squeaks. "Um… calm down. Are you calm? You need to be calm. You're *driving*. Through enemy territory. So be calm."

"I'm calm," I snap. "*What does this mean?*" Why is he waffling on about me being calm, for fuck's sake, when I'm having a personal love crisis and need his support!

"It's a good thing," he assures me. "Right? You like Aidan. Ah… I'm guessing that you guys had sex? No details," he adds quickly. "I don't need any details. But it's nice that you feel a connection to him. It's growth. It shows you're getting over your, uh, past trauma."

Yeah. Yeah. I'm growing. Healing, and all that other crap. I'm ready to try relationships again. So me thinking of Aidan as my… what? I need a word for what we're doing. It's not a hookup; I've had plenty of those. This is different. Fling? That sounds so emotionless.

"What do you call the person you feel affection and lust for?" I ask Sam.

"Is it mutual?" He sounds cautious.

I think of the way Aidan initiated a goodbye kiss this morning, even though he was grumpy with me. "Yeah." The warmth is back in my chest. It's nice to get a goodbye kiss from someone you respect and like and want to fuck through a mattress before you go on a potentially dangerous drive through enemy territory.

"Well… if you're not ready for a relationship label like partner or boyfriend, but there's more to it than friends with bennies, I guess… I have no idea. The person you're seeing? Your lover?"

Delight runs through me. "Ooooh, lover sounds so illicit! It's perfect. Aidan will love it!"

"I don't know Aidan that well," Sam says doubtfully, "but I'm pretty sure he won't love it."

"Clearly I know him better than you. What with being his *lover* and all." This is perfect. I can't wait to get back and tell him we're officially lovers.

I mean, he knows that already after last night, but he doesn't know that it's our official label. He's going to be thrilled; I just know it.

CHAPTER ELEVEN

Aidan

It's after eight by the time Alistair gets back. I've run out of food in the stupid bathroom, and I'm hungry. He better have brought dinner.

I don't smell anything edible.

"Aidan?" he says, still downstairs. "You can come out now."

I narrow my eyes at the door. He'd better feckin' have a feast on the way. And maybe greet me naked and on his knees.

Leaving my laptop, the armchair, and the empty coolers where they are—he can put everything away later. I'm never stepping foot into this damn bathroom again—I unlock the door and make my way out into the rest of the house. The sense of freedom is like nothing I've ever experienced before. Shifters are definitely not meant to be locked up for fourteen hours at a time.

When I get downstairs, Alistair is leaning over his laptop at the island—fully dressed, unfortunately. Fortunately (for him), the first thing he says is "I ordered dinner about fifteen minutes ago—it should be here soon. And Sam ordered more groceries for us, too—they'll be delivered between six and nine tomorrow morning. That'll tide us over until we know how long we're staying."

Well… I suppose that's acceptable. But I still had to spend fourteen hours in a bathroom, so I'm not letting go of my grudge.

He straightens and turns, smiling at me with genuine happiness, and it gets a little harder to hold on to that grudge.

"I'm sorry I wasn't back sooner—was your day too awful? I wish you hadn't been stuck in the bathroom all day."

And there goes my grudge. Dammit.

"It's not an experience I'd like to repeat," I say dryly, even as I take in the dark smudges under his eyes. He's spent almost the whole day driving, with few breaks. That couldn't have been a picnic either. "How about you?"

He shrugs. "I'm hungry, cramped, and dying for a shower. I think I'm going to eat standing up. I'd forgotten how annoying it is to be in a car for a long time."

Softening even more, I close the distance between us and go up on tiptoe to offer my mouth. He still has to bend his head to kiss me, but I like it. I like that outwardly he's the bigger one, but that our dynamic is much more equal. And honestly, that kiss is the best part of this day.

"Do you have time to shower before the food gets here?" I murmur against his lips. I feel them curve in a smile before we separate.

"If I hurry. And I think I will. I had the car windows

open for hours, and I can smell all sorts of shit on myself now."

I take a step back. "I wasn't going to say anything, but yeah." I inhale and wrinkle my nose. "It's hard to tell because you stink of farms, exhaust, and other hell-hounds, but that weird grassy tang—is that the elves?"

He nods, once again doing that thing where he tries to lift an eyebrow and ends up with both rising lopsid-edly. It's so adorable. "I'm impressed that you can smell it at all, mixed in with everything else and as faint as it was."

I sniff again. My nose will never be as good as a hell-hound's, and Alistair's had some pretty specific training on top of that, but the elvish smell stands out. "It's pretty distinctive." I shake my head to clear it. "Go shower, or that's all we'll be able to smell while we eat."

He drops another kiss on my mouth—aww—then walks past me, saying, "The team waited at the office to do a full debrief. They'll be calling in about fifteen minutes."

"No problem. We can talk while we eat." I walk a circuit around the living room and island, just so pleased to be out of the bathroom.

He's halfway up the stairs when he stops and turns around. "Oh—and you should know that you're my lover now."

I blink a few times. "Yeah, I know. I was there, remember?" Maybe being stuck in the car all day addled his brain a bit.

He chuckles. "No, silly. I mean it's our official label. We're lovers. You can tell people I'm your lover."

Uh...

He's nearly to the top of the stairs before I manage

to ask, "Alistair, you haven't called me your lover to anyone, have you?"

"Of course!"

I'm left staring at the top of the stairs. The weirdest part is how enchanting and charming I find this—it's mixed with horror, but I can't deny it: Alistair's foibles are adorable to me.

A wide grin spreads across my face.

SOMETHING IS DRAWING me out of sleep, something not right, even before Alistair whispers my name. I open my eyes, blinking away sleep, and it hits me immediately: the faint scent that clung to Alistair when he got home is back.

Elf.

It's not that close—not in the house—but close enough. The unusualness of its scent really stands out. I sit up slowly as Alistair gets out of bed and—

Someone's knocking.

We both look toward the open bedroom door, then at each other. Is this a trick of some kind?

The knock comes again. It's firm enough that even a human would be able to hear it at this distance.

Alistair inhales deeply, and a peculiar look crosses his face. He turns to meet my gaze, then points toward the bathroom.

He's got to be feckin' kidding me. I shake my head vehemently. He crosses his arms and nods.

The knock sounds for the third time. If we want to maintain any kind of advantage, we need to act.

I flip Alistair the bird and go into the bathroom,

buck naked, and ease the door closed. But I don't lock it or open the window, instead concentrating on listening.

There's a rustle—Alistair putting on pants?—then footsteps so light that no other species could hear them as Alistair leaves the room. By the time he gets to the stairs, I can't even hear them, and I'm not certain if he's even still moving or has stopped.

Then I hear the locks on the front door click open, and I brace. If it's a trick, this would be the perfect time to spring it—shove the door open, throwing Alistair off-balance, and overwhelm him with… I don't know what. I can still only smell elf, and I'm pretty sure it's just one. There's no variation in scent that would indicate more.

Why didn't Alistair go out the back door and circle around? Or even out a window?

The door opens, a hinge squeaking slightly.

"Who are you, and what do you want?" Alistair asks, a lot of growl in his voice. I can just picture him looming in the doorway, half-naked, looking all intimidating.

Focus.

Whatever the elf says in response is so low, I can't hear the individual words.

"Are you alone?" Alistair demands.

There's another low murmur of sound.

"Do you intend us any harm? I can smell it if you lie," he warns.

The tone of the murmur changes—surprise? Maybe Tish and the CCA have been keeping secrets from their allies.

"Aidan!"

I guess that's my cue. I pause in the bedroom only long enough to put on my pants and make it down the stairs in record time.

Alistair's got the elf inside and the door closed by the time I get there, but he still hasn't turned the lights on. We don't know much about the elves, but shifters are the only high-intelligence species on Earth with the ability to see perfectly in the dark, so presumably he wants to use any advantage we might have.

"Who's this?" I ask, and based on the way the elf startles, they don't have shifter-level sight or hearing. I was quiet coming downstairs, but not that quiet.

To my surprise, the elf answers. "My name is Caolan of Ebenkreis, and I believe we have a mutual enemy." Their voice is even, slightly accented, and really very pleasant to listen to.

I glance over at Alistair, who hasn't taken his eyes off our visitor. I smirk a little when I notice he didn't put on pants, just his boxer briefs—the ones with bright yellow smiley faces all over them. "Keel-an?" I confirm, a little surprised they have an Irish name. Or perhaps we Irish adopted it from their species? They nod. "And who is this mutual enemy?"

They blink and widen their eyes, presumably trying to see better in the darkness, but otherwise don't move. "Éibhear of Kesmegan."

"Don't know 'em, sorry," I say lightly. Alistair seems content to let me handle this for now. He's braced on the balls of his feet, slightly crouched, which I recognize as being a defensive position, and he's breathing evenly, taking in as much scent as he can.

"He has allied himself with one of your people," the elf says. "Francis Tish."

I swallow my excitement. This could be the source of information we've been looking for.

Or it could be a trap.

"You know we can smell lies?" I ask. It's not strictly true. Alistair can because he's been trained to do so. I—and most other shifters—can smell biochemical changes that indicate stress and certain other emotions, but that doesn't mean I can tell whether that's due to a lie or just that aforementioned stress. And in this case, without knowing the biochemical baseline for elves, even Alistair would only know that the scent had changed, not what that meant.

But we need every advantage we can scrape together. If this elf turns out to be on our side—or at the very least an enemy of our enemy—we can apologize for misleading them later.

"Yes. Your companion told me." They still seem composed—a little tense, maybe, but given they're in a dark room with two beings who are treating them like an enemy, that's to be expected.

"Are you an enemy of Tish?" It's not the question I most want to ask, but how the elf answers will tell us a lot.

They hesitate. "I don't know Tish," they say at last. "I am reluctant to declare enmity without knowing his purpose and goals. But I am an enemy to his ally, Éibhear, and for so long as Tish works with Éibhear, I could not ally myself with him."

"So you don't share the purpose and goals of Éibhear?" Whoever that is. Another Irish name, although the place names they mentioned don't have Gaelic language roots.

"I do not." There's a definite shift in tone this time —the disgust is clear.

"What are Éibhear's purposes and goals?"

"The enslavement or extinction of all higher-intelligence beings on this planet."

Well, shite. I look over at Alistair again, and he nods slightly. Either this elf is able to completely control their own biochemistry or they believe what they just said strongly enough to cause no change to their scent.

"Why do you believe we are enemies of Tish, and thus of Éibhear?" Although we'd have to be pretty feckin' dumb not to be enemies of the person who wants to eradicate us.

"He…" The elf trails off. "Is he still here? The one who opened the door?"

"I'm here," Alistair says.

"You were there today, near the place where Éibhear and Tish are. I sensed your energy when I was scouting."

"I was" is all Alistair replies, and it clicks. An elf who opened a portal in the middle of nowhere, then just stayed still… as though assessing a strange and potentially hostile environment.

"The living force surrounds you strongly. It protects you; protected you today. It showed me clearly that you are an ally."

I groan. I am so fucking stupid.

"Aidan?" Alistair sounds on edge.

"I'm fine. Just… hang on."

I open myself completely to the magic, but I don't need to. Ever since the magic chose me to be species leader, it's looked out for me. It's warned me every time I've been in danger and guided me to make the right decisions. Not once since I woke up ten minutes ago has it given any indication that this elf is a risk. It didn't even wake me—as far as the magic is concerned, this elf is nothing to worry about.

Reaching out, I feel the familiar warmth of it around me. *Can we trust this elf?*

All I get in return is assurance and confidence.

Still… I'm not willing to risk Alistair and, ultimately, the lives of all my people so lightly.

"Wait here," I instruct and run back up the stairs to find my phone.

Percy answers on the second ring. "Aidan?" he asks calmly, and that's an instant reassurance. It's a call from someone in a potential danger zone at three in the morning—you don't answer it calmly unless the existential magic that makes up the universe has assured you there's no problem.

"Sorry to wake you, but we have a situation here, and I need your take. You have a closer bond to the magic than me."

He hesitates. "I'm only getting reassurance and positive vibes. What kind of situation? Is everything okay?"

"Well…" How to put this? "What does the magic tell you when I say there's an elf downstairs with Alistair right now?"

Percy makes a startled noise, and there's a clatter—him dropping his phone, maybe. It's followed by a very un-Percy-like curse and a scrabbling sound, then he's breathlessly demanding to know if I'm still here.

"Yes, I'm here."

"There's an *elf* with Alistair?"

"They knocked on the door about ten minutes ago," I confirm.

"I was not expecting this," he mutters.

"Neither were we. Alistair's only wearing underwear."

He chuckles. "Well, the magic is still all happy about this, even if it's not giving me any more information. The surprise is purely my own. Has the elf said anything yet?"

I give him a quick rundown on the story so far, and he makes a thoughtful sound. "I think it's safe to treat them like a tentative ally for now. The magic doesn't seem concerned at all, so I'm guessing our motives and goals at least partly align."

"I'll tell Alistair we can turn on the lights, then," I say dryly, aware that Alistair's listening to everything I say. Sure enough, a moment later a light switch clicks. The elf makes a startled sound, and through the bedroom doorway, I see the faint glow of light reflecting up on the landing.

"I'm going to wake everyone up and brief them," Percy continues. "Do you think there's any value in you and Alistair staying there?"

"I'm... not sure." Even if Caolan can't tell us exactly what Tish's plan is, they can give us information about the elves' capabilities and potentially lend us a fighting force... well, maybe. We really know nothing about them except their name and that they're on the other side from Tish right now. For all we know, they might be acting completely alone. "Let us ask Caolan a few more questions. I don't think we've got anything further to gain by talking to the local pack, so it's really just if we need to ferret out more information on the elves."

"I'll expect to hear from you in the next couple hours, then," he concludes. "Depending on what you learn from... what name did you say?"

"Caolan," I repeat. "Sorry for waking you so early."

"My alarm is going to go off soon anyway," he says, and my tired brain remembers the time difference. "Once I hear back from you, we'll decide what to do next."

"Thanks, Percy."

We end the call, and I take an extra second to pull on a shirt and grab Alistair some clothes and his phone before heading downstairs again.

Neither Alistair nor Caolan has moved, although now Caolan can see Alistair and is staring at him with a slightly furrowed brow.

"Catch," I tell Alistair while I'm still halfway across the room and toss his shirt and pants at him. He dutifully catches and begins to get dressed.

"May I ask…?" Caolan begins hesitantly, and we both look at them.

"Of course," I say. "But we won't promise to answer." Percy and the magic may be convinced Caolan is, if not on our side, at least not working against us, but that doesn't mean I'm going to agree to tell them anything they want to know.

"Are… Do the faces reflect mood?"

For a second, I think we have a language issue, which is surprising because their English has been fantastic so far. Then they gesture toward Alistair's underwear, still showing a little where he hasn't zipped his pants, and it's all I can do not to laugh.

"Ah…" The quiver in my voice is the only giveaway of my amusement, and I'm so proud of myself. Especially when Alistair hurries to zip up and nearly catches himself in the zipper. "No. That's just a picture. It's supposed to be humorous."

Their face relaxes, and they smile a little. I'm relieved to see that they have so many mannerisms like ours—that will make communication a lot easier and prevent us accidentally starting an interdimensional war.

Although, if this Éibhear person plans to wipe us out, that war has probably already begun. We just don't officially know about it yet.

"Why don't we sit down?" I suggest, nodding toward the couch and armchairs we haven't used since we got here. I lead the way and gesture for Caolan to take one of the chairs. If Alistair and I sit beside each other on the couch, we'll be able to speak subvocally without it hearing us.

Alistair seems to have the same idea, because he joins me on the couch without me even having to glance at him, and immediately asks, in a tone too low for anyone but a shifter to hear, "Magic okay?"

"Yes," I mutter back. "Percy says tentative ally."

Alistair turns his full attention to Caolan, who's sitting calmly in the armchair, watching us. When I read the report about Noah's encounter, his description of the elf he saw frustrated me. Looks mostly human, but not? Like a fantasy movie elf, but not? What kind of description was that?

But now, looking at Caolan, I get it. From behind, with hair covering their ears, they would look completely like a tall, slender human. But a single glance at their face dispels that idea completely. Shifters, sorcerers, and incubi/succubae can pass for human without even trying as long as we're not actively using our abilities. Vampires need to keep their fangs retracted, and demons need to hide their horns, but other than that, they too can pass for human. But there's just no way to mistake Caolan for human. Aside from the sharply pointed ears, the bone structure of their face is just too different. Heavier around the brow and eye sockets, extremely sharp at the cheekbones, and almost pointed at the chin. I try not to stare but study closely. The bottom half of the face, while more dramatically shaped than I've ever seen, is not too different from the structure you see in some Celtic and Slavic features, but the top is very clearly *other*.

The overall result is remarkably attractive, although I'm not really sure why. I've always preferred bulkier builds—Alistair ticks all my boxes.

Speaking of Alistair…

"Why are you here?" he asks bluntly.

"For information," Caolan says promptly. "And to search out potential allies."

That's promising.

"Are you here on your own behalf or someone else's?"

It seems confused by that. "Both?" they ask more than tell. "I serve at the pleasure of my king. It is my will and his."

There's a lot to untangle there, but I want to take a different tack for now.

"We understand that you came here from a different dimension, but it seems we speak the same language. How is this so?" If we can believe what folklore tells us, the elves were frequent visitors before the species wars— perhaps even semipermanent residents. But modern English wasn't the language spoken then, and Caolan speaks it just as well as we do.

"We do not. I am using a translator spell. It is somewhat awkward now but will learn and attune more as it hears more of your language."

"Get out. No fucking way!" Alistair leans forward, face alight. "Is that spell something you can only do for yourself?"

Before he demands that the elf from another dimension begin experimenting on him with magic we don't understand, I step in. Caolan is looking confused, possibly because Alistair told them to get out but also seems to want them to stay.

"Could you, uh, turn it off so we can hear what your language sounds like?" I suggest, and they smile and rattle off something that sounds mostly like gibberish to me, although there's something familiar about a few syllables. It might be that the Irish language borrowed from the elven one back in the day.

"Was that acceptable?" they ask, and I nod.

"Thank you. This is a very useful spell."

Alistair, maybe remembering that this is serious stuff, not a new toy for him to play with, leans back again. "Perhaps you could tell us your story from the beginning. Who you are, who your king is, what happened to bring you here, and why you followed me."

"Yes, of course. I'm not quite sure where to begin— it's been a long time since my people had contact with yours. Are you aware of our existence?"

"Your existence, yes," I tell them, choosing my words carefully, "but not with many details."

"Our dimensions exist parallel to each other, reachable only through portals. At one time, there was a great deal of contact and trade between our peoples. I am here now to seek information and offer aid."

Beside me, Alistair lifts his head sharply, and Caolan stops. In the next second, Alistair's off the couch. "You were followed. Come on."

CHAPTER TWELVE

Aidan

CAOLAN and I get up and follow him toward the stairs. I inhale deeply, but I'm not getting anything. Still, I trust Alistair. The magic is still calm, so it obviously doesn't consider me to be under threat.

Does that mean whoever Alistair can smell is on our side?

I no sooner think it than the magic rears up, clanging warnings through my head.

Okay, so maybe the intruders are dangerous, but the magic is confident that Alistair has things in hand?

The magic settles again, and I marvel over how… *interactive* it's become. It never used to be like this. A sign that times are changing?

"How many?" I ask Alistair softly as we go up the stairs.

"Around a dozen. They're still hanging back, so it's hard to tell."

"It's impossible," Caolan says in a hushed tone. "The spell I used to follow you would work only for me, and I portal-jumped. There is no way I could have been followed. They did not even know I was there."

"Maybe not immediately, but they would have smelled you and your magic," I tell them softly. "We can sort out the details later, but either you or Alistair were followed, and they seem to have been right behind you."

They look startled. "*Smell* me?" They shake their head. "I thought that was a myth."

Alistair and I exchange glances. "We'll need to talk about myths later," he says. "For now, I need to know if you can use your magic to support yourself physically." He leads the way into the master bedroom but leaves the lights off.

"Yes… it depends on what exactly is required," Caolan replies. While Alistair explains our escape route, I grab our laptops and other essentials that would be hard to replace—or dangerous in enemy hands—and pack them into bags with cross-body straps. Anything attached to our bodies goes wherever our clothes end up when we shift. So if I've got a laptop bag full of stuff strapped to me when I shift, it'll still be there when I change back, but I can forget about it completely while I'm in cat form.

Pretty cool, huh?

"I can do that," Caolan says. "And I can make it so the spell is not visible, also."

"Great," Alistair declares. "Aidan will go first. You're next, and I'll bring up the rear. If I fall behind, you keep going." He meets my gaze in the dimness as fear clutches my stomach. Leave him behind? No feckin' way. "You keep going, Aidan. I'll catch up or the special ops team will come back for me."

"What special ops team? There isn't one here!" I

hiss. I know he's being sensible, but every fiber of me is going nuts at the idea of leaving him behind.

"They're going to be on standby just as soon as I make this call," he says, holding up his phone. "Open the window in the bathroom, would you? And show Caolan where they'll be going, but keep the light off and be as quiet as possible. Let's not give the details of our plan away."

I want to argue with him, but now really isn't the time, so instead I take Caolan's elbow and guide them into the bathroom. While I open the window and help them climb up on the vanity to poke their head out, I listen to Alistair's call. It's to Gideon, and at least part of it seems to be in code or shorthand. When he's done, he locks the bedroom door, then joins us in the bathroom and locks that door too.

"We're going to wait a bit," he says. "We don't want to move and then be stuck in the backup location because they haven't closed in. As soon as they start to move closer, I'll send a message to Gideon and we'll go out the window. Hopefully, by the time we're in the other house and they're searching this one, local enforcement will be nearly here."

I start to nod, then realize something. "How are you going to get out the window?" He's too big. He *might* fit in hellhound form, but hellhounds don't have the type of claws needed to climb a sheer wall. He'd get out the window and basically fall two stories to the ground.

"With a lot of luck and a very carefully timed shift," he says, and maybe I'm imagining it, but he doesn't sound as confident as usual.

"I don't understand," Caolan says. "Shift… you mean change to your other form?"

I freeze. Did we mention that we were shifters?

"My other form?" Alistair asks, and I know he's picked up on that too.

"You have a twin soul, correct? I can see it when I look at you. Yours is canine. Aidan's is feline."

"You can *see* it?"

They wave a hand in frustration. "Not see with my eyes. My magic sees it. Senses it!"

I have so many questions—so, so many—but now is not the time. "Yes. We will change forms to go out the window. My cat will be able to scale the side of the building, but Alistair's…" I hesitate, unsure how his translator spell will cope with the word "hellhound." "…canine can't do that. He'll need hands." And even then, it might be a problem. As I recall, one of the things he liked about this window was that it was more than an arm's length from the edge of the roof.

Caolan squints at Alistair in the faint light from outside, then turns and looks up at the window. "You won't fit this way. I can help."

Alistair does his lopsided eyebrow thing, and I bite back a smile. "You can?"

Caolan nods. "I don't have claws like a cat either. I will create a shelf outside the window to stand on, then climb up to the roof." It shrugs. "I can leave the shelf long enough for you to use it too."

In this moment, I could kiss them. A tiny part of me warns that they could very easily not follow through, causing Alistair to plunge to the ground, but the magic is still projecting calm rainbows through my mind, and honestly, even if Caolan is on our enemies' side, they would gain far more by helping us now than by maiming Alistair and losing our trust.

"Thank you," Alistair says. "That's very kind of you. I accept your offer."

And then we stand in the bathroom, listening and smelling for intruders. Well, that's what Alistair and I are doing. Not sure about Caolan. Maybe they're wondering if this is all some kind of weird scheme to test their trust?

"May I ask a question?" they say abruptly, breaking the silence.

"Yes," I tell them, this time not bothering to add any caveat. I'm pretty sure it would be okay with me declining to answer.

"Earlier, when Alistair told you to bring me in here, I was referred to as 'them.' Is there a local or cultural custom by which gender pronouns are not assigned until after a ritual?"

I look at Alistair. He's looking at me. Neither one of us wants to take on this potential minefield. Contact with a new species is *hard*.

In the end, I do it. After all, I'm the closest to a diplomatic representative of the two of us. Alistair's my muscle.

"No, there's no such custom. We merely didn't want to assume your gender and, uh, we weren't sure if there were any cultural or societal taboos against us asking." I grimace, glad they can't see me clearly in the dim light. "It's been a long time since our peoples interacted, and a lot has been forgotten. We weren't even sure whether your species has assigned genders and didn't want to begin again by causing offense."

Caolan nods. "That is reasonable. I have also been concerned about this. Perhaps we can agree that amongst the three of us, there will be no offense to any question asked with respect and a genuine desire to learn? We can be envoys and… interpreters for our respective people."

"That's an excellent idea. Thank you, Caolan. This will enable us to share information much more quickly."

"You're welcome. And my pronouns are he/him."

"So are mine," I tell him. "Alistair's, also."

"Hush," Alistair whispers, and a second later, I catch my first whiff of what he's been smelling. Hellhounds. A group, although I can't quite tell how many—mostly because they have the same underlying base scents, which tells me they're from the same geographic area and family groups.

They approach steadily, not speaking, trying to be quiet, although it's clear from the way they occasionally scuff or mutter that they haven't had the kind of training Alistair has.

"Let's go," Alistair murmurs subvocally, and I lay my hand on Caolan's arm and turn him toward the window so he knows what we're doing. Alistair already dismantled the stool-and-blanket shelf that was in here with me all day, but I can manage without it.

I shift and leap up onto the vanity. Caolan sucks in a breath, but I don't look back, pushing up off my hindlegs and twisting halfway so I can catch myself on the windowsill but be in the right position to latch on to the exterior wall.

It's only been about thirty hours since the last time I did this, but it still feels amazing to let my felid instincts take control. The cat in me knows how to do this, and he won't let me down—even if he is pissed that I don't shift more often.

Balancing half in and half out of the window, I

extend my claws and latch on to the wall above the narrow window, giving myself a moment to make sure my grip is secure before shifting my weight and pulling the rest of my body out. The window embrasure on the outside is just a few inches deep, but it's enough for me to regain my balance and push upwards. Within moments, I've climbed up to the roof. I pull myself over the edge and move a few feet along, allowing room for Caolan to join me while I smell and listen for the intruders.

They're at the front door. What is it with people and the front door? I know the back courtyard is fenced, but it's not that much more effort to get over the fence. And there are plenty of windows too.

I hear the bang of a body colliding with the door— guess they've given up on being quiet—just as Caolan reaches over the edge of the roof and pulls himself up. He crawls over to me, and a moment later, Alistair's huge hellhound form bounds up after him. It belatedly occurs to me that I could have done that too if I'd asked Caolan to create his magic shelf early, instead of literally clawing my way up the building.

My felid self wonders why I'd want to rely on someone else's magic instead of my own claws and wits. He's a little disappointed that I'd even consider it.

A crash from the front of the house tells me our intruders have made it inside. They're not even trying to be subtle anymore. Do they know we're on the move?

Pushing the thought aside, I creep along the flat part of the roof, keeping half an ear on Caolan and Alistair behind me and the intruders going through the house.

Interestingly, there are sounds of people waking in the other condos, and I gently nudge the magic, making sure it's aware of the situation. We can't have humans getting involved in this.

I reach what I think is the right spot and peer over the edge of the roof. There's a narrow bathroom window beneath me, wide open. For a second, I consider shifting back and asking Caolan to lend me his magic shelf, but my cat does *not* like that idea, and given the precarious situation, I need him onside. So I unsheathe my claws and turn around to back over the edge of the roof. Because, like most cats, the way my claws curve means I can't go down while facing that way.

It's a little trickier getting back in through the window than coming out was, but I manage, and soon I'm on the bathroom floor, shifting back and shaking out my muscles. I look up at the window in time to see Caolan lower himself to stand on what looks like thin air just outside it, then duck down and clamber in. He's slender enough to fit, but because of his height he has to fold himself up and looks very awkward. I reach up to grab his feet and guide them to the vanity, and he shoots a grateful smile over his shoulder—though not quite in the right direction. He's really putting a lot of trust in us, following us through the dark without complaint.

We move back from the window as Alistair leaps down onto the shelf, then wiggles through the window— it's tight for him even in hellhound form—and jumps to the floor. He shifts back and reaches up to quietly slide the window closed, making it tougher for anyone trying to pursue us that way, although they'd have to be real idiots to not just get off the roof and try the front door.

"Is the shelf gone?" Alistair whispers very softly to Caolan, who nods. "Come on then." He leads the way out of the bathroom and through the house, leaving the lights off. I guide Caolan, taking an extra second to place his hand on the banister before we go down the stairs. The last thing our very delicate nascent accord needs is a broken elf.

In the garage is parked a nondescript four-door sedan, backed in to facilitate a quick departure. Alistair has us get in but leave the doors open—to minimize noise—and then he makes a whispered phone call.

There are shouts from the direction of our condo, although I can't make out the actual words.

"They've realized we're not there," Alistair murmurs, just loud enough for Caolan to hear. "It took them way too long. Amateurs. Enforcement is two minutes away and will arrest them. The special ops team is in the air to take them into custody and transfer them to the secure facility outside Seattle. We need to hang tight here for a bit, and then we'll decide on our next step."

We sit mostly in silence, Alistair and I trying to listen to what's going on outside and occasionally updating Caolan. Alistair also has Gideon on the line, providing updates on what the local enforcement team is doing. Almost an hour passes before the last of them are gone.

"Okay," Alistair says, finally speaking at a normal decibel and reaching up to turn on the car's interior light for Caolan. "We should be clear. Gideon, I'm putting you on speaker. Aidan and Caolan are here with me. Can you give them a full update? Caolan, this is Gideon, one of the people I work with."

"I am happy to speak with you," Caolan says politely.

"And I you," Gideon replies with a courteous

formality I've never heard from him. I shouldn't be surprised, though—I'm acquainted with his family, and demons have some of the most convoluted courtesies of any of the species, even if Gideon is usually taciturn. "Andrew's in contact with local enforcement until the spec ops team takes over. There are thirteen hellhounds in custody—"

Caolan turns his head to look at me, an arrested expression on his face, and I interrupt.

"Sorry, Gideon, just a second. Caolan, hellhound is the nickname for canid shifters like Alistair."

There's a weird sound from Gideon as Caolan smiles with relief and nods. "That makes much more sense than what the translator spell suggested. Thank you."

"My apologies," Gideon says smoothly. "I forgot that you haven't been subjected to the peculiar humor of canid shifters before. It can take some adjustment."

"Our humor is not peculiar," Alistair huffs. "It makes perfect sense for us to be called hellhounds." He turns to Caolan. "You see—"

"Perhaps that can wait?" I suggest, and the big, tough ex-special ops hellhound who just guided us safely out of danger subsides in his seat, pouting. If Caolan weren't sitting beside me, I'd kiss that pout off his face.

"Thank you, Aidan," Gideon says, and to give him credit, he doesn't add anything to mock Alistair. "As I was saying, there are thirteen canids in custody. None of them was particularly well trained for this type of event, which fits with what we believe we know." He sounds a little sour there, probably because we don't "know" very much for certain. "None of them seem willing to talk, but the spec ops team is going to transfer them over here, and we'll see if we have better luck. We're trying to keep details quiet, so we haven't given enforcement information that might allow them to gain answers."

"That works for me," Alistair says. "I'd like to bring Aidan back. Now that they know we're here and that we pose a danger to them, I want him better protected."

I open my mouth to protest, mostly on principle, but Gideon's already talking.

"Agreed. Although, they may not know specifically about you and Aidan yet. Their phones—which were the only communication devices they had with them—showed no calls or messages for the last few hours. If they followed Caolan like we think and didn't know where he was going or to whom until they got to you, they hadn't reported back yet."

"Amateurs," Alistair sniffs, and Gideon makes a grumbly agreeing sound. I bite back a smile.

"Apologies for interrupting," Caolan says. "But if they had none of my people with them, how did they follow me? I was portal jumping."

Alistair and I exchange a glance. "What does that mean, exactly?" I ask. "Did you sense where Alistair was and open a portal to that place?" Because if the elves have that kind of ability, we're pretty much fucked.

He shakes his head. "No, that's not possible. Living beings have unique energy patterns and leave a trail everywhere they go. It's possible to sense an individual's pattern, as I did today with Alistair. I then reached out as far as I could sense him and opened a portal to that place. From there, I reached out again and did the same, opening a series of sequential portals in the direction he was going until I found him."

That's... fecking amazing.

"What kind of distance was between the portals?"

Alistair asks, sounding fascinated. "Were you mostly following the highway?"

Caolan frowns. "I don't know how you measure distance here," he admits. "It took almost thirty portals. And yes, I followed you along the big road."

"They followed your scent," Alistair says. "Once they realized you were on the highway, they wouldn't have had to be so careful about tracking, especially if they'd already heard we were here in Portland. Possibly they also caught my scent going in the same direction and thought we were together."

Caolan's eyes widen. "That is impressive."

"It makes it even more important to get you all back here," Gideon says. "I'll have Sam arrange a flight for you all. It will likely have to be a private plane, as Caolan doesn't have any ID."

I study our new elf friend. "We'll need to stop and get him a hat and sunglasses," I say, trying to choose my words carefully. "Your appearance is quite distinctly not of Earth," I add, "and until we are prepared to let the greater population know of the return of your people, we'd like to keep your presence here private."

"Of course," he agrees politely. "Forgive me, but this flight you speak of—is it literally flying? As birds do?"

"Not quite like birds. We have machines—" I hesitate for a second to see if his translator spell can handle that word, and he nods. "—that are capable of flight. We sit inside them and they carry us from one place to another. It's considerably faster than traveling over land."

It's his turn to hesitate.

"It's safe," I hurry to add. "There are very rarely any problems."

He shakes his head. "Of course. But… you mention that it's faster. How much faster?"

"Much," Alistair says. "Driving on land in a vehicle like this"—he pats the steering wheel—"would take two or three days. Flying in a plane will take about five hours."

Feck—hours and days would almost have to be different in his dimension. Do we need to count out time for him and then explain how many seconds go into a minute, hour, and day? I open my mouth to ask, feeling a little overwhelmed by the thought—teaching is not my strong point—but then he starts counting on his fingers and muttering.

"Okay," he says dubiously. "I believe I have converted your time correctly. Five hours is still a considerable portion of the day." He turns to look at me. "Isn't it?"

"Yes. There are twenty-four hours in a day here."

"I think I remember learning that. It was a long time ago. So five hours to travel from here to where your workmates are will take a substantial part of the day."

"Yes," I agree. "But it's our only option."

He hesitates, and like a ton of bricks, it hits me what he's so worried about saying. In my defense, I've only had about three hours of sleep and my brain has been busy with other things.

"Would it be rude," I say slowly, again choosing my words with care, "if we were to ask you how your portals work?"

He smiles, his relief obvious. "Not rude at all. We channel the life force to open a gateway into the void and from there another to the place we want to go."

That explains… absolutely nothing.

"I don't understand," Alistair says. "What's the void? Noah didn't mention anything about a void."

Caolan tips his head in question. "Noah?"

"A friend of ours was taken by Tish and one of your people who's working with him," I explain. "They took him through a portal to your world." I look at Alistair. "Maybe he didn't notice? It all happened pretty fast, and just the existence of a portal is pretty shocking… for us."

"He likely didn't notice," Caolan agrees. "With practice and experience, we are able to position the two gateways in such proximity that crossing from one place to another takes a single step, thus creating a portal. There is nothing in the void, and it is too easy to become lost there. It's safer to minimize our time in it."

"Can all of your people use portals?" I'm glad I can keep calling them portals. For a second, when Caolan called them gateways, I thought I'd have to change terminology.

Caolan shakes his head. "No. Only a very small percentage of the population." He seems sad. "This is why Éibhear wishes to invade here."

"That sounds like something we all need to hear," Gideon says, and I startle slightly. I forgot he was still on the line. "Would you be willing to bring Aidan and Alistair here via portal? We can finish this conversation in person, and you can meet the lucifer—our leader."

A nervous thrill shoots through me at the idea of traveling by portal. I can smell Alistair's rising excitement and know he feels the same.

"It would be my honor," Caolan says. "I need an image of the place we are going, if that's possible. I can do without, but it increases the risk."

"I'll text a photo," Gideon says. "We'll do this at

Sam's and my place. There's too much chance of someone else seeing Caolan at the office. We would be honored to host you, Caolan."

"That's very kind of you," Caolan says but looks at me uncertainly. I look at Alistair, since he's the one who's actually been to Gideon and Sam's house and has a home of his own in the area. I'll be staying in a hotel.

"If you're not commuting back to your dimension, that's a great idea," he confirms. "Their guest suite is fantastic, and my apartment is only a short distance from there. I'd offer for you to stay with me, but there's no bed in my extra bedroom. Believe me, you want the king-size bed instead of my couch."

Caolan grins, and the magic settles around me in a way that makes me think it's happy with how things are going.

"That's settled, then," Gideon affirms. "Get your things together while I run home and take that picture, and we'll see you soon."

Alistair ends the call, and we get out of the car and slam the doors.

"We can go through doors to get back, right?" I ask. As much as my cat would love the challenge of scaling walls and creeping over rooftops again, my tired body is cringing at the thought.

"Yep," Alistair declares. "But Caolan needs to keep his head down, just in case any humans are looking out their windows. People will start getting up for work soon."

We go back into the main part of the condo, out the front door, and then down the street to the condo we've been living in. The door has been pulled closed, but it doesn't latch anymore. "That's gonna cost us," I grumble. Sure, I'm not personally paying for it, but it still chafes my thrifty soul.

"Sam will take care of it," Alistair says confidently, then grins. "And it's not my fault this time, so he can't even yell at me for it."

He's positively gleeful about that, and once again, I feel a rush of affection. He can be so adorable when he's not being dangerously competent. Is it wrong that I find the two sides of him sexy? Like… he's a complete badass, but also so playful. It allows me to be the mature adult but also feel secure in the knowledge that he can look after me.

I pinch the bridge of my nose as I head up the stairs. That might be a little deep, seeing as we've only had two nights together and I'm running on minimal sleep.

But maybe I'll find a place over here in the States—for a while at least. It's not like there isn't a lot of shit happening right now that I want to keep an eye on. And I'm strangely reluctant to leave Alistair—it can't hurt to see how things go, right?

If he even wants that.

Pushing those thoughts aside before they give me a headache, I pack up all my stuff, then jog downstairs again to help Alistair clear out the kitchen. There's not much left there—

"Oh, fuck! Weren't we getting a grocery delivery this morning?"

Alistair looks at his watch. "I'll call Sam."

It takes literally fifteen seconds to ascertain that Sam's already fixed it. I don't know how, since it's not even six in the morning here, but he assures Alistair it's been taken care of.

No sooner does that call end than Alistair's phone

beeps with a text. "It's Gideon," he says, then looks over at Caolan, who's been sitting patiently on the couch while we dithered over the potential grocery delivery. "Are you ready?"

He gets up and smiles. "You have the picture?"

Alistair hands over his phone, and Caolan studies the screen carefully. After a moment, he begins to glow a deep emerald green.

"Feck me!" I take an involuntary step back, then shake my head when he and Alistair look at me. "Apologies. I was just startled." Noah said the elf he encountered had glowed—although it was purple, if I remember right. So the color depends on the individual? Or the family? It could be anything, really—I add it to my mental list of things to ask Caolan. I also need to apologize to Noah for doubting him. This is no trick of the light—Caolan's glow is bright enough to read by, as long as you don't mind the green.

"I have it," he says confidently, and a second later a motherfeckin' *portal* opens in front of us.

I knew it was going to happen, but part of me still didn't really believe it.

"I must go last," Caolan says. "It's too difficult to maintain from the other side."

Before I even get my wits together enough to step forward, Alistair is there, *sticking his head through the portal.*

I've never had a heart attack before, but I imagine it feels somewhat like the way my chest does now as I watch my... whatever he is (I am *not* saying lover) poke his head through a portal created by elf magic as though it's a window.

He pulls back and smiles. "All good. You first, Aidan."

Huh? Why didn't he just go—

He flicks a glance at Caolan, and I resist the urge to roll my eyes as I get it. He doesn't want to leave me here alone with an elf. Damn overprotective hellhound.

This does *not* make me feel special and cared for. Not at all. Really, it doesn't.

"I'll see you on the other side," I say, grabbing my overnight bag and stepping forward. I'm not going to lie; I hesitate before walking through. I can't help it. Just wait until you're faced with a portal that will take you across the country in a single step and see how you react.

Actually going through, though? No problem. I was expecting to feel something, but there's nothing. No resistance. No tingle. It's just another step, and then I'm in what looks like an entranceway in a private home.

Gideon's there, and he grabs my arm and pulls me away from the portal before I can get a word out. "Into the living room." He gives me a little push in that direction. That's the Gideon we all know and tolerate.

I go through to the living room, nearly staggering as I cross through some ridiculously strong wards, and find David waiting for me.

"Aidan—you're all right?" He looks me up and down somewhat anxiously.

"I'm fine," I assure him and gesture behind me. "Did you put that ward up?"

"Yes. The entranceway is now warded off from the rest of the house. Just a temporary precaution. We trust your and Alistair's assessment of Caolan, but we still don't know his story."

Well, I can't blame any of them for that.

"Are the others on their way?"

"They will be in a moment. I need to ask you—how much do you trust your assistant?"

I frown. "Manoj? Very much. He has access to almost everything. In fact, before this current situation, I can't even remember the last time I kept something from him. Why?"

"He arrived at the office this morning, demanding to know exactly where you are."

That can't be right. "But he knew I was in Portland." I pull my phone out of my pocket and check the call register, my messages, and my emails. "He hasn't tried to contact me."

David makes a face, then as the sound of voices drifts in from the entranceway, he lowers his voice and says, "But you didn't give him the exact location you were at. I'm not sure why he hasn't called you, but he seems pretty frantic. Is he trustworthy?"

"Yes," I say automatically, then take a second to really think about it and reach out to the magic. "Yes," I repeat with more confidence. "I don't know what's going on, but I trust him."

"Enough to bring him into the loop on this?" David waves toward the door behind me.

I hesitate, and the magic surges around me. "The magic says yes," I tell him dryly, and he rolls his eyes.

"Yeah, that's what Percy said. I guess I'm just being paranoid." He pulls out his phone and sends a text. "Percy told him they'd bring him to see you—which freaked him out, by the way, since he thought you were in Portland still—"

"Well, I was a minute ago." I can't quite get my head wrapped around that still. One step took me across the breadth of the country.

"—but the rest of us wanted to be sure, so Andrew's had the drivers circling the block while I checked with you."

I don't even have time to laugh at that image before I hear the sound of a door banging open and Manoj shouting my name. I turn toward the doorway as he rushes in and grabs me in a tight hug.

CHAPTER THIRTEEN

Alistair

WHAT THE ACTUAL FUCK! Who is this guy and why is he all over my lover?

Hands curling into fists, holding back my shift by a thread, I—

Find myself being held back by Gideon.

"Let me go!" I snarl, trying to yank my arm free from his grip. Damn fucking demons and their strength.

"Sam will kill us both if I do," he says. "That's Aidan's assistant. He turned up this morning."

"I don't think kissing is part of his job description," I grit out as the fucker leans back and dips his head to smack a kiss on Aidan's mouth. Why hasn't he let go of Aidan yet? "What's he doing here anyway? I thought this was going to be top-level clearance only."

"Percy and Aidan both said the magic gave him the all-clear," Andrew says, coming up beside me. "So relax. Aidan's safe."

I'd glare at him, but I don't want to take my eyes off the slimy fucker groping *my* lover.

That's right. He's *mine*.

"They're awfully touchy-feely for what's supposed to be a professional relationship." I yank my arm again, and Gideon responds by tightening his grip to bruising proportions.

Andrew turns fully to stare at me. "Are you…?" A slow grin spreads across his face. "You're jealous!"

"I'm not jealous," I snap. "I'm infuriated! Look at that leech."

My asshole secondary best friend doesn't bother to look. "Is there something going on with you and Aidan?" He leans forward. "You can trust me. I won't tell everyone I know." The gleam of delight in his eyes makes me wish I can partially change so I could claw them out.

Well… almost. I'd threaten to, anyway.

Surprisingly, Caolan speaks up. "You have nothing to fear," he assures me, looking at my lover and the leech and then dismissively waving a hand. "You and Aidan have paired souls. With that one, there is nothing."

Uh…

"What?" My voice squeaks just a little. "Did you…? Are you saying Aidan and I are *soul mates*?"

"Do soul mates really exist?" Andrew adds, and Gideon's grip on me loosens.

All three of us stare at Caolan, and he takes a step back.

"Soul mates? I don't… oh, two people meant only for each other? No. There's no such thing."

"But you just said," Andrew whines. Caolan cuts him off with a shake of the head.

"I said paired souls. It's different."

We lean forward in anticipation, but he appears to be done.

"Well?" Gideon barks. "Tell us!"

Caolan tries to peer around us, seemingly a bit nervous. I don't know why. Maybe it's Gideon—he can be a scary motherfucker. "There are some souls with greater compatibility. Relationships change as people grow, and sometimes that means a connection between two souls comes to a natural end. When people with paired souls are in a relationship, they always grow in the same direction. Their souls will always complement each other."

I sneak a glance over my shoulder into the living room. Aidan's still talking to the leech, but it doesn't bother me so much anymore.

"That's lovely," Sam says, appearing out of nowhere, and I choke down a shriek. "Is this an abstract conversation or are we talking about someone in particular?"

Andrew opens his mouth. I jam my elbow into his solar plexus.

"Sam, you haven't met Caolan yet," I say quickly as my secondary best friend bends over and gasps for breath. "Caolan, this is Sam Tiller, one of my close colleagues and my dearest friend."

Caolan smiles and looks from Sam to Gideon and back. "I'm very pleased to meet you."

"We're so excited to have you here," Sam tells him. "We have many questions, but we'd like you to feel welcome and comfortable. Is there anything in particular that you need? Food, for instance. Are there specific foods I can get for you?"

The consternation on Caolan's face is almost comical. "I'm not certain," he confesses. "As far as I'm aware, your native foods are safe for me to eat, but things have changed considerably since last my people were here."

"We'll stick to fresh produce, then, and ask Percy to check in with the magic before you eat anything," Sam says soothingly. "Just to go back to the previous topic of conversation, do you mean a relationship between paired souls doesn't end?" He shoots me a sideways smirk that tells me he knows exactly how this came up.

Caolan spreads his hands. "Everything can end. Anyone can choose to end a relationship. But when it's between paired souls, it would take a lot. Compatibility is assured, forever. The only breakups between paired souls that I've heard of are when one decides they no longer wish to be in a relationship—or if they meet another paired soul and decide to pursue a relationship with them."

Sam looks fascinated. "So let's say you met someone, got along really well with them, started a casual sexual thing, and thought it might be more but worried that it was too soon. If you were paired souls, that worry would be groundless, wouldn't it?"

"Yes." Caolan smiles. "There is no such thing as 'too soon' with paired souls. If they feel the connection and choose to accept it, it won't fade simply because they've only known each other for a short time."

"That's incredible," Andrew says. "And you can see by looking at a couple if they have paired souls?"

"Not literally see." Caolan looks at me. "This is the same as the twin soul. 'See' is a dangerous word in your language."

"He senses it with his magic," I tell the others.

"What's a twin soul?" Gideon wants to know.

"Shifters."

"I'm a twin soul?" Sam sounds way too excited about that. "That's so cool."

Caolan hesitates, then says, "You are also a paired soul."

The joy that breaks across Sam's face is almost painful to see. "I knew it!" he shrieks, throwing himself at Gideon and climbing to wrap his arms and legs around him. "You're mine forever!"

Gideon buries his face against Sam's hair, but not before I get a glimpse of his massive grin.

"Just checking," I say to Caolan, "Sam's soul is paired with Gideon's, right?"

Snapping his head back up, Gideon growls at me, and I take a sideways step behind Andrew.

Caolan looks from me to Gideon and back, then says, "Yes. Of course."

Andrew, the tool, can't stop himself from asking, "You'd say that even if they weren't, right? Because Gideon's got his scary face on."

Sam detangles himself and drops his feet back to the floor, laughing. "Ignore them, Caolan. Thank you so much for telling us. We appreciate it more than we can say."

I squint at my bestie and then ask Andrew, "Do people in relationships become a joint entity? Are Sam and Gideon no longer able to speak for themselves individually, only for the collective Sameon?"

"What the fuck are you all blithering on about now?" Noah pushes past Andrew, and I look over to see Percy and Elinor behind him. "We let you out of our sight for two minutes, and— Oh." He catches sight of Caolan, pales, and steps back. "Uh, s-sorry about the swearing." He swallows hard and reaches for Andrew's hand.

Fuck. I didn't think that meeting an elf might bring

up some bad memories for Noah, especially since he's still recovering from what happened the last time he met an elf.

Lucky for me, Sam swoops in. "Caolan, we'd like for you to meet the lucifer, Percy Caraway. Why don't we all go into the living room? We have a lot to talk about."

Percy comes forward, smiling in that way that makes everything feel better, and says, "Welcome to Earth. I hope Alistair and Aidan have been taking good care of you."

I sniff and open my mouth, but Andrew steps on my foot, so I close it again.

Caolan smiles back at Percy. "They have, although I will confess this morning has been more exciting than I anticipated."

"For us, too," Percy commiserates. "Come and sit, and I'll introduce you to everybody properly." He gestures toward the living room doorway and then leads the way in, Caolan falling into step beside him. Before I can follow, Sam grabs my arm.

"Did you hear that?" he hisses. "I'm going to be with Gideon forever!"

"I heard," I say, looking toward the others. "Shouldn't we—"

"And you and Aidan are *meant to be.*"

I grin before I can stop myself. "That's not what he said," I caution.

Sam raises an eyebrow.

"But yeah," I continue, "Aidan's probably stuck with me forever. Our wedding is going to be a glorious event. We'll both wear white to symbolize the purity of our paired souls, but I'll be draped with a sash of vividly colored fresh flowers as I walk down the aisle. Thousands will stand and bow their heads in reverence as I pass, and—"

"Thousands?" Sam's skepticism is a knife through my heart. "Also, *reverence*?"

I pout. "People revere me, Sammy. Lots of people."

"Uh-huh. I'd hold off on sharing those wedding plans with Aidan, just—"

The front door opens, and a guy I recognize from Percy's security sticks his head in. "Food delivery?"

My stomach rumbles in appreciation. "Oh, thank fuck. I haven't eaten in hours."

"I'll take care of this. You go in there—Caolan will probably feel more comfortable with you around."

I obey, because only an idiot gets on Sam's bad side—especially when he controls the food—and stroll into the living room. Percy and Caolan are seated in the armchairs that flank the fireplace, while Noah, Andrew, and Elinor have taken the couch. Gideon's hovering near the door—he won't settle until Sam comes in. Extra chairs have been brought in and spaced around the coffee table, making the area an actual conversation circle. Aidan and the leech are in the two opposite the fireplace, while David is sitting beside Percy.

"Hey," Gideon mutters subvocally, "is it just me, or is Caolan being weird?"

I can't answer him without the others possibly hearing—demon ears are good, but not as good as shifter—so I turn my attention to Caolan.

It only takes me a few moments to see Gideon's right. Caolan's gaze keeps sliding across to David. He'll jerk it back to Percy, who seems to be giving him an abbreviated rundown about our situation with Tish, but then a few seconds later, it's right back to David.

David's noticed, of course. He always notices details, and having a diplomatic envoy stare at him during talks is a pretty big detail. Being David, the only giveaway that he's concerned and unsettled is the slight twitch of his index finger.

Then his whole right hand flexes, and Gideon and I exchange an alarmed look. That's akin to a public tantrum.

Before we can find a way to step in, though, Percy pauses, and Caolan seizes the chance.

"Please forgive me for interrupting," he says politely to Percy, then turns to David. "You are the most beautiful being I have ever seen in my life."

My jaw drops.

It's not the only one.

And David, calm, unflappable David, begins to sputter.

Nobody seems to know what to say.

Except Caolan. He's got plenty to say.

"From the instant I laid eyes on you, my soul has been crying out for yours. Never did I dream that in this world I would find such perfection as you."

Whoa, this guy has some smooth lines. I make a mental note of that soul crying out one—I can use it on Aidan when I tell him we're almost soul mates—then turn to look at David.

Honestly? I don't see what Caolan sees.

I'm not being an ass, I swear. Objectively, sure, David's good-looking. Black hair and blue eyes is a combination that appeals to a lot of people. His nose is on the bold side, but the rest of his features are even and attractive. He's fit, intelligent, and kindhearted, and the kind of friend who, as the humans say, I would take a bullet for gladly.

But to call him perfection… I don't see it.

I guess I don't have to, though.

"Dare I hope that a person so wonderful is unattached?"

There's a moment of silence as we all stare at him, then I realize what he's asked.

"Yes!" I shout. "He's single. He'd love to date you. How about tonight?"

"Alistair!" David snaps, seeming to come out of his shock. "That's a decision for me to make, not you!"

"Actually," Percy says smoothly, "at this stage, I'm going to make it. Caolan, I'm deeply sorry—more than you can possibly imagine—but until we've had more time to talk and rebuild relations between our people, I cannot allow an intimate connection between you and David—or anyone else here."

David looks relieved. Caolan bows his head in acknowledgment. "Of course, I understand. Truthfully, my king would say the same if he was here. I will wait patiently and put my effort into diplomatic matters in the meantime."

"Thank you. I appreciate your understanding." Percy's voice is solemn, but there's a twinkle in his eye that makes me think he's not so much "saving" David as genuinely trying to get the diplomatic stuff out of the way first.

"I wish we had popcorn," Ellie says just as Sam comes in, directing two of Percy's security team who are carrying trays of food.

"What do you need popcorn for?" he asks as the food is set on the coffee table. I abandon my post beside the door and join the conversation circle so I can make up a plate.

Ellie fills him in, and Sam's face lights up. "Oh! Are you paired souls?" he asks Caolan excitedly.

"What are paired souls?" Noah demands. Andrew hands him a plate loaded high. I guess that means he's still obsessively trying to feed him up.

Sam explains, then glances at Caolan. "Did I get it right?"

He nods. "Yes. But it is a sad fact that I cannot see —*sense* when I meet a soul paired with my own."

"Oh, what a shame. Well, we'll just have to set up some kind of exchange program and bring more of your people over here so they can tell you."

David sputters some more. We ignore him.

"How does it work?" Noah leans forward and sets his still mostly full plate on the coffee table, seemingly intrigued. Andrew makes a sound of protest, picks up the plate, and lifts a strawberry. "Andrew, I swear to god, if you try to feed me that, I'm going to shove it some-where very uncomfortable for you."

Andrew puts the strawberry down. Too bad. I would have liked to see that.

Noah turns back to Caolan. "Are all elv— I'm sorry, how do you collectively refer to your people?"

Caolan opens his mouth, then closes it. "I'm not certain which word to use," he admits. "The translation spell has suggested several. In my language, it's—" He says something that has too many consonant sounds for me to easily understand. "The spell says fae, elf, sídhe... there are others too. I apologize for not being able to answer clearly."

"That sounds like a problem we created," Andrew

says. "If I remember correctly, elf is of Germanic origin, and sídhe is Irish—right, Aidan?"

"Oh, aye. Folk still speak of the sídhe, especially in the countryside."

"And fae is French—I was around when that one crossed the language barrier. So I'd say we English speakers adopted terminology from other languages that mean more or less the same thing."

Noah looks back at Caolan. "Do you have a preference?" he asks politely. "We've been using elf, but we wouldn't want to cause any offense."

Caolan inclines his head. "Elf is agreeable. Thank you for asking."

"You're welcome," Noah replies, a little awkwardly. "Uh, are all elves able to sense paired souls?"

"No." Caolan shakes his head. "It is a… specialized skill? But cannot be learned by all. One must have the basic ability."

"Well," I say, putting the pastry I was about to devour back on my plate. "It seems your king sent a highly trained and skilled envoy, since opening portals and sensing paired souls are such niche abilities." That makes sense and makes me wonder exactly how high in the ranks Caolan is. Pretty high, I'm guessing.

He inclines his head. "Thank you. I do my best to serve my king well—as you do to serve your leader." He looks around the group. "It is unsurprising to find so many paired souls here. Paired souls arc more stable, and the life force often rewards those who serve faithfully."

The warm glow of his compliment is still spreading through me when Ellie says, "You mean there's more than just Sam and Gideon paired here?"

He nods.

As one, we all lean toward him.

"Who?" Surprisingly, it's David who asks. He's been unusually quiet, no doubt not wanting to inspire any more heartfelt declarations.

Caolan gazes at him sappily, then sighs and tears his gaze away. I'm loving this. Like… really loving it.

"Andrew and Noah," he says, looking at them, and Andrew leaps to his feet, fist-pumping the air.

"YES! I fucking *knew it*!"

"You did not." Noah grabs his arm and yanks him back down. "But now you're stuck with me for the next sixty or so years. Finding someone else whose soul is compatible with mine sounds like too much work."

Andrew leans in and kisses him. It's sweet.

I look back at Caolan, wondering if I can give him a sign not to mention that Aidan and I are paired souls. I'd rather reveal it myself. He's frowning at Noah and Andrew.

He can't be homophobic, can he? Not after the way he gushed over David. Maybe he doesn't like PDA? But he was fine when Sam climbed Gideon like a tree.

His gaze shifts down the couch to Ellie, and he smiles. "And you have a paired soul also, although your match is not here."

The sound that bursts from my throat is a little embarrassing, but I sweep past it. "You're dating someone? And you didn't tell me? I'm your favorite cousin! How could you so malign the bond between us?"

She rolls her eyes, smirking. "You're not my favorite cousin. Danielle is my favorite cousin."

I gasp and fall back in my chair, my hand rising to my throat. She didn't… did she?

"And yes, I've been seeing someone. I didn't tell any of you because I didn't want to subject them to… well, to this." She waves her hand in my direction. What's that supposed to mean?

"I get it," David says, nodding. "Take all the time you need to make sure they're truly invested before you introduce them to us."

Now wait a second!

I stand and spread my arms wide. "How can you say such a thing?" I cry. "How can you denigrate the love I have for you all? Keep this up, and none of you will be invited to my wedding!"

There's a beat of silence.

"What wedding?" Ellie asks. "You're getting married? You haven't even been in a relationship since… well, not in this century *or* the last."

Oh. Whoops. I should probably have proposed before announcing my wedding.

Well, no time like the present.

I turn to where Aidan and the leech (who's far too close to my lover, by the way) are sitting. My plan is to drop to one knee for an incredibly romantic declaration, but first…

I narrow my eyes into my most intimidating glare. "I'm Aidan's *lover*." I savor the word as it rolls off my tongue, lingering on the *r*. There are a couple of gasps, and someone squeaks in surprise. "Who the fuck are you?"

"Alistair!" Aidan protests, his skin flushing that flaming red color that I now know for a fact goes all the way down to his chest. My cock twitches at the memory.

The leech stares up at me, seemingly taken aback, but then his eyes narrow and he stands. He's a hellhound too and almost my height, but I'm confident I can take him.

"Did you just call yourself Aidan's lover?"

"I did and I am. Who are you?"

The guy turns his head to look down at Aidan. "Is he missing a few screws?"

I growl, and Aidan stands up fast.

"Okay, this is… I have no idea what this is, but it's getting out of hand. Manoj, this is Alistair Smythe, and yes, we're… uh, seeing each other." The look he shoots me clearly says he's not calling us lovers. Even though we are. "Alistair, this is my assistant, Manoj. He keeps my life running smoothly, and I'll be pissed all the way off if you scare him away."

The leech—Manoj—scoffs. "As if I could be scared away by *him*."

"We won't know if we don't try," I sneer. I love a good sneer.

"Alistair," Aidan warns. "Manoj is an old friend and an exceptional assistant. I don't know what bug got up your ass, but this stops now."

I turn all my attention on him and pout. "He's all over you," I complain. "I don't like the touchy stuff."

He sighs and looks at Manoj with a raised brow. For a second, Manoj just stands there with a smug expression, but then Aidan clears his throat, and he sighs too. "We're not usually this touchy," he admits. "I'm just relieved Aidan's okay. I have a contact who brokers odd jobs on the dark web, and he told me a couple weeks back that unidentified people have been asking leading questions about some of you—Aidan included. Then late yesterday I realized that none of my emails and messages to Aidan are going through."

"What?" I look at Aidan, and he nods grimly.

"I'm not sure what's happening, but we should probably assume my phone and email are compromised. David's already taken my electronics."

That must have happened while I was in the entranceway.

"I'm going to need to check yours too, Al," David interjects. I nod and wave him off.

"So you're not trying to steal him from me?" I ask Manoj suspiciously.

"I didn't even know he was yours for me to steal," he exclaims, and I growl again, because that was *not* the right answer. "But no," he adds. "Aidan's my boss and dear friend. I'm not interested in him that way."

I give a satisfied nod and extend my hand for him to shake. "We'll probably be seeing a lot of each other, what with Aidan being my lover and all."

"Does anyone else feel creepy when he says that word?" Noah asks. "It makes me feel creepy."

I flip him off without looking.

"Sure," Manoj says. "I… look forward to it."

With that taken care of, I take both of Aidan's hands in mine. He promptly pulls them away. "I don't know what the feckin' bloody hell is going through your head, but you can't just be announcing to all and sundry that we're lovers. And stop using that word!" He's all flushed and flustered, his eyes flashing with emotion. Anger, probably, but that's okay.

"Caolan?" I call, not taking my eyes off Aidan.

"Yes, Alistair?"

"Were there any other paired souls here?"

Aidan's jaw drops.

"You and Aidan," Caolan says, and if I'm reading

his tone correctly, he's utterly delighted by this whole situation.

I go down on one knee in front of Aidan, and Ellie says, "Where's my phone? I need to record this!"

"Gotcha covered," Andrew declares. I block them all out.

"Up until a few days ago," I begin, "I hadn't been in a romantic relationship for a hundred and fifty years. I got burned—literally—when I was young, and I never wanted to risk a broken heart like that again." I see the sudden awareness in his gaze as he realizes the story I told him was about me. "Spending time with you changed that. I wanted more time with you. I wanted more than just sex with you. I wanted you, always. That scared me, because how could I possibly have gone from being afraid of getting hurt to being willing to expose myself completely to you… and in just a few days?

"But then Caolan told me our souls are paired, and Aidan, it makes more sense to me than anything else ever has. Part of me recognizes that we can be happy together forever—my soul recognizes yours. I know we still have so much to learn about each other, but I want you to know I'm fully committed to us, and one day, I'm going to marry you."

"Aww," Sam murmurs tearily.

Aidan blinks a few times, then looks past me. "Paired souls never grow apart?"

"Never," Caolan confirms. "What you feel for him now is what you will always feel."

Aidan starts to laugh. "Get up," he tells me. "I want a kiss."

I leap to my feet and grab him, then dip him back

over my arm, classic-movie-style, and kiss him amidst cheers and jeers from my friends and colleagues.

When we straighten, he lifts a hand to my cheek, smiling. "It's nice to know we're not actually taking it too fast," he murmurs, "but I was willing to commit anyway."

I kiss him again, more thoroughly this time.

Sometime later, hands pry me away from Aidan and reality crashes back in.

"…got a lot to get through, and this is getting kind of uncomfortable for the rest of us," Sam's saying. It sounds like he's trying not to laugh. I open my eyes to see that Aidan is now three feet away, flanked by David and Manoj. A glance around shows that the vise grip on my arms is courtesy of Gideon and Andrew. My secondary best friend is outright chuckling, and even Gideon has a sparkle of mirth in his eye.

"How dare you keep me from my lover?" I demand, yanking at their grip. Andrew's loosens a little, but Gideon's is like iron. I'm going to have so many bruises tomorrow.

"We're in the middle of diplomatic talks between dimensions for the first time in nine thousand years," Percy says dryly. "Not to mention the threat to our secrecy and existence. I dare to keep you from your lover because your relationship isn't right at the top of my priority list."

Oh. I guess he has a point.

"But it *is* on your priority list? Just not at the top," I ask hopefully.

"Alistair," Aidan groans, but Percy's grinning.

"Most assuredly. And as soon as our current situation is resolved, I want to hear all about the plans for your wedding."

"Even I know you'll regret that," Noah mutters, "and I haven't known him that long."

Smiling sweetly at him, I say, "You look tired. Have you been getting enough rest and food?" Instantly, Andrew drops my arm and leaps over the coffee table. I'm impressed by how cleanly he clears it. In the next second, he's on the couch beside Noah, babbling about how he needs to rest.

Noah glares at me. I smirk back. And while he threatens his boyfriend with grievous bodily harm if he doesn't sit down and shut up, I grab Aidan's hand, sit, and pull him onto my lap.

He jabs me in the ribs with his pointy elbow, scrambles off my lap, and sits in the chair beside me. Before I can work up a good pout, he grabs my hand and laces our fingers together.

Compromise is very important in a relationship. We're going to rock this shit.

It takes a few more minutes to get everyone settled, and then Percy turns his smile on Caolan. "My apologies for the distraction. You were saying that your king sent you here to offer assistance."

Caolan nods. "Yes. We offer whatever aid we can to stop Éibhear and his accomplice, Tish. Your people should not have to suffer for what happened to us."

"I don't understand. What happened to you?" Sam asks. "I thought this Éibhear person was just out for personal gain."

"He is. But this is not a new thing for him. His quest for personal gain has been ongoing for millennia, and now, after causing the destruction of our dimension and the eventual annihilation of our people, he is attempting to twist the situation for his gain again."

Whoa.

I'm not the only one who needs a minute to take that in. Aidan's hand tightens in mine.

David looks around the group. When his eyes land on me, I feel as though he wants me to speak, but what do you even say when someone brings up the destruction of their entire dimension and the genocide of their species?

Finally, he seems to get fed up waiting for someone else to step in and clears his throat.

"Perhaps you could tell us exactly what Éibhear has done. From the beginning of his exploits. We'd like to understand what has happened."

Caolan's eyes go all soft as he smiles at David. "For you, anything."

David's hand flexes, but he forces a smile in return.

"The ban on travel to this dimension caused a lot of things to change for us. Your world had long been a popular destination for those wishing to experience new things—the atmosphere and native foodstuffs are close enough to ours to be safe, and your diverse people have abilities and skills similar enough to ours that we were not deified or persecuted. Those among us with the power and skill to open portals were able to amass vast fortunes for little work and use those resources to further their own research."

"Like an artist or scientist taking a side job to pay the bills so they can focus on what they really love," Ellie says. "Cool."

"But then came the species wars…," Percy adds, and Caolan nods sadly.

"Your species wars shocked us. This planet was deemed too risky for our general populace to travel to, and a ban was implemented that prevented portals to here from being opened without the king's permission. Over the next few centuries, the king sent scouts, hoping for an end to the strife, but once the fighting was done, the largest part of your population was suddenly blind to its own power—and remembered nothing of the other species, nor us." He shrugs. "The king deemed it safest for our people to ban all travel here until he could be certain of our people's safety. Every few centuries, a scout will visit and report back."

David, who's been taking notes like the nerd he is, asks, "So your current king continued this practice when he took the throne?"

Caolan frowns, looking confused. "I don't understand. My king, the current king, is the one who decided to ban interdimensional travel."

David's pen freezes.

"I beg your pardon." Percy leans forward. "Your current king was the king at the time of our species wars?"

"Yes."

"I... uh... how different is time in your dimension?" Percy sounds completely thrown. I don't blame him. We're long-lived, but if the king was ruling nine thousand years ago and is still going strong, that takes long life to a new level.

"Not so different," Caolan says. "Our day is a little longer than yours, but we don't break time down into such small increments as you do. We have morning, midday, afternoon, early night, midnight, and late night, following the cycles of the sun and moon. If we were to apply your measures of time to our daily cycles, I believe our day would be approximately twenty-six of your hours."

"Wait," David says, a look of abject horror on his face. "Are you saying you don't keep time? So if you were supposed to meet someone, the most accurate timeframe you could give would be 'in the morning,' which spans around four or five hours?"

Caolan shrugs. "Time will pass regardless of how we measure it. If a situation is not so urgent that it must be dealt with 'now,' then what does it matter if it is attended to at the beginning, middle, or end of a morning?"

I'm pretty sure David just had an aneurysm. He's opening and closing his mouth like a demented goldfish, and his face is red.

"That's certainly a much more relaxed perspective than what we have," Percy says diplomatically while Sam gets up and brings David a glass of water. "But returning to what you were saying, it seems to me that your species is much longer-lived than ours are."

There's a moment of silence, then Caolan says, "Forgive me, the spell struggled to translate that. You are saying that my species lives longer than yours does. This is true, but also not true. We live as long as we choose to, unless we are killed."

The glass slips from David's hand. Fortunately, the rug is thick enough that it doesn't break. Poor David. He likes order and rules, and it seems that the elves don't care about any of that.

I look over at Andrew. He's looking back, a wicked gleam in his eyes. Caolan might be a good match for David, after all—help him loosen up. And I've always fancied myself a matchmaker… after all, I didn't kill Gideon when he hooked up with Sam.

Aidan squeezes my hand, and I glance over to see him shake his head warningly.

"What?" I mouth, widening my eyes innocently, and he just shakes his head again. I guess he doesn't want to be part of my super awesome plan to get David laid by an elf from another dimension.

Too bad.

"That's fascinating." Noah's fully engaged, seemingly past his initial wariness of Caolan. "If you don't mind me asking, were you alive when the travel ban was implemented? Had you visited Earth back then?"

Caolan tears his gaze reluctantly from David and shakes his head. "I was born some centuries later. This is my third visit to this dimension—I have scouted here previously."

"Oh. I was hoping you could answer some questions for us about humans of that time. Our records tend to leave them out. They're also very sketchy in reference to your people."

"There are others who may be able to answer your questions," Caolan assures Noah. "Perhaps if you make a list? We would be happy to do this as a gesture of good faith. We can also consult the living archive."

Noah grins, and even David comes out of his shocked stupor somewhat at the thought of getting some answers, but Percy says, "I'm going to ask that we put that on hold for the moment. We keep getting side-tracked, and the magic is telling me we really need to hear your story. You were saying that after the species wars, those who had made money from opening portals were faced with change."

"Yes. Éibhear was one of those. He had amassed a vast fortune and resented not being permitted to continue. Some turned their attention to locating alternative destinations in other dimensions, but finding inhabited dimensions that also contain planets with suitable environments amongst the many millions that exist is painstaking and dangerous work. To this day, only one other has been located, and it currently does not have an evolved higher-intelligence species." He smiles. "Which makes it a boring place to vacation."

"Éibhear wasn't one of those people, was he?"

Caolan shakes his head. "No. Exploring new dimensions is time consuming and dangerous, and Éibhear has ever been someone who wanted a quick, easy result. We're not sure what his thought process was, how he discovered it was possible, or even if he understood from the outset what the dangers were, but what he chose to do instead began the destruction of our dimension.

"He began opening portals through time."

CHAPTER FOURTEEN

Aidan

THROUGH TIME? Does he mean…?

Alistair yelps and yanks his hand away from mine, and I belatedly realize I've been squeezing. "Sorry, love," I murmur, and his face lights up at the endearment.

"I'm sorry," Elinor says, shaking her head. "Are you saying it's possible to travel through time?"

"Possible, but not advisable unless you wish to end life," Caolan says, and if I wasn't already sitting, my knees would have given out.

David, frantically scribbling on his notepad, says, "Let's save the questions for later. I have many. But we need to hear this." He doesn't look up from what he's writing, so he misses the look of fond longing Caolan gives him. This is so weird… yet fascinating.

"We knew nothing then of the consequences of his actions," Caolan continues. "The wealthy flocked to him for his service. They wished to visit times long past or once again visit with those now dead. He guarded jealously the knowledge of how to create these portals, which caused much furor for millennia, but in retrospect was beneficial. If there had been hundreds or thousands of others doing the same, the process would have been speeded up.

"It was only five thousand years ago that the anomalies began. Random blips in the fabric of time, and anything that had occurred in that blip ceased to exist. People who'd lived for tens of thousands of years would just vanish as the moment of their conception was erased."

"Holy fuck." I'm not sure who whispers it, but it's imbued with all the horror I feel.

"As it continued, natural catastrophes became the norm. Millions—billions—of moments of sediment settling or of erosion or of rainfall were gradually wiped away, and so over time mountains collapsed, shorelines disappeared, and weather patterns changed drastically. By the time we identified the source, our population had dwindled from tens of millions to less than five million, and we lived in constant fear. His Majesty advised Éibhear immediately that his temporal portals were the cause of the disasters and asked that he cease using them. The hope was that our universe would begin to heal if no further timeline anomalies were created. Éibhear demanded compensation."

"He did *what*?" Sam shouts, leaping to his feet. "What an asshole!"

Caolan seems to consider that—the translator spell is clearly working overtime—then inclines his head in agreement. "He very much is, but with our existence at stake, his majesty felt it prudent not to quibble. Éibhear was compensated for giving up his business, and it was communicated far and wide that temporal portals were responsible for the ills that were befalling us, just in case anyone else should happen upon how to create one."

"We can certainly understand why your king feels the need to intercede here, if Éibhear is involved," Percy says. "We thank you greatly for bringing this to our attention."

A sad smile twists Caolan's mouth. "I wish that was all, but my story is not yet over."

I reach out and grab Alistair's hand again. He'll just have to live with it if I squeeze too hard—I need something to hold on to. I've been trying to calculate where the safest place would be to gather everyone if something similar was to happen here, and the answer is nowhere. Where could we possibly be safe from the destruction of *time*?

"Despite our hopes, the issues not only continued, but in fact became worse. It was several more centuries before the life force directed his majesty to the realization that Éibhear was still opening temporal portals, doing further damage to the fabric of time. With the aid of the life force, his majesty was able to strip this ability from him, a most traumatizing and arduous feat." A shiver runs down my spine. I thought my magic-granted power to compel members of my species was grave, but to strip away an ability? I can't imagine the impact that would have on someone's psyche.

"In light of the severity of the event, and with Éibhear's solemn oath to dedicate himself to researching ways to stabilize our dimension, his majesty allowed him to retain his life." Caolan's tone indicates very clearly what he thinks of that. "However, at the first opportunity, he fled and declared himself to be the true king of our people. He claims that he alone can save those remaining."

"I mean no offense by this question," I say slowly, "but is there any chance he can?"

Caolan shakes his head. "We wondered the same at first, but no. He doesn't have any way of reversing the damage done or even preventing further damage. The fabric of time in our dimension is too ravaged now, and there are only a few seasons remaining before it collapses entirely and the dimension is destroyed. And to answer the question you are too polite to ask, no, he has no claim whatsoever on the throne. Our king is selected by the life force—in much the same way your lucifer and you yourself are, Aidan." He inclines his head to Percy and smiles. "I can sense it in you like I can in him. It is a great comfort while I'm so far from home."

So the life force he's been speaking of is existential magic. It transcends dimensions… which means we know even less about it than we thought.

"I'm glad to be able to give you comfort," Percy replies gently. "How many of your people remain? Is it possible to bring them all through portals to here before your dimension collapses?"

For the first time, Caolan looks uneasy. "I am not here for that," he says firmly. "My king feels that he owes a duty to the life force to ensure Éibhear cannot do harm to more people and places. Éibhear has drawn a small group of like-minded followers, and the souls of our people, both those lost and those preparing for the end, will not rest until he and his followers have been dealt with." He draws a deep breath. "For his sins, Éibhear has earned soul death."

"Soul death?" David asks as Percy gasps. I squeeze

Alistair's hand harder. I'm not sure exactly what it is, but it makes the magic unbearably sad.

Caolan nods gravely. "It can only be carried out with the permission and assistance of the life force. The spell has been cast, and unless Éibhear performs some deed of such merit that the life force grants him clemency, upon his death, his soul will end. There will be no rebirth."

This time, I feel my hand clench around Alistair's, but it's okay, because his is squeezing back. Our whole lives are built around the notion that we move to the spiritual plane upon our death and then can choose to be reborn. Those of us who want to can undergo ceremonies to remember our past lives and our time in the spiritual plane. When our loved ones die, the knowledge that they go on, that our souls can one day be reunited, helps to ease our pain at their passing.

No rebirth? There could be no punishment worse than that.

Of course, given what he's done, he certainly deserves it.

"We will certainly do all we can to assist you in your mission," Percy tells him, "especially given the vested interest we have ourselves. However, whether it was your aim or not, I offer your people sanctuary here on Earth."

Caolan swallows hard. "I—" His voice cracks. "Thank you. There aren't many of us left, and… thank you."

The magic flares around me, happy and… filled with a sense of the inevitable? I have no doubt that Percy has made the right decision. The elves need to live on, and them doing so on Earth is what the magic wants.

"I imagine you'll want to speak to your king as soon as possible," David says, "but could I ask a few questions first? So we can begin planning."

"Of course. Anything you wish to know."

"How many of you are there, and what is your preferred climate? Do you live in family groups or larger clusters, and how many to each?"

"We are adaptable to climate. Our planet is not dissimilar to yours—or what our records of yours show. The polar ice caps are largely uninhabited, but there are several clans among our survivors who hail from a desert region and would be glad to return to that environment. His majesty has all survivors living within an energy shield on the plains, and some have found it a trial."

"That's fine," David says, taking notes. "We can easily manage that. It might be best to set up several large settlements in different environments for the initial few years. I imagine once people become comfortable being here, they'll travel a bit and find their own places."

Caolan nods. "As a species, we enjoy discovering new things and places. I believe once everyone begins to feel safe again, they will return to normal behaviors."

"And how many of you are there?"

"We are down to just under two hundred thousand."

I bite down hard on my tongue to keep from making a sound.

"So few?" Elinor looks like she's going to cry. Caolan nods sadly.

"It is only due to the energy shield that we have that many. Animal life has been all but wiped out—we have some few left for meat, but nothing lives outside the shield. The same for plants—only what we have cultivated remains."

"Okay," David says. "Okay. The animals are going to make things harder. I didn't want to bring this up just yet, but does your spellcasting ability allow you to disguise yourselves? Since the species wars, our continued existence has depended on our ability to hide in plain sight."

"Some of the smallest children may have difficulty, but their families will assist them," Caolan says confidently. "Changing one's appearance is a simple thing."

I blink several times as he changes in an instant from an elf to a human. It's still him—eye and hair color and most of his face are the same, but the elements that made him so distinctly "other" have been softened. I'd walk past this guy on the street and not give him a second glance—except maybe to admire his attractiveness.

From the way David clears his throat, he's noticed the same thing. Alistair chuckles beside me, a gleeful little *hehehe*, and I make a mental note to keep a close eye on him. David and Caolan can manage their own… whatever it turns out to be. They don't need his interference.

"Thank you," Percy says. "As you can see, amongst ourselves we don't bother with such glamor, but when with humans, it's our first priority."

"I understand." Caolan changes back to his elfin self, then, while I'm marveling at how his features can be so much the same and yet so different, says, "There may be some problems with the dragons."

…

…

…

Noah breaks the stunned silence. "I beg your pardon," he says politely. "Did you just say dragons?"

"Yes." He suddenly looks anxious. "They can come too, yes? They're the only other higher-intelligence species in our dimension."

"Dragons," Gideon repeats. "Like… dragons."

Andrew holds out his phone to Caolan. "This kind of dragon?"

Caolan takes it and examines the image closely. "There are some differences," he says at last, "but for the most part, yes. Do you have dragons here still? I thought they all returned to our dimension when the travel ban was instituted."

Alistair begins to laugh wildly. "Motherfucking *dragons!*" he cries. "Yessssssss. I'm going to make friends with the dragons. My tertiary best friend will be a dragon—you better lift your game, Andrew, or they'll replace you as secondary best friend."

I'm not exactly sure what he's talking about, but as long as he's not planning to replace *me* with a dragon, it's fine.

"Dragons," David whispers. "Okay. Okay. I can…. We need to talk about what the dragons will need. They don't eat people, do they?"

"Well," Caolan begins, and David makes a whimpering sound. "No, no," Caolan hurries on. "They *can* eat people when they're in dragon form, but they don't. Not anymore, anyway. Not for hundreds of thousands of years. They mostly eat while they're in biped form now."

"They're shifters?" Noah's grinning widely. "Dragon shifters? That's awesome!"

Alistair slumps a little and mutters something, and I know without asking that he's not happy about hellhounds no longer being the largest subspecies of shifter. I roll my eyes but let him have his sulk.

David's looking a little less pale now. "Would the dragons be able to remain in biped form for the most part? We can try to find a remote area where they can shift… Oh fuck, the satellites… Wait—do they fly?"

Caolan nods, seemingly fascinated by David's semi-meltdown.

"They fly. How am I going to hide giant flying dragons from the humans?" David mutters.

"They can make themselves undetectable in their dragon forms," Caolan volunteers, and David perks up. "But they can be… stubborn sometimes. And they like pranks."

As one, we all turn to look at Alistair. "What?" he demands. "I'm not a dragon."

"They sound an awful lot like hellhounds," Sam muses. "Can they be distracted with cookies?" he asks Caolan, who shrugs.

"As a rule, they have a sweet tooth. And they're stubborn and sometimes… exuberant, but they're not stupid. Once we explain how important it is to remain hidden from humans, there will be only rare episodes of foolishness."

"Like hellhounds weren't bad enough," David grumbles, and in unison, Alistair and Manoj say, "Hey!"

"Don't be jealous of our awesomeness, David. It's not our fault you're stuck in one form."

David ignores him and asks Caolan, "How many dragons are there?"

"Not many. They were always few in number, and the deterioration of our dimension affected them disproportionately. There are fewer than five thousand left."

"Dragons," Noah whispers. "Five thousand dragons."

My stomach rumbles, reminding me I didn't eat enough of the food Sam provided, and I feel my face getting hot with embarrassment.

Andrew makes a tsking sound. "Honestly, Alistair, if you can't look after your man better than that, there's no way he's going to marry you."

Alistair opens his mouth to reply, but Percy hastily says, "I think it might be time for a break. It's been a long and busy morning—and night, for some of you. Caolan needs to confer with his king, plus, I want to check in at the office, and I'm sure David wants to start planning for the migration. Shall we reconvene here in three hours?"

There's a general murmur of assent, but as we all get to our feet, Gideon says, "Just one more thing. You said earlier that Éibhear had declared himself king, even though the magic—life force—selects your king. Presumably his followers know this. What reason do they have for following him?"

Caolan sits back down, and my stomach sinks. The rest of us follow suit.

"Our best intelligence is that they do so for personal gain and survival. Éibhear has proclaimed that he will save our species, but only for those who follow him. That is further indication of his unfitness to rule, but for most of us, the fact that the life force does not support him is all we need to know. Some of our people did at first wonder if he might have a solution and joined his ranks, but they returned upon hearing of his plan. He has no way to save our dimension. His plan to save his followers is to bring them here. But his followers are few, a mere ten thousand or so, and he wishes to rule over many, not remain hidden."

"Ah." Gideon closes his eyes briefly. "Hence the enslavement and eradication of our people."

Nodding, Caolan continues. "As best we know, he found a way to circumvent the travel ban sometime within the last century, came here, and sought someone amongst your people who would support his goals."

"Tish." It's said by multiple voices.

"Indeed. Together they plan to enslave humanity and murder any of your species that attempt to gainsay them. Then Tish will rule over his own kind, and Éibhear will have dominion over humanity."

"I'm not doubting you," Sam says slowly, "but that doesn't seem like something Tish would agree to. Giving up power like that, I mean."

"It fits his actions, though," Noah adds bitterly. "When he took me through the portal, he seemed subordinate to whoever was in charge—Éibhear, presumably. Which reminds me, they all seemed really intent on stealing Percy's seal of office. Why?"

Caolan frowns. "A seal of office? An insignia? I have no idea. Perhaps they think having it would sway some of your people to their side?"

Noah doesn't seem convinced. "It didn't feel like Tish cared that much. He was doing it to fulfill a bargain with Éibhear." He thinks about it, then shakes his head. "I don't know."

"And none of what we know explains how either of them plans to get around the magic—life force," Andrew says. "They may have been able to run their plans in the background until now, but the collapse of a dimension and the dodgy dealings here have definitely got the magic's attention. For now, it seems content to let us try to handle things, but eventually it's going to act… right?"

Percy shrugs. "It won't give me a commitment on that either way, but given the way it's stepped in previously when genocide loomed, it's a safe assumption."

"Especially since it's so pleased we've invited the elves—and dragons—to live here," I add, feeling the warm comfort of the magic around me as I say it. "Why would it be happy to have saved them, only to let Tish and Éibhear wipe them out or enslave them?"

"So the life force is just as elusive with you as it is with us," Caolan says dryly. "That's both good to know and incredibly frustrating." He turns his gaze on Noah. "You were taken through a portal to my dimension?"

Noah nods. "Yes. They took me to a large building made from something similar to our stone and locked me in a linen cupboard."

"Why would they have a lock on a linen cupboard?" Caolan asks in puzzlement, and Noah jabs a finger in the air.

"Yes! That's what I want to know."

"My best assumption is that you were at Éibhear's base of operations. He and his senior spellcasters have managed to create their own energy shield, although it is much smaller and less stable. It's just as well for you that they brought you back here."

"They didn't," Andrew says. "Noah teleported himself home."

"*Teleported?*" Caolan's shock is a physical force in the room.

Noah sighs. "So that's not something humans could do back before the species wars?"

Caolan shakes his head, apparently too stunned to find words.

"And on that note," Sam says, "I think it's time for that break Percy mentioned. Anyone who wants to stay here is welcome. I'm having more food brought in, and the Wi-Fi password is on the fridge. Otherwise, we'll see you in a few hours."

I turn to Manoj as the group begins to disperse. "Could you find me a hotel near here? Have you sorted out a place to stay?"

He opens his mouth to respond, but Alistair gets in first.

"Are you trying to hurt me? Why don't I just give you a knife so you can jam it into my gut?" He brings his wide, sad puppy eyes to bear. "My lover would rather stay in a hotel than with me. It's like you've brought my deepest, darkest fear to life."

I bite back a smile at his dramatics. "Really? That's your deepest, darkest fear? That I'd stay at a hotel?" I hold up a hand before he can reply. "Never mind. Of course I'll stay with you—I just didn't think of it because I'm tired and used to staying in hotels."

He sniffs and grabs my hand. "Good. Let's go."

I yank him back. "Hold on." Turning back to

Manoj, I ask, "Have you made arrangements for yourself?"

He shakes his head. "No. I just got in a few hours ago and planned to fly directly on to Portland as soon as I found out where you were staying. Don't worry—I'll find somewhere to crash."

I look over my shoulder at Alistair, who manages to growl and pout at the same time.

"You can stay on my couch," he mutters reluctantly, and Manoj laughs outright.

"Thanks, but unless you have top-notch sound-proofing wards, that's a hard pass. There are some things I really don't want to hear my boss doing."

My face gets really, really hot, both from embarrass-ment and at the thought of doing those things with Alis-tair. I've had skin this fair for hundreds of years—my whole life—and yet I still hate how my face becomes a beacon so easily.

"Good point!" Alistair sounds far too cheerful. "Well, there's a decent hotel a couple blocks from here. We can share a ride—it's on the way to my place." He frowns. "Did you say David has your phone now?"

"Yeah." That's going to be a bitch. Not just that David has my electronics, but that my accounts are compromised. I can't even log in to my email from another computer—it's just not worth the risk right now.

"Let's stop and get you a burner, then. I don't like the idea of you not having a phone, just in case we're separated."

Aww. Is it any wonder I have all the warm feelings for him?

Part of me still thinks this is too fast and that I should be practical, but the rest of me—and the magic

—know it's right. Alistair fits with me, and I only regret I didn't make an effort to get to know him better sooner. We could have been together six months ago.

"C'mon, lover!"

It's probably going to take me six months to train him to stop using that word.

ALISTAIR'S PLACE IS NICE. In a barely-lived-in kind of way. Maybe I should say it has the potential to be nice. Spacious rooms, open-plan living, big windows. Hardwood floors, high ceilings.

A lone recliner pointed at a midsize television, with a two-seat sofa off to the side—lucky Manoj opted for the hotel, because he wouldn't have been comfortable on that. No coffee table, but rather a folding chair placed beside the recliner with the remote and an empty beer bottle on it—and yes, the bottle smells. It's clearly been there for some time. A collection of flattened cardboard boxes and empty bottles and jars litters the kitchen counter, awaiting a trip to the recycling dumpster. And there's dust everywhere. I almost expect to see a giant dust ball roll past.

Maybe I would have been better off in a hotel too.

"Sorry about the mess," Alistair declares. "It's been a busy few weeks… months, and I spend a lot of time at Sam's place, anyway. I've been concentrating on essential cleaning only."

I'm about to ask him what that means when I realize that the kitchen is clean despite the clutter on the counter. Sparkling clean. Sink, oven, stovetop—not even a water stain in sight. The counter, underneath the recyclables, is spotless. And the empties here don't smell at all, so clearly he rinsed them.

No sooner do I think it than he passes me with the bottle from the folding chair in hand, headed for the sink.

Okay. This might not be as bad as I thought. He doesn't care about dust, but there's no mold, and I'm not allergic to dust.

"Is it okay if I grab a shower?" I ask, and he grins at me over his shoulder.

"Of course. Down the hall, first door. There are towels under the sink. I'm going to order some food—there was nothing here before I left."

I leave him to it and go in search of the bathroom. It, too, is immaculate. If he's willing to clean the bathroom and kitchen, I have no issue doing the dusting and vacuuming.

The hot water is amazing, and I spend a few moments just letting it beat down on me and wash away all my exhaustion. There's a lot more to get through today.

I hear Alistair coming long before he opens the shower door, and a thrill of excitement runs through me. It's been a long time since I've indulged in shower shenanigans, and right now, I want every second with Alistair that I can get.

"Well, hello," he says, lounging in the doorway and letting all the steam out. "Does the owner know you're here?"

Choking back a laugh, I decide to play along. "Are you going to tell him?"

His face lights up with delight, and he steps into the giant stall and closes the glass door. "That would be the right thing to do. If you're not supposed to be here…" He shrugs and tries to look conflicted.

"Is there anything I can do to change your mind? I've heard the owner is a horrid man, and I'm so—" I cough to cover my laughter. "—I'm so vulnerable. I need someone to protect me."

Alistair puffs out his chest. He's getting way too into this. "I would gladly protect you from the evils of the world! For I am a fierce protector." I bite my lip. Hard. "But if you're here without the owner's knowledge—and I hear he's a *wonderful* man, not at all horrid—then I'm not sure I can help you. It would be a great cost to me, you know, and while I've always been selfless and giving, I *do* need to consider myself sometimes."

I decide to move this along before he turns it into a three-act play. Sinking to my knees on the slippery tile, I look up at him and say, "You need someone to give to you. Let me." Without waiting for an overdramatic bull-shit response, I lean forward and wrap my mouth around the head of his cock.

He gasps. "No, wait," he protests halfheartedly. "I couldn't take advantage of you this way." One hand comes to rest on the back of my head, adjusting the angle, and I huff through my nose.

Time to shut him up.

Alistair's dick is in proportion to the rest of him, and there's no way I can get all of him in, but I do my level best to try. From the sounds he's making, he appreciates it. I give myself over to my task, using every lick, suck, and nibble to push him closer to the edge, loving the tang of precum that seeps from him, until suddenly he clenches his hand in my hair.

"Aidan," he warns gutturally, and I take that as a sign to go deep again.

I feel the gentle scrape of his barbs against the back of my throat. He shouts, and my mouth fills with his hot, salty cum.

I pull back, spit, and as he leans shakily against the shower wall, I say, "I can take care of you like that all the time if you'll protect me from the owner."

"What owner?"

CHAPTER FIFTEEN

Alistair

It's edging into evening, and my stomach reminds me that dinner is needed, yet it feels as though we've barely made a dent in the to-do list.

I glance up at the wall David's covered in paper and written said list (and all the sub-lists) on. There are only a few items crossed off.

Things should start moving a little faster now, though. A big part of what we did today was establishing what needed to be on the list and then deciding who would handle what. One positive is that Caolan came back from his dimension with reinforcements: a warfare specialist who can work with us on where the elves will best integrate into our plans to stop Tish and Éibhear, and a historian who was actually alive and on Earth during the species wars. She and Noah have been tucked in a corner talking and poring over notes nonstop for hours, with David drifting over there every time he can pull himself away from the rest of the planning.

Our shared intelligence has helped to fill in a lot of gaps. As best we can tell without hearing it from the horse's mouth, Tish's species-segregated compounds are his way of growing his follower base. Elf magic and specifically the use of portals gives their side an advantage over humans, but the numbers are still against them, especially since Éibhear only has about ten thousand followers. They needed more beings from the community on their side—something Tish would be particularly eager for, since ultimately he would end up being their leader. As a rule, people look askance at cults—it's why the CCA never before got as big a foothold in the population as it has now. The general public doesn't like the idea of living in a compound away from creature comforts, and definitely doesn't like going against the mainstream. By integrating with existing communities—albeit taking them over and ousting any who don't conform—the CCA shows itself to be accessible and ordinary.

And thus, dangerous. Add to that Tish's experiments with DNA and the resulting chance of increased fertility, and there's a strong chance many could be swayed, at least for the short time he needs to take over.

The one factor we can't work out is how they plan to get around the magic. Surely they must be aware that their plan can only go so far. Unlike at the onset of the species wars, the magic is fully aware of what is happening. They might succeed in killing my team, Percy, and the elf king, and in establishing themselves as leaders. But that will still leave a huge number of community members, and no matter how we crunch the numbers, they always show that most will fight back. Widespread killing on that scale, plus an attempt to enslave humanity, can't fail to induce the magic to step in. We don't know what will happen then, but I doubt it will end well for Tish or Éibhear.

Through the doorway into the kitchen, I spy Aidan and Percy sitting at the kitchen table in front of Percy's laptop. With the migration of the elves and dragons imminent, they're reaching out to the other species leaders to share that information and come up with a safe and sane way to communicate it to the community at large… along with the fact that elves exist. And dragons. This has given them an excuse for our investigation into Tish—nobody needs to know about his research; we can just tell them he's in league with a rogue elf who destroyed his own dimension and now wants to take over ours.

And that's a sentence I never thought could be used outside of a superhero movie. All those times I thought humans were overly imaginative… who knew it would be the Community of Species that ended up causing the drama?

Caolan and the warfare specialist, Garin, are confident that they can take out Éibhear. According to them, it would have been done already, except they were distracted by their forthcoming annihilation and trying to prevent it. I can understand how that would have been uppermost in their minds. Éibhear has already been convicted of his crimes and sentenced to death, so all anyone needs is a clear shot. Tish is a different story, since he's yet to be formally tried. Percy and Elinor are dealing with that, working with a judge to see if he can be tried in absentia. If not, we'll manage. While I know it would just be easier for us all if we could take Tish out with a well-aimed sniper shot, part of me really wants to be able to see him tried in court and have to face sentencing. I'm vindictive like that. He needs to suffer.

So our next steps... well, the priority is to get the elves and dragons safe. Not only is that an ethical decision, it also gives us back the ground we lost when we discovered Tish had elves on his side. We also gain an edge, since we have far more elves who are better trained for war than the wealthy dilettantes Éibhear has attracted. Plus, we have dragons. Not a single dragon joined Éibhear, and from the smirks Caolan and Garin exchanged when they told us that, it gives us a huge advantage. I can't wait to meet a dragon. They sound like super cool beings—we're going to get along like spaghetti and meatballs. I'll need to teach my new dragon tertiary BFF the lyrics and choreography to every Spice Girls song ever written.

Another benefit of the migration is that, as I said before, we have a public reason for declaring Tish a wanted criminal... and we can involve more people in the hunt for him. Now that we don't need to keep things under wraps, Andrew is putting together an interspecies task force with specialist agents worldwide. We'll be able to dig through the data faster, locate Tish sooner, and get him arrested, tried, and convicted. He'll be working closely with Ellie and the judiciary, and he's definitely motivated now that Tish knows Noah is still alive.

My stomach growls again, and I glance toward the kitchen. Are they on a call right now, or can I sneak in and grab a snack while Gideon and Garin discuss different hand-to-hand combat tactics?

The doorbell rings, and Sam, who's been circulating amongst every strategy group all afternoon, facilitating our action plans, goes to answer it. In a few days, once news of the elves and dragons has been circulated, we'll be moving back to the office, and I'm sure Sam and Gideon will be glad to get their house back.

Sam comes back with two of the interns from the office and the head of the CSG security team, and David excuses himself from the group to go over to them. I watch idly, glancing occasionally back toward the kitchen doorway. If Percy and Aidan weren't cats, I might be able to sneak in using my super-stealth abilities. I guess I can wait a few minutes more—how much longer can those calls possibly take?

When I look back over at the group by the entranceway, the head of security is gone, Sam is directing the interns to do something with the files they brought over, and David is coming toward me with what looks like Aidan's laptop and phone in his hands.

I stand and go to meet him. "Well?"

"They're clean now, but there were some very interesting weaves attached. Security wants to talk to Aidan and see if they can work out when someone would have had the chance to place them."

"What did they do? Should he be checked by a doctor?" Sorcery is so woven (no pun intended) into our everyday lives that most of the community couldn't live without it, but that doesn't mean it's not fucking dangerous. A knife is a household implement used to prepare many common meals, but it can also harm and kill.

David shakes his head. "No, the weaves were for spying. They were supposed to send copies of all Aidan's emails and messages to a third party—they're tracing that back now, but one of Tish's people is a safe bet— and allow that person to listen in on his calls. Security says one of the weaves was a little sloppy and came loose, fucking the overall functionality, which is why Aidan stopped getting anything at all. They want to check all our electronics just in case, but they're pretty confident that the new security measures we introduced after the leak last year would have caught something like this."

"Have they upgraded Aidan's security? Maybe we should look at rolling out the new measures to all the species leaders as well. We can't have the CCA listening in—"

As one, David and I turn to look into the kitchen, where Percy and Aidan have been contacting species leaders all afternoon. If the CCA got to any of those leaders, they've just learned exactly what our plans are.

"Fuck," David mutters, heading in that direction. I follow. There's not a lot we can do about it now, but the kitchen is where my gorgeous lover is… and the food.

I miss a step and almost fall, distracted by the thought of Aidan and food together. I could eat off his body.

What a delightful thought. We'll need to stop by the grocery store on the way home and stock up for a late supper in bed.

By the time I drag myself away from my thoughts and catch up with David, he's already handed over Aidan's electronics and is explaining the situation. I pretend to be absorbed in what he's saying as I edge toward the pantry. Sam's gotta have some cookies or something.

"Have security contact the species leaders and make arrangements," Percy says as I ease the pantry door open a few inches. Cookies normally live on the third shelf… yes! I widen the gap enough for my hand to—

"Alistair, just open the door properly like a normal person," Aidan says in exasperation. "I doubt Sam will care if you eat some of his food."

Caught! Dammit. I might need to review my stealth skills.

Pouting, I pull the door wide and grab the package of cookies—and a container of almonds—then join the three of them at the table.

"How did the calls go?" I ask. Aidan makes a face, and Percy sighs.

"They could have been better," he admits. "Everybody's in agreement that we need to offer sanctuary to the elves and dragons, but there's a lot of shock about that fact that they exist, that portal travel exists, and that the CCA is not just an irritating cult but is in league with an attempt to take over the world. Ideally, we'd give the leaders time to process and find a way to slowly and gently share this information with the wider community, but…" He shrugs. "They'll just have to process on the go. We can't put living beings at further risk because we need time."

David nods, but he's frowning. "I know their numbers are shockingly low when you consider that's all that remains of entire species, but it's still not going to be easy to find places for them on such short notice. I don't want to traumatize or isolate them by making them spread out, but a sudden influx of population will be noticed by humans in most places… not to mention we need to find housing for them. Our priority has to be to keep families together, and I thought we could put out a call for host families for singles and couples. See if we can get people to volunteer their spare bedrooms and/or vacation homes. That might give us a bit of a cushion."

"You can have my place," Aidan offers, leaning over to grab one of my cookies before I can slap his hand away. "I'm staying here with Alistair for now anyway, so that's four bedrooms going empty."

"And I've got an empty room," I volunteer through cookie crumbs. "It doesn't have a bed, but I can order one." Even if that means Aidan and I have to be quiet during sex.

Percy's smile is a reward for my sacrifice. "Thank you both. Let's have PR come up with a campaign to attract host families while we look into long-term arrangements. I might be fooling myself, but I think our community will step up to help people displaced from their homes under threat of extinction."

"Tish and Éibhear are going to find out about this really soon," I warn, then glance at Percy's laptop. "If they don't know already."

"Then we'll just have to deal with it. There's no way to safely keep it secret."

"Let's be as vigilant as possible over the next few days," David adds. "Once there's a substantial number of elves here, we'll be in a stronger position to deal with an uprising. Tish has to know that, so if they can, they'll strike immediately."

I nod. "Gideon and Garin have already discussed that. They're making contingency plans. The first priority is keeping civilians safe, and the second is keeping the humans ignorant."

Aidan steals a handful of my almonds. Is this the future I have to look forward to? A lifetime of guarding my food?

There's a small commotion in the other room, and

we all look in that direction. A moment later, Andrew appears in the doorway, face grim. "Percy, David."

I bring what's left of the cookies with me as I follow them out of the kitchen. Back in the living room, everyone's standing tensely. The ruckus seems to be centered on Eerika, the elf historian, although a few people are looking at an intern standing by David's wall of data. No—not at the intern (who looks like she'd like to shit her pants and cry), at the picture tacked to the wall beside her head.

I study it. It's of a stylized design that's vaguely familiar, and after a second, I realize it's the official sigil of the lucifer. It's not something I've seen often—the lucifer *is* the government, so on the rare occasions he has cause to affix a seal to something, the CSG sigil is the one used. Most people probably don't even know this one exists. It's been purely symbolic for more years than I've been alive.

But this is the design of the seal that we believe Tish and the elves are after.

"What seems to be the problem?" Percy asks calmly, drawing my attention to where he and David are now standing beside Eerika and Noah.

She raises a shaking hand and points to the picture. The intern, face crumpling in terror, ducks away, and Sam hurries over to her. In mere seconds, he ushers her and the other intern into the kitchen and comes back.

"What is that?" Eerika asks.

I don't know about you, but I have strong feelings that this is not good.

Percy looks at the image, and from the way his face tightens, I know he has the same bad feeling. "That's the design on the seal Éibhear and Tish were trying to steal," he tells her, then glances over at Caolan. "Did that come up when you were briefing the king?"

He nods. "I did mention it, but he had no insight."

"Did you show him this image?" Eerika demands, and Caolan blinks at her.

"No. I didn't have this image. This is the first time I've seen it."

She sucks in a deep breath. "I apologize. I am… shaken."

"Come and sit," Noah urges, taking her arm. "I'll get you some water."

We wait while Noah settles her and makes her comfortable. I'm not the only one feeling impatient, but she's genuinely shaking, so we'd all be assholes to not let her have a minute to collect herself.

"Thank you," she says at last, handing Noah her empty glass and turning to Percy. "I-I have some questions."

"Ask anything you wish," he says immediately.

"The seal… what is it made of?"

"I'm not entirely certain," Percy admits. "We've never had cause to check. The handle and base are wood of some kind, but I know they've been replaced at least once due to decay—the most recent instance was around three thousand years ago. The sigil itself is some kind of metal—brassy in color, but I don't think it's brass or gold. As far as I know, it's the original sigil used by the first lucifer."

She leans forward. "How did the first lucifer come to have it?"

Percy makes a face. "I'm sorry, that's unclear. It seems to be more legend than fact. The story is that the magic itself gifted it to him as a symbol of its faith in him. Although… if I recall correctly, there was also something about the gifting being witnessed by a dragon, so it might be that the story is completely factual and we just didn't know it." He rubs his brow. "This is going to take some getting used to."

I'll fucking say. Aidan comes up beside me and takes the last cookie from the package, then slips his free hand into mine. His touch and the highly tense scene playing out before us are the only things that stop me from demanding to know how he can guiltlessly deprive me of food like that.

Eerika closes her eyes briefly. "This seal—it is safe? You have it secure?"

"Yes," he says immediately. "When Noah told us Tish had promised it to Éibhear, we took steps to ensure it wouldn't be stolen. We don't know why he wants it, but it seemed the wisest course of action." He hesitates, watching her. "You know why he wants it, don't you?"

She nods.

We wait.

She sighs. "When existence began, it was willed out of nothingness by the life force—the magic. The essence of life itself. It willed itself to be and is the consciousness of all existence."

I close one eye and try to make sense of that. For something to will itself, it must first exist, right? Nothing can't be something. This is a chicken and egg thing all over again, and Sam and I nearly ended our friendship debating that one time.

The safest thing for me to do is just trust that the existential magic knew what it was doing, however it came about.

"It created dimensions, universes, and worlds. From

there, single-cell organisms came about and evolved. The life force guided it all, part of it all. As higher-intelligence species came to be, it found delight in their—our—existence and antics, and often made itself corporeal to take part."

Someone drops something, someone makes a startled sound, and my knees wobble. Only Aidan's quick reflexes save me from tumbling to the floor. I look down at his stunned face, then around the room to see similar expressions on the faces of my friends and the other elves.

The magic can make itself corporeal?

It can take physical shape and walk the world?

Fuck. Me. Dead.

"But taking the forms of its children changed the life force. It is impossible to live as a corporeal being and not have the experiences and emotions of one. It found itself forming bonds with others, and when those others entered into conflict, it joined them in a show of friendship."

"Oh, man," Noah mutters. "That can't be good."

Eerika smiles, but it's little more than a movement of her lips. "No, indeed not. It was only when its comrade was wounded and the life force found itself preparing to wreak havoc in response that it realized the implications of its actions. It immediately called an end to the conflict and forced both parties to the negotiating table. The primary debate was of leadership—both were strong leaders in their own right, and both felt they would best serve as overall leader to the elves. The life force heard them out, and in its corporeal form, it wanted most of all to endorse its friend. It recognized then that it could not remain, that in this form, its judgment was swayed by emotional bonds. Its power was limited to what could be contained by its physical body, and while that was still vastly more than any other, it did not allow for the true impartiality of its ethereal form."

That kind of makes sense. Nobody says a word. We're all waiting for her to continue and the other shoe to drop.

"It proclaimed that it would return to its natural state and that forthwith, it would select leaders for all peoples, making the selection based on the needs of the people at any given time. In that way, there would be no need for conflict, as all would know the best choice had been made."

Is it just me, or is the magic arrogant? I mean, it's not wrong, and the plan clearly worked for I don't even know how many years, but still… it sounds like the magic was the kind of person who wouldn't enter a karaoke contest because it already knew it was the best.

"But although it knew the decision was sound, the ties of emotion made leaving its corporeal form difficult. It found it could not bear to leave forever the sensation of touch, the joys of taste and smell, and the complexity of feelings that are not apparent to those without form. And its friend saw this hesitation, but instead of preying upon those vulnerabilities to his own advantage, he performed a single great act of friendship and suggested the life force should leave itself a path back. A way to recreate its corporeal form and once again walk amongst its creations."

"Feck," Aidan whispers, his grip on my hand getting unbearably tight. "The seal."

Eerika nods. "Yes. The life force created in that moment a sigil of metal never before and never after found anywhere within the known worlds. It cast a spell of elven magic and bound it to the sigil, and declared that forever after, it could be drawn to physical form when the spell was cast over the sigil by an elf, in the presence of willing ambassadors of all species across the two known dimensions and sealed by dragon flame. It then dissolved its physical self and, within moments, had invested the leaders of our people and yours. The sigil was taken up by the first elven king and delivered through a portal to the first lucifer on behalf of the life force and witnessed by the first wing leader of the dragons. He was told to keep it close and safe and pass it through the generations—as the king would the spell."

There's a long pause as we all wait to see if that's the whole story. When Eerika sinks back in her chair, Garin lets out an explosive sigh.

"Did you know this?" he asks Caolan, who shakes his head. Garin turns to Eerika. "Does the king know this?"

She spreads her hands. "To some extent, perhaps. The spell has been passed to each new king over the millennia, although I believe its exact purpose may have been forgotten. The living archive is the only place the full story still exists—and now you all know."

"I'm going to come back to that living archive thing," Andrew says, "but can we talk about this spell? I'm guessing the magic can't do anything to save your dimension or it would have, but it might still be able to help us avert a major conflict here. Our biggest drawback has always been that we're bumbling along without all the facts, and it's not possible to get answers out of the magic in its ethereal form. It would solve so many problems if we could just *ask* instead of having it occasionally feed Percy—and your king—trickles of incomplete information. What if we cast the spell and—"

"No!" Eerika and David shout in unison.

Andrew stops. "Okay. May I ask why?"

"Isn't that what Tish and Éibhear want? I can't imagine why else they'd be after the seal," Gideon says. "They think casting the spell and making the magic corporeal will help them in some way."

"But how?" Andrew asks. "And why can't we leverage that for ourselves?"

"How is what I want to know," Ellie says. "How would drawing the magic into a physical body advance Tish and Éibhear's cause?"

"Maybe because a body limits its power? Maybe Tish and Éibhear think they can pull off their coup while the magic is limited by a body," Noah suggests.

Sam shakes his head. "And then what? Even with the limits of a body, it was able to end that war last time. And the second it leaves the body, its full power would be restored."

"Maybe it could be trapped in the body," Caolan says, but he sounds doubtful.

"Uh…" David half-raises his hand like a schoolboy. It's shaking. "If I could interrupt?" He turns to Eerika. "When you said its power was limited by its physical body… do you mean the magic became mortal?"

She nods, and David sinks into an armchair. "What… what would happen if Tish and Éibhear cast the spell, drawing the magic to corporeal form, and then killed that body?"

Black dots appear in front of my eyes, and I blink hard. Passing out in shock won't help anything. For a long moment, nobody speaks. It's as if we're all trying to process the horror of what David is suggesting.

"The magic would just return to its noncorporeal state, right?" Ellie asks uncertainly.

Eerika shakes her head. "Nobody knows. There is no mention of that possibility in the archive. Theoretically…" She trails off, and David gets up and moves to crouch beside her chair.

"Please finish. Any theory you have might give us insight."

She shrugs a little helplessly. "Over the millennia, several scholars have posited theories. The general consensus is that the spell is based on elf spellcasting and was created by an elf—more or less. The body that the life force would return to would therefore be that of an elf. When elves are slain, our souls continue to the ether and reside there until we are ready to be reborn."

"Yes." Percy sinks down into the chair beside her. "That's very similar to our own experience—our eternal souls transition to the spiritual plane and then are reincarnated. I imagine it's the same thing but in different dimensions."

"The question is, does the life force have a soul? Is it a soul? If so, it could return to its ethereal state, which would be the best outcome. Or it could, due to the nature of the spell that made it an elf, continue to the ether and await rebirth, essentially trapped in elf-soul form. Whether it would be able to dissolve its next body is uncertain. It may be able to but need to wait for adulthood. It may instead be destined to remain an elf for eternity."

Not much of that sounds good, if being corporeal limits the magic's power.

"And if it doesn't have a soul?" David asks.

"If there is no soul in the body, its death could well result in the extinction of the life force."

Aidan makes a sound beside me, and I look over. His face is deathly pale, and considering how pale he normally is, that's really saying something. He's still clutching my hand, but I've long since lost feeling in it.

"We must not allow the spell to be cast," he whispers, his tone and words oddly formal.

"We must not," Percy agrees with the same formality, rising, and with a start, I realize the magic must be communicating with them. "Under no circumstances should the spell be cast while Tish and Éibhear roam free."

"Can we consider that to be confirmation that they plan to kill the magic?" Gideon asks, face set.

Aidan shakes his head, and Percy says, "I don't know. All I know is that the magic unequivocally does not want the spell cast."

"So we don't let that happen," Noah declares. "But I'm still not sure what Tish and Éibhear hope to gain exactly. Let's say they somehow manage to cast the spell and then kill the magic permanently. What happens then? I'm guessing they don't think it'll be the destruction of the world."

"I suppose that would be possible," Eerika says thoughtfully. "The life force is part of every living molecule. But the overriding theory is that once something exists, the destruction of its creator doesn't necessarily result in its destruction. Many spells can continue to exist after their caster has died."

"So we're talking about an existence without the magic," Noah concludes. "Tish and Éibhear could legitimately declare themselves leaders, and anybody saying otherwise would have to fight for it, because there'd be no magic to invest leaders."

"That's why they haven't been teaching their young about the magic," I realize. "They're planning for a time when it doesn't exist. And if it doesn't exist, we'd struggle to stop them. Even if we gave up on trying to keep hidden from the humans, how could we protect them all?"

"It's only theory," David says grimly, "but it fits too well to ignore it. What are our best options? Can we destroy the sigil and the spell?"

"No!" Eerika presses a hand to her chest. "It is a spell like no other, and we don't even know what the sigil is truly made of. Destroying them might bring on the disaster we're trying to avoid."

"The magic is strongly against destroying the spell and the sigil," Percy says. "I'm not sure if that's because it would kill it or if it just wants to keep its gateway to being a person open. Either way, I don't think it's a risk we want to take."

"No," David agrees, regaining his feet and beginning to pace. Caolan watches him closely, concern on his face, and I remember that I had plans to matchmake them. That was so long ago, before the revelations that just turned my world inside out. "Okay. Okay. So we increase security on the sigil. Maybe the elves can add a layer of protection, mix it in with what we've already got and make it trickier for anyone to get through."

Caolan agrees immediately.

"We get word to your king and have the spell placed under the strongest protections possible. Éibhear clearly believes he can access it when he needs to. We need to change that."

Caolan agrees again. "I will go to the king now," he says.

"If I remember right," David continues, turning to look at Eerika, "for success, the spell needs to be cast in the presence of willing witnesses of all species… and there was something about dragon flame?"

"Yes." She nods. "The spell must be sealed by the flame of a dragon."

"Well, between them, Tish and Éibhear have gathered followers of all other species, but you said none of the dragons had joined Éibhear's efforts. Are you certain?"

"Absolutely certain," Garin swears. "There are so few dragons that all are accounted for, in life and death."

That sounds kind of morbid, but this isn't the time to ask what he means.

"Then all dragons must be protected. We make sure their leader is fully aware of the situation and that every dragon must be accounted for at all times. Éibhear and Tish cannot be permitted to get their hands on one."

A murmur of agreement runs through the room.

"I don't think that will be necessary," Eerika says. "The archive is clear that all witnesses to the spell must be willing. In order to gain a willing dragon witness, Éibhear would need to resort to trickery, and even foolish young dragons have the ability to sense a lie."

"Are you willing to stake the existence of everything on that?"

She sighs. "I suppose it's best to take precautions."

David makes a sound that might be a laugh if the

person laughing was having a mental breakdown, but in the next second he's pulled himself together again.

"We migrate your people safely, we hunt down Éibhear and Tish, and we keep everything secret from the humans. Those are the priorities. We can worry about the rest later."

I suck in a deep breath, gently pry my hand loose from Aidan's, and draw him within the circle of my arm. Not gonna lie: I'm scared. Being at the forefront of the battle to save existence was never in my life plan. But that shit's gotta get done, and I'm not about to shy away from the job and leave the fate of my lover in someone else's hands.

The meeting begins to break up. Caolan goes out to the entranceway to open a portal and report back to his king. Sam invites everyone to stay for dinner, and David's in a huddle with Eerika and Garin, his phone at his ear. Andrew sinks down beside Noah and wraps him in a hug, and for once, Noah just snuggles in, even though they're in public.

I look down at Aidan. He's pale and looks drawn. No doubt he's worrying about all the shifters in the world. He's planning the best way to tell them about the elves and dragons and warn them about the danger of Tish. He's fretting over those who have been assimilated by the CCA, especially the children. And he's thinking about the challenges ahead.

I am too. But that's for tomorrow. Tonight, I'm taking my lover home and basking in the joy of being with him.

Thanks for reading! Want an Alistair and Aidan bonus scene? Subscribe to my monthly newsletter (bit.ly/ LouisaMBonus)

We talk spoilers in my Facebook group, RoMMance with Becca & Louisa.

If you're an "extras" kind of person, check out my Patreon (patreon.com/louisamasters) for early access to chapters, artwork, and other bonus material!

ALSO BY LOUISA MASTERS

Saddles & Suits

Alistair's Extraordinaries

Grave Situation

Elemental Men: The Complete Series

Style Me

Rebrand

Couture

Elf Magic

Wooing the Wiccan

Enticing the Elf

The Collective

Higher Demon

Demon Hunter

Demons-In-Law

Asher

Micah

Zachary

Franklin U

Mr. Romance

The Holigay Hookup *related novella

Batting Style

Ghostly Guardians

Spirited Situation

Vortex Conundrum

Conduit Crisis

Gateway Catastrophe

Here Be Dragons

Dragon Ever After

The Professor's Dragon

The Dragon Experiment

Conspiracy of Dragons

Hidden Species

Demons Do It Better

One Bite With A Vampire

Hijinks With A Hellhound

Sorcerers Always Satisfy

Hidden Species Box Set

Met His Match

Charming Him

Offside Rules

A Christmas Chance (novella)

Between the Covers (M/F)

Joy Universe

I've Got This

Follow My Lead

In Your Hands

Take Us There

Novellas

Fake It 'Til You Make It (permafree)

One Golden Night

O Hell, All Ye Shoppers

Out of the Office

After the Blaze

Blokes Down Under Novella Collection

ABOUT THE AUTHOR

Louisa Masters started reading romance much earlier than her mother thought she should. As an adult, she feeds her addiction in every spare second. She spent years trying to build a "sensible" career, working in bookstores, recruitment, resource management, administration, and as a travel agent before finally conceding defeat and devoting herself to the world of romance novels.

Louisa has a long list of places first discovered in books that she wants to visit, and every so often she overcomes her loathing of jet lag and takes a trip that charges her imagination. She lives in Melbourne, Australia, where she whines about the weather for most of the year while secretly admitting she'll probably never move.

http://www.louisamasters.com

www.ingramcontent.com/pod-product-compliance
Lightning Source LLC
Chambersburg PA
CBHW021242060726
47590CB00005B/1862

* 9 7 8 0 6 4 8 9 7 7 6 2 9 *